MW00444919

Nisha,

Happy reading!

Take Hart
F. J. Talley
©2017

Thank you for reading *Take Hart*! If you enjoy this book, please leave a review or connect with the author.

Acknowledgements

Thanks to my family -- Ellen, Mark and Rosa -- for their patience and support during the production of *Take Hart*, my second novel. Thanks for everything!

Also thanks to *Take Hart*'s awesome launch team!

Ziv Ball
Ashantee Barnwell
Robyn Baumann
Alex Cantor
Joanna Colvin
Michelle DiMenna
Cody Dorsey
Mary Dorsey
Simmone Francis
Kyla Hasemeier
Devin Holt-Zimmerman
Marie Keller
Toni Kruszka
Kelly Martin
Kezia-Alean Osunsade
Jordan Parker
Twinkle Raheja
Morgan Smith
Ellen P. Servetnick
Rosa Talley-Servetnick
Elizabeth Williams
Jeanni Winston-Muir

Prologue

"Is this how it ends?" She could taste the gunpowder as she tried to keep her focus on the task ahead. The tunnel felt dank and closed in claustrophobic.

One member of her team shot, and the other injured and in a lot of pain. She glanced back at him, and thought she could see the strain in his eyes as he sat. Still, she knew he would back her up, his weapon at the ready.

The weapon in her arms suddenly felt heavier than before and she could feel beads of sweat under her helmet. But, she had a job to do.

"This is what I trained for."

She brought strength to her arms and hands and took a deep breath. She focused her gaze down the tunnel.

"Let 'em come."

Chapter One

The hallway to Captain Andrew Shoemaker's office was well-lit, and the two officers approaching it walked with sure steps. The male officer was a sergeant, confident and a bit arrogant. His female companion was equally confident and wore the blue shield of a probationary officer in the Port Angel Police Department. The sergeant looked briefly at his female companion, smirked, then raised his hand to knock on the office door.

"Come in." The sergeant opened the door, and held it for the female officer. Captain Shoemaker looked up as they entered. "O.C., Hart," said Captain Shoemaker. He gestured toward the two seats in front of this desk. "Come in and sit." Shoemaker waited for a moment, then looked again at Sgt. O.C. Boyd.

"So, O.C.," the captain began. "You've just finished with Officer Hart, here." He paused briefly. "While I wonder if I'll regret this," he said. "What is your evaluation?"

Sgt. Boyd smiled again at Officer Stephanie Hart, then returned his gaze to his commanding officer. "Officer Hart is just fine, Shoe," Boyd said, using the captain's well known nickname. "She seems to be getting the hang of things around here." Boyd leaned forward toward his captain. "Of course," he continued, "She could be a bit more social -- you know, with the guys."

As Boyd spoke, Captain Shoemaker looked quickly to see if Hart had a reaction. She seemed to have none; she just looked ahead with a very slight smile on her face, but was otherwise neutral. Shoemaker shook his head.

"Anything else, O.C.?"

"Captain," Boyd began "I think I've gone about as far with Probationary Officer Hart as I can. Now it's up to her final field training officer."

That it is, O.C.," Shoemaker agreed. "That it is." Shoemaker turned his gaze again toward Hart.

"Officer Hart," he said. "You've been through three of our knucklehead FTOs." While Shoemaker spoke, Boyd humphed into his moustache. Shoemaker glanced briefly at Boyd then continued. "Any comments on our little 'burg' of Port Angel?" Shoemaker sat back in his chair, as Stephanie Hart leaned slightly forward.

"Hardly a little burg, sir," she said. "Port Angel is the biggest city I've lived in besides Philly." She paused. "There's nothing little about it." Both Boyd and Shoemaker laughed, as Hart smiled.

"Really, sir," Hart continued. "These months in the field have been very helpful." She glanced briefly at Sgt. Boyd, then continued. "Sgt. Boyd has really shown me the ropes, and I'm looking forward to my last rotation."

"Nothing else?"

"No, sir," Hart replied. "Just ready to meet my last FTO."

Shoemaker looked at her, then briefly at Boyd before replying. "Very well, Hart," he said. "Stick around here. Officer Novak should be on the way." He turned his attention once again to Boyd. "Go out and take care of the world, O.C."

Boyd rose, looked for a second at Hart, and said, "See you later, Stephie." Shoemaker locked eyes with Hart as he heard "Stephie," and again seeing no reaction, returned his gaze to Boyd. "Thanks, O.C., he said. "If you see Novak out there, please send him in."

"Got it, Shoe," said Boyd. And he opened the door and left the room.

As Boyd left, Shoemaker let out a long breath, then looked again at Hart, a slight smile on his face.

"He can be infuriating at times, I know, Hart."

Hart was quiet before shaking her head slightly and smiling. "I spent a lot of years in the MPs working for people just as infuriating, sir." she said. "I can handle it."

"Oh, I know you can handle it Hart," Shoemaker said, leaning forward again in his chair. "But I know how you feel about being called 'Stephie.' I was seriously worried you were going to smack him upside the head."

"Not in front of a witness, sir," Hart said. Finally, Hart relaxed a bit and continued. "Infuriating doesn't quite do him justice, Captain," she said. "But I have to tell you, I learned a tremendous amount from Sgt. Boyd. He knows the city, knows officers from everywhere, and gave me lots of feedback to help me adjust to Port Angel." Hart lifted her palms toward the ceiling slightly. "And if sometimes those lessons come in a somewhat crude and unsophisticated package, I guess I'm okay with that."

At this, Shoemaker laughed out loud. He took out a pen and jotted notes on his blotter.

"Let's see -- somewhat crude and unsophisticated package -- was that it?"

"Actually sir," she began, her eyes widening, "I was just talking out of turn, I…."

Shoemaker shook his head. "Nope. Sorry, Hart," he replied, raising his index finger. "That's about the best way of describing Boyd I've ever heard." He made a placating gesture with his palm. "I promise not to ascribe it to you." He laughed again, saying, *sotto voce* "crude and unsophisticated package -- that's really good."

Hart, sensing the humor in the situation, relaxed again. "I can think of others, sir."

Shoemaker waved her off. "Don't bother, Hart," he said, as he tapped his blotter. "This is already good." Finally, Shoemaker regained his composure and looked directly at Officer Stephanie Hart again. "Here's a question, Hart: how do you think Sgt. Boyd evaluated you? Do you think he believes you to be a good upcoming officer -- your honest sense of what he thought."

Hart first smiled then shook her head slightly. "To be honest, sir, I really don't have a clue what Sgt. Boyd thinks. Actually, I thought I did on many occasions, then he would surprise me." She looked up to Shoemaker who made a "please continue" gesture.

"Most of the time," she continued, "I felt like a complete rookie who didn't know anything about law enforcement with him, which is the infuriating part," she said. "Then something would occur where he had me make a traffic stop or something else, and he wouldn't say a thing. Then we'd get back in the cruiser and I'd keep looking at him for feedback. Then he'd say "What? You need somebody to tell you you did the right thing? Not my style, Stephie." Hart finally chuckled again. "You were right," she began, "infuriating *is* probably the best way of describing him."

Shoemaker had listened to Hart patiently, and not without a little amusement. Then he nodded slowly and spoke. "Well, I will tell you Hart that Boyd has a very high opinion of you as a probationary officer." Shoemaker could see that his words had the expected impact on Hart, who leaned back as if smacked by a blow. Before she could speak, Shoemaker used his palm to calm her again. "Oh, I know he can be a pain in the ass and tries to keep all of you guessing," Shoemaker continued. "But he told me on several occasions, that your judgement was sound, you were resilient, and you could think for yourself, which probably led to at least some of your clashes with him."

"There seems to be a conflict here, sir," Hart said. "Sgt. Boyd tries to get people to think his way, yet you're saying that he likes the way I think for myself; that doesn't make sense."

Shoemaker smiled again. "Actually, it does, Hart. The fact is that Boyd likes to get new officers to think like him because he really *does* know how to be an effective cop in Port Angel for all the reasons you cited. Any officer would be successful if they thought like Boyd -- however crude or unsophisticated he may be." Both Shoemaker and Hart chuckled at this.

Shoemaker continued. "It seems to me that you didn't need to learn how to be a cop, Hart. As a matter of fact, Boyd thinks you're much more advanced than the usual probationary officer, and he just wasn't used to someone with your" -- he searched for a word, before smiling widely -- "sophistication."

Shoemaker and Hart laughed again before Shoemaker became serious again. "Now," he began. "A little about what to expect during your last rotation." Shoemaker indicated Hart's notepad with his eyes, and began talking about expectations for the final rotation for probationary officers in the Port Angel Police Department. As one of the largest and most diverse departments in the state, Port Angel had a particularly rigorous system for vetting its probationary officers. Twenty percent of officers who complete academy training fail to complete their probationary periods successfully, which was a testament to the rigor of the system and the high performance level of Port Angel police officers. As he spoke, Shoemaker reflected that he had no doubt that Probationary Officer Hart -- who preferred 'Stephanie' if not just 'Hart" would complete her probationary period successfully, as she had been an especially good find and a mysterious one at that.

Moving to Port Angel after serving for years in the Military Police both stateside and deployed in three countries, Hart had a spotless record and several commendations, so much so that Shoemaker wondered why she didn't continue in and retire from the Army. When he interviewed Hart, she talked about how excited she was to start a new chapter in her life, and that she wanted to get started on a civilian law enforcement career as soon as possible. She also suggested that she had done all she wanted to do as an MP. While Shoemaker still wondered about her background, all her records and recommendations were without blemish, and he happily chose her as a probationary officer to join his precinct.

Hart took quick notes and asked a few excellent questions, and just as Shoemaker was finishing her briefing, they heard a firm step in the hallway, then a knock at the Captain's door.

"Come in," said Shoemaker.

Hart rose and turned to face the man opening the door, seeing a ruddy faced man of about 6 feet entering the office. Hart stepped aside to let the captain greet the officer.

"Danny," said Shoemaker. "Come in and meet Officer Hart."

Hart quickly took in the tall figure: red hair, what looked like blue eyes and a strong chin along with a ready smile. Hart smiled back and shook his hand firmly. "Nice to meet you Officer Novak," Hart said.

Novak returned the handshake. "Nice to meet you as well, Officer Hart." Both officers turned their attention to Captain Shoemaker.

"This is Officer Novak's first time as a FTO, Officer Hart," Shoemaker said. "So be gentle with him."

"Understood, sir."

Shoemaker sat back down at this desk. "I don't have anything else for either of you now," he said. "So, you're free to go out and catch the bad guys."

Novak and Hart, standing at attention, each said,

"Thank you, sir," though not quite in unison, then turned to leave the office.

Novak closed the door behind them and began walking down the hallway. He stopped and looked briefly over his shoulder.

"By the way, I don't need the Officer Novak stuff, Hart. Just 'Danny' is fine with me," he said. Leaning forward, he continued. "And I promise not to call you 'Stephie.'"

Hart's eyes briefly went skyward before she returned the smile.

"Fair enough," she said.

Chapter Two

Hart followed slightly behind Novak as they walked down the hallway, noticing his strong but not overdone build. He seemed to be about her age -- 31 -- a few inches taller than her 5'9", and moved with an easy grace. Moving next to him, she noticed that officers and administrative staff all greeted Officer Danny Novak warmly. He was clearly someone people liked, and Hart felt herself relax in his presence, though she didn't even know him, or much about him. She was so engrossed in her thinking that she failed to notice Novak step to his left down a new hallway.

Novak called to her. "Hart?" he said. "We're going this way." He pointed with his finger.

"Sorry, Danny," she said, and gave him an embarrassed smile. "I guess I was a little distracted."

Novak smiled at her, then squinted playfully. "Are you always this cerebral?" he asked.

"What do you mean?"

"Well," Novak began "You've had your head in the clouds since we left the captain's office." Seeing Hart stiffen, Novak quickly added. "Not a problem -- just something I noticed." Novak's manner became more inviting. "Is there something I should know about?"

"No, Danny," Hart said. "I often have a lot on my mind, but I'm back now." Seeking to draw attention away from herself, she added, "Just where are we going, anyway?"

"Motor pool. We have to pick up a new cruiser from 'Wheels.'" With that, Novak led the way to the rear of the precinct main building, past evidence rooms, and other areas that Hart remembered seeing in her previous rotations. After descending another flight of stairs, they ended up near the dingy but neatly organized motor pool. Novak stopped to let Hart examine the area.

"Obviously, this is the motor pool," he said. "The last couple of cruisers I've had have given me trouble, so I was sent to get a new one."

It seemed to Hart that Novak was holding something back, so she gave him a look and said "And…?"

"And," Novak added sheepishly, "I've sometimes been known for having more problems with my cruisers than other officers." As Hart smiled, Novak added "That's not to say I'm not a good driver, mind you, just that some people believe…" Novak shook his head. "You know Hart, I don't really have to explain this to you right now."

Taking his comment in good humor, Hart replied, "Nope. You don't. But I do like to know who I'm driving with."

"Right. And just remember who is the supervising officer here."

Hart stood up straight, saying, "Got it."

Novak noticed her change in demeanor and winced. "And just so you know, I'm not O.C. Boyd, so please don't give me any of that fake respect he likes so much."

Hart laughed. "Is he like that with everybody?"

"Oh yeah," Novak said. "O.C. supervises every probationary officer. To be honest, because he really is that good, but he can be an arrogant son of a bitch." Novak paused, and looked at Hart, who shrugged.

"Hey, you get no argument from me," she said.

"Well anyway," Novak continued, "just know that I'm not like him. I know your record, and know that this is really only a formality with you."

"What do you mean?"

Novak laughed. "Are you *serious*?" Hart continued to shake her head in confusion, so Novak continued.

"Look, you were an MP in the Army for what -- 12 years -- right?"

"Yep."

"And during that time you were involved in investigations, firefights, regular patrols of teenage soldiers, stuff like that?"

Slightly exasperated, Hart interrupted. "Right. I've done all of that," she said. "But what about the formality thing? I heard that only about eighty percent or four fifths of officers make it through probation, and given how I felt around Boyd, and how I thought he felt about me, I didn't know if I wasn't going to be part of the one fifth."

Novak laughed out loud again. "Captain Shoemaker would feel like a total idiot against Boyd, that's just what O.C. does to people." Novak leaned closer to Hart. "Don't let that ever bother you. If Boyd really didn't think you could do it, he would have made that clear to the captain." Novak stood straighter again. "To be honest, I think he likes you." To this Hart smirked.

"Oh yeah," she said. "I can really see that."

Novak dismissed her comment. "Well," he said. "In any case, he thinks you're an excellent cop, even better than some veterans of the department. All you need to do is to learn how to channel your Army policing to civilian policing and learn the neighborhood and Port Angel."

Novak kept smiling, which prompted Hart once again. "And I guess you're the one to teach me that?" she asked.

Novak, who had presented himself as more of a peer than a supervisor suddenly changed his manner. "Actually, Hart, I am. I'm from Port Angel, and I like to think I'm one of the best in the precinct -- maybe even in the entire department -- at community policing." He smiled and became more humble again. "And I know you're going to get this just fine like O.C. said."

As he finished speaking, he noticed a large man with a determined look approaching them. Indicating the man with his head, Novak added "Now, let's go see about our new ride."

* * *

The man approaching them was dressed in neat, but worn coveralls, and he had a swagger that suggested that he owned the motor pool and didn't just work there. As dominant as he appeared, he gave a genuine smile as he approached Novak. "Danny," the man said, and he extended his hand.

"Good to see you, Wheels," said Novak as he shook the man's hand. He turned toward Hart, "And this…."

"And this must be Probationary Officer Hart, am I right?"

Hart smiled and extended her hand. "Stephanie Hart," she said. "And did I hear the name 'Wheels?'"

"Yep. The full name is Mickey Rom, but for some unknown reason, people call me 'Wheels.'" As he spoke, Rom smiled.

"Yeah," Hart laughed. "I wonder where that could have come from." Rom and Hart turned their gazes to Novak, who was waiting impatiently.

"Please don't encourage him, Hart," Novak said. "He doesn't need any of that."

Rom rolled his eyes, then looked again at Hart. "Trust me, Officer Hart. Novak is one officer I never want to see in my motor pool. He is the hardest man I know on a police cruiser."

"You know I'm still standing here, right?" asked Novak. "And I'm not any harder on the cruisers than anybody else."

"Sure, Danny," Rom said. "You just keep believing that."

Hart looked back and forth to the two men. "So, is there something I need to know here?"

"No!" Novak replied quickly. "Wheels seems to have a little, umm, *challenge* in keeping our vehicles in shape. I just try to keep him on his toes." Novak paused then added, "It's a really important job, Hart."

Rom kept quiet while Novak spoke, then he turned to Hart and asked, "So Hart, I've heard that you've got some experience in evasive driving and high speed chases."

"Right," she said. "I spent 12 years in the Military Police and led convoys and transported dangerous people, mostly from behind the wheel."

"Ha!" Rom said, as he looked to Novak. "Finally someone who can keep you from ruining my cars." Returning his gaze to Hart, he added "Are you going to be driving -- please?" Rom made a pleading gesture.

"Can't say that for sure, Wheels," Hart said. "I am only a little probationary officer, after all."

"Right. A little probationary officer. Forget it Hart; I already know all about you." Rom turned again to Novak. "I'm giving you #9 today, Danny, so please don't screw it up."

Novak smiled when he heard the number. "Really, Wheels," Novak said. "You're giving me your 'baby?'"

"Against my better judgement," Rom said. "But I don't have a lot of options today since #7 is out of commission."

"Out of everything, you mean." Turning quickly toward # 9, Novak motioned for Hart to follow him. "But I'm not going to look a gift horse in the mouth, Wheels. Number 9 will do just fine for us." He looked to Hart again. "Let's head out, Hart."

Hart turned again to Rom, extended her hand and said "Nice to meet you, Wheels."

Hart continued into the hot July sun toward the cruiser's passenger door as Novak started the engine. She quickly opened the door and sat down, checking her watch and the shotgun mount as she did so. As Novak checked other gauges, Hart squinted and tilted her head. Novak didn't notice her and started to shift the car out of drive when Hart put her hand over his. "Wait, Danny, she said. "Put it in gear slowly, but don't do anything else." Novak was confused, but did as she asked. He placed the car in gear and waited, while Hart listened.

"Rev it a little, Danny," Hart said. Novak complied and revved it for Hart who listened, then got out of the cruiser. She crossed over the garage and approached Rom, who had just noticed that Novak and Hart hadn't left the garage yet. "Wheels?"

"What is it?"

"Not sure," Hart said. "It's just an odd sound that I heard." Hart noticed that Rom leaned back slightly, as though offended. She reached out her hand. "I mean, I don't know what it is, it just sounded odd to me." Rom shrugged, turned toward #9 and started toward the car. As he got to the hood, he stopped, listened, and then got closer. He turned toward Novak and said,

"Pop the hood, Danny." Novak complied, and Rom stuck his head into the engine cavity. His hand raised above the level of the hood, and he gestured to Novak, saying, "Rev it a bit, Danny." Novak lowered his foot on the accelerator, and revved the car slowly. Rom listened again, then gestured for Novak to stop.

"Put it in park, Danny." Rom said. He turned his attention again to Hart. "Are you saying you heard that?" he asked.

"I heard *something*. What is it?"

Rom shook his head. "I think it's one of the lifters, but I'm not sure." He nodded with a slight smile. "Nice catch, Hart" Rom said.

Rom leaned into the cruiser to speak with Novak. "We'll get you another unit, Novak," he said. "But make sure that Hart drives it -- if you don't mind." Rom turned back to the garage, checking his clipboard for the next cruiser to issue to Novak and Hart. He returned quickly and guided Novak and Hart to another unit, giving Hart the keys. The two officers opened the cruiser doors, got in and went through their usual check, pausing so Hart could listen to the engine. She nodded and turned to Novak before putting the cruiser into gear.

"Sounds fine to me, Danny," Hart said.

"Is this how it's going to be all day, Hart?" Novak asked.

Hart was unmoved.. "Not sure what you're talking about, Danny," she said.

Novak shook his head and added, "Never mind," he said. "Let's head out." Hart put the car in gear before leaving the garage and going on patrol.

Chapter Three

Novak and Hart drove down Pike Street, then turned left onto Market Ave. For the first few minutes of their drive, they were silent, Hart following the route often given to her by her Field Training Officers. As they stopped at the third traffic light on Vine, she turned to Novak.

"Just where are we going?" she asked.

Novak squinted slightly, then pointed toward the left. "Let's turn left at Slocum, then head up to the plateau."

Hart thought a moment, then remembered the rise up toward a mesa overlooking the southern tip of the precinct. As the light turned green, she headed into traffic then signaled to turn left at Slocum, the next large thoroughfare. Turning, she drove at moderate speed up the street.

As Hart drove, Novak looked at her out of the corner of his eye. She was as attractive as the other officers said she was, he thought. And she seems confident and what was the word? Settled. Yes, that's what she was, settled -- and secure. He could see why they were impressed with her as an officer. Novak also noticed how her eyes shifted and examined the people on the sidewalks and the traffic coming and going. *She has a cop's vision*, Novak thought.

As they got near the top of the hill, Novak pointed toward the left. "Make this last left, and we'll head to the crest," he said.

"Okay," said Hart. She guided the car into the turn and to the top of the hill, stopping in a small parking area by the guard rails. She turned off the car and looked at her partner. "Okay," she began. She looked out over the hood of the car. "Is there something you wanted to show me?"

Novak opened the car door, saying, "Sure. Come over here with me."

Hart complied, getting out of the car but leaving her club inside. She followed Novak over toward the edge of the plateau, still safely away from danger. She noticed that Novak was smiling. He took a deep breath, savored it a little bit, then turned to Hart. "Hart. What do you see down there?"

Novak seemed serious, so Hart decided not to use her trademark dry humor. She looked over at the city before answering. "Well, I see the city, even the whole shape as it bends toward the docks." Her voice trailed off.

"That's what I see, too," Novak said. smiling. "But of course I see more." He pointed toward the east. "Over there. That's where I saw my first dead body, and it wasn't while I had a badge. It was a guy who used to bully me all the time. He got into a fight while we were in high school and somebody shot him." Novak turned to his partner. "His mother called me to be a pallbearer, because her son said I was one of his best friends. I didn't have the heart to tell her that her son was an asshole who tried to beat me up every day." Novak's body shook like he had a sudden chill. "And down by the docks?" he continued, after a pause, "that's where we had a big shootout between residents who were being pushed out and the developers who were trying to gentrify the area. Nobody died, but it left a really bad taste in the mouths of people from the Auburn section right next door." He turned again to Hart. "I grew up in Auburn."

"Right," answered Hart.

"Well anyway," Novak continued. "I can point to every part of the city, particularly in Lexington and Auburn and tell you about the people I know there. It can be rough growing up in Port Angel if you're from the wrong side of the tracks." He chuckled briefly. "And that would be me."

"Well, me too."

Novak raised his fist playfully in salute. "Well I guess we have that in common then." He returned his gaze to the city. "When I think about the people I grew up with, there are some like me who made the right decisions, went to college or got good jobs -- some moved away, of course. But we've done what we would all agree are the right things and we're happy about that. Then, there are those who were never really on the right side of the law in the first place, and they've been just as successful at doing that. I grew up with drugs dealers, murderers, robbers, teachers, rapists, doctors, preachers -- all kinds of people, some of whom went to the same church I went to, and were in Cub Scouts and Boy Scouts with me."

"Were…" began Hart.

"Stop!" Novak said. "Yes, I *am* an eagle scout, thank you very much."

"And I guess you can read minds, too," said Hart.

"Please keep that in mind, Hart," Novak said. "I have to tell you something though. I go to church every week when I can -- the same church, and some of these guys, the good *and* the bad they go to church with me. And we still talk, you know -- about our kids, about baseball, elections -- all that stuff. And it's like nothing's ever changed from high school, except if I catch one of them doing what they do for a living now, I'm going to try like hell to put him in jail. They know it and I know it."

"Does that ever scare you?" Hart asked after a pause.

Novak was silent for a moment, then said, resolutely, "Not really. I know the danger is there, and there are plenty of people I didn't grow up with who wouldn't give two shits for my life, but the guys I grew up with wouldn't gun for me, and I guess if anything happened to me by their hands it would be an accident." Seeing Hart looking puzzled, he continued. "One of the reasons is that these guys know that if they needed the help of a cop, they could always call me. If their kid was being bullied, and they wanted somebody to talk to the bully, they wouldn't do it, they would call me. In those situations that aren't related to what they do for a living, I have their back and they actually have mine." He turned again to Hart. "And if you think that's complicated and hard to explain to some, you'd be right. And while I am accepted as a cop in our precinct and beyond, there are a few -- just a few mind you -- who wonder if I'm just as bad as those guys from high school, just that I'm wearing a badge now, you know? Novak sat on the guard rail, and indicated a section for Hart to sit on.

"So tell me a little bit more about yourself, Hart," Novak said. "People don't move more than halfway across the country just for a change of scenery after a strong military career." He noticed Hart stiffen, but waited patiently for her.

"Actually, Danny," Hart began, "That is pretty much what happened." She paused, gathering her thoughts. "I mean, I am originally from Philadelphia, but after the Army, I really didn't want to go home, especially since my family wasn't there anymore. I mean, didn't you ever think of moving away from Port Angel?"

"No, because this has always been home to me."

"But it seems to me that you could fit in anywhere you went," Hart said. "You're obviously competent enough, people like you, and you must be a good cop if you're an FTO. You could take this anywhere."

"I could," Novak agreed. "But it wouldn't be the same. I still fit in because I choose to fit in. Plus there are some things I can do or can access that few other cops can in Port Angel, and that sometimes can make a difference." He stretched out his legs. "And I'm happy here." He turned to Hart again. "Plus, my wife Sheryl is happy here, and that's really important."

"I hear that," agreed Hart, and she started to rise.

Novak laid a hand across her arm. "But we were talking about you -- or a least I was trying to get to know you a little better." He tilted his head. "Partners do need to know more than name, rank and service number, you know."

Novak noticed Hart's chest rise and fall slightly, before she smiled again. "Fair enough," she said. "As I said, I'm from Philadelphia, and went to a really good public high school for girls." She noticed

Novak's eyebrows rising, but ignored him. "Almost everyone in my high school class went to college, and I was one of only 10 who didn't, and chose the Army. My father had been an MP, and I thought that would be a good career." She chuckled. "Of course, he preferred that I served as an officer, rather than enlisted, but I didn't want to wait that long, so I enlisted on my birthday."

"Did he ever come around?" Novak asked.

"Oh yeah," Hart replied. "You should have seen him at my graduation from basic, and even more after my special training. They traveled all the way to Missouri when I graduated from MP school, so yes, he's very proud of me." She paused then as she continued, Novak could detect a different tone in her voice. "Serving in the MPs was great. I traveled, had the chance to be involved in basic patrol, do a little bit of investigating, get command experience with a platoon -- you know the things they always tell you when they want you to enlist. Eventually, though, I wanted to come home, yet Philly wasn't really home anymore. So I wondered where else I could live that was big but not too big, had a good police force, was diverse, plus I always wanted to learn how to sail. Then, somebody told me about Port Angel." She turned again to Novak. "That's pretty much all I am these days, Danny," she said.

Novak smiled at her and said, "Something tells me there are more layers to Stephanie Hart than that, but I'm okay with it for now." He rose from the guard rail and looked at his partner. "Let's head back out -- and *I'll* drive."

Hart laughed, and fished the keys from her pocket. "You're the boss," she said. They got back into the cruiser, and after closing the door, she turned to Novak. "And just so you know," she began, "My friends call me 'Steve.'"

"Steve it is."

Chapter Four

After cruising through the neighborhood and showing Hart some features of this sector of the 9th precinct, Novak turned down Lexington Avenue and stopped in front of the Heaven's Home Restaurant. As he turned off the engine, Novak turned to Hart.

"Call in lunch, Steve," he said.

Hart smiled at hearing her nickname, and picked up the microphone.

"Unit 224 to 9-base." Hart heard slight crackling, then a voice.

"Go ahead, 224," the voice said.

"Unit 224 is out of service for lunch, 9-base," Hart said.

"Out of service, Roger, 224."

"224 out," Hart concluded, and hung up the microphone. She turned to Novak. "I've never been here before," she said. "So, can I assume it's good food?"

"The best," Novak said. "I know O.C. comes here a lot, but he wasn't working with you in this sector very much."

Both officers exited the cruiser, and started toward the door of the restaurant. Novak stopped before entering. "What did you and O.C. do for lunches?"

"We'd usually eat out one or two times a week; the rest of the time we packed."

"Sounds like a good system," Novak replied. "We can just agree on one day what we'll do the next day." Novak turned again toward the door. "First day is on me."

Novak opened the door, and Steve's eyes opened wide as she took in the rich colors and strong, but delightful smells. She slowed down as she walked in, and Novak glanced at her before smiling. "It's quite an experience, isn't it?" asked Novak.

"That it is," said Hart. She turned around looking at all the walls as she spoke. "But actually, it reminds me of my grandmother's house on Sunday afternoons after church."

"You have no idea how close you got that, Steve," said Novak. "Let's head in and meet the Williams.'" He led the way toward the kitchen, clearing his throat so he wouldn't scare his friends. A clear woman's voice pierced the silence.

"You know, Danny Novak," the voice said, "I already saw you and your partner getting out of your cruiser. It's about time you paid your respects." As she spoke, the woman attached to the voice stepped from beside the oven. She was slightly taller than average and of medium build. About sixty or sixty-five years old, Hart thought. She smiled and approached Novak, giving him a big hug. Novak smiled and returned the hug.

"Yes, Ma'am, Ms. Williams," he said. "You know I always do." He leaned back from the hug, indicating his partner with his hand.

"Ms. Williams, this is Stephanie Hart, a new probationary officer for the department. Steve, Ruth Williams."

Out of habit, Hart stood practically at attention as she smiled at the older woman. She extended her hand, but Ruth Williams looked at Hart's outstretched hand, smiled, then embraced the taller woman in a hug.

"Handshakes don't work here, Child," she said. "Only hugs for Danny's friends. "

"Thank you, Ma'am," said Hart, as she broke the embrace. "I'll remember that." She moved back from the embrace, and was surprised when Ruth Williams took her hand and led both her and Novak to a table in the restaurant. Hart could sense that Ruth Williams was accustomed to being obeyed.

"So, Stephanie," Williams began. "How have you enjoyed Port Angel, and how much of it have you seen?" Ruth Williams' eyes, a deep brown, drew Hart in.

"Ms. Williams, I've seen a lot of it, though I can't say I know it very well yet," Hart said. She looked up at her FTO, who seemed to be enjoying the exchange. "But I think Danny is going to show me a lot more during this rotation."

"He'd better," the older woman said. "That's something he has to do if we're going to keep this city together." Williams noticed Hart's puzzled reaction and added, "That may take you awhile to understand, but you will."

"I look forward to it, Ma'am," Hart said, as she returned the smile.

Ruth Williams turned again to Novak. "Danny, what do you think we ought to cook up for Stephanie, here?"

"That's up to you, Ms. Williams," Novak said. " When have I ever been able to order and get exactly what I ask for?"

"Now I know you don't mean that, Danny," Ruth Williams said. Williams looked again at Stephanie. "Is there anything you don't eat, Stephanie, like red meat or dairy -- anything?"

"No, Ma'am," Hart replied. "I was telling Danny that your place smells just like my grandmother's on Sunday afternoon."

Williams smiled at the comparison.

"You know, Ms. Williams," Novak said. "One thing Stephanie really should have is your cornbread, if you have some made."

At this, Hart sat back. "And I'm sure I'd love it Ms. Williams, but I can't eat too much cornbread before it goes right to my hips."

Williams laughed. "I understand, she said. "Tell you what -- just try it this time. You'll be surprised how light it is."

"Sounds good to me," Hart said.

"Good," said Williams. Glancing back at Novak, she added, "And since Danny has seen fit not to make any other suggestions, I'll just make up something for the both of you." She rose and turned to the kitchen

"Thank you, Ms. Williams," Hart said. Ruth Williams returned to the kitchen and Novak and Hart could hear the sounds of pans and spoons.

Hart looked back at her partner. "There must be a story here between the two of you," she said.

"Not really," Novak replied. I mean, *some* I guess. The fact is, I've known Ms. Williams all my life. I grew up about six blocks from here, and my parents would often come by and pick up food from the Williams' when they didn't want to cook." He smiled at the memory. "We were probably the only Irish Catholic family who that collard greens on Thanksgiving and sweet potato pie instead of pumpkin."

Hart laughed. "Well not surprisingly, that's what my family *always* had, notwithstanding my Dad's side of the family. I didn't even know pumpkin pie was a real thing until I went into the Army; I thought it was just something people talked about in old stories."

"And," Novak added, suddenly more serious. "I come in here for both the food *and* to get a pulse on the neighborhood." He sat forward again. "The Williams' are leaders in Lexington, and theirs is one of those businesses that *everybody* patronizes. If something bad is brewing around here, they hear about it early, and always let us -- usually me -- know about it."

"'Salt of the Earth' people?"

"Exactly," Novak said. "Kind, very loving, and supportive of the neighborhood even as it's been hit so hard by drugs and other stupid shit."

"So very much a part of *your* city?"

Hart's eyes twinkled as she spoke, and Novak caught the sentiment.
"Yes," he said. "And they can always help me re-center and
remember why I decided to put on this badge." He looked up again.
"Plus the food is out of this world, and at about the most reasonable
cost anywhere. When we eat out, we'll probably do it half the time
here."

"Given how everything smells here, that works for me."

Just then, Ruth Williams came out of the kitchen, carrying a tray
with two plates of food and glasses of water. She placed them on the
table in front of Novak and Hart, noting the officers' reactions.
"Yes," Williams said. "You can take some home in boxes." She
turned to Hart, adding, "But make sure you taste the cornbread first."

"Happy to, Ma'am," Hart said.

Williams sat down and was serious for a moment. "You know,
Stephanie, Danny talks a lot about what people do for him, but not
much about what he does for everybody else." Hart glanced briefly
at Novak and saw him begin to blush.

Williams continued. "Danny has helped our son Harold stay on the
right path through high school and now at college, and it's given
Harold the strength and support he needed."

"You can pay it forward or pay it back," Novak said quietly. "It
really doesn't make any difference. We're all family, and we have
to help each other."

Williams clicked her tongue as she shook her head. "If only more
people felt that way," she said. She turned again and addressed
Stephanie. "You learn from him, Stephanie," said Williams. "We
need more police like Danny in Port Angel."

Hart looked at her partner -- still red around the face and neck and
said, "I'll do that, Ma'am."

Chapter Five

The ceiling lights were down low as Louis Gray always liked them. He lifted his hand from his desk, rubbing his smooth head before setting his eyes again on the four men seated in front of him. They could tell by his demeanor and by how slowly he was speaking that he was not happy. He looked directly at Emilio Cabral, his main lieutenant, but his words were meant for all four.

"You are not bringing me good news, gentlemen," Gray said. "How are we going to grow this business if we can't get these low level dealers to work for us?"

Cabral opened his mouth to speak but was cut off by Gray.

"I'll tell you when it's time for you to speak Emilio," Gray snapped. He surveyed the four men in front of him again. "We are trying to keep ourselves strong, and all I hear is how we don't have the strength to stop a few little piss ant dealers from working our territory." Gray leaned forward in his chair. "Is that what you're telling me?" Shifting his eyes once again to Cabral, he asked again. "Do you have a new plan, Griffin? Something that will work this time?

"Yes sir," Cabral said. He gestured with his hands to his companions. "We talked about that before coming to see you. Pepe said that we should take out a few of them in a big way, like in a drive by outside of our territory, so they know that we own everything." Cabral licked his lips as he finished speaking.

"Is that the best you could come up with?" Gray asked, annoyed. "A drive-by?" He stood quickly. "We are not trying to hurt innocents, gentlemen," he said. "We are running a business, and the last thing we want to do is to bring the wrong kind of attention to our operation. If we want to target one of these stupid independents, we have to do so without anyone else getting hurt *and* staying under the radar of the gang unit."

"Now, do you think you could handle something as precise as that?"

"Yes, sir," Cabral began, sounding hurt. "We can handle that, and that's what we were talking about." Surveying his companions once again, he added, "We just think it needs to be public enough that other guys sit up and take notice, you know, to shock them into either giving up or joining us."

Gray let out a slow breath. "Well, that is wise, I suppose." Gray turned and looked out the window again. "The only way we can grow this operation and change how we distribute is to get the small operators out of our way. Our partners in Texas and Arizona are not interested in working with a tiny operation, and if we don't grow, we don't eat, understood?" A chorus of "Yes, sirs," followed. Gray turned again to his lieutenants, then sat down behind his desk.

"You say that, but I don't think you understand what we're trying to accomplish," Gray began. "We are bringing opportunity and clean operations to what has been a very messy business. The Spino and Parker gangs have made a mess of the drug business in this city, and we are going to clean it up."

"Why are we talking about them?" Ricky Sayles asked "I thought we had agreed to leave each other alone, you know, to divide up the city." He looked to his companions for support. "I mean, we already have the biggest territory, right?" A few of his fellow lieutenants gave non-committal nods. Sayles turned to face Gray again. "Cobra, don't I have that right?" Sayles was almost pleading now.

"Calm down, Ricky," said an exasperated Gray. "You should know enough by now to realize that business is business." He pressed his thumb and forefinger to his temples, then raised his head again. "The agreement with Spino and Parker is in force now, but no agreement is forever," said Gray. "Our new operation will expand our territory so that it is practically all of Port Angel. That will allow us to keep our prices where they need to be so our dealers can get the percentage we want them to have." He nodded as if agreeing with himself. "It's all about the business model gentlemen, and empowering our people so they want to stay with us rather than work with anyone else. Let's be honest. Spino and Parker couldn't take us on now if they tried. We're just making it happen a little faster that it would have anyway."

While he didn't want to respond, Cabral, as Gray's primary lieutenant felt compelled. "Are we going to take on both of those gangs, sir?"

Gray leaned forward as he answered. "Only if you -- *all of you* -- can make it happen," he replied. "We can't continue to have those groups make the drug trade a nasty and uneven business. We're going to fix it, which will benefit everyone." Looking each of his people in the eye in turn, he continued. "Are each of you ready to make that happen?"

Stunned though they were, each of the lieutenants nodded their assent.

After they did so, Gray sat back again with a slight smile. Good," he said. "Now, perhaps I have given you the idea that taking them out will be easy; it will not, but I know that they could never take us on. Eventually, we'll be in control of the trafficking in this city and can finally bring some order to it." He looked in their eyes again. "What other obstacles do we have?" He turned to Cabral.

"Emilio?" Gray asked.

Cabral was silent for a moment before speaking. "Well, we have several cops in Lexington and Auburn who make it tough for our people." Gray made an impatient gesture.

"We don't take out police, Emilio," Gray said, dismissively. "We're neither barbarians nor stupid. What else do you have?"

"There are a couple of churches, especially Greater AME Zion that's always trying to get our people to repent or some such shit," Cabral said contemptuously. "And I don't want to take out a damn preacher either, but he's making it tough for us."

"I agree," said Gray. "But as you say, taking out a preacher is more trouble than it's worth. Gray nodded his head slowly. "And I think his influence isn't what he thinks it is, anyway. But you're right, Emilio, we would be in far better shape if Greater AME Zion would focus on souls and feeding the homeless rather than on our business.

Silent up until now, Tommy Burch spoke up. He was a tall burly man, with sandy brown hair. "We're still trying to get Harold Williams to give us some time, Sir."

"Ugh." Gray said. "We've been trying to enlist Williams for years, Tommy, and he is almost more trouble than he's worth." Gray gave a cool smile. "Now *him* I would like to take out." His eyes widened slightly then returned to their regular size. "But as I think about it, his parents are a bigger problem than he is. I can just imagine the trouble they'd make for us if we did something to Harold."

"Ricky," Cabral interrupted. "Who was working on Williams to get him to chill?"

Sayles thought for a moment. "I think it was T-Wright, but he is kinda young."

"Then get somebody else to do it," said Cabral, then realizing where he was, turned again to Gray. "That okay?"

"Yes, Emilio," said Gray. "Is there any weakening of Williams, or are we just wasting our time?"

"I can't say," Cabral said. "We don't seem to be able to find a hook to make him roll."

Gray listened carefully. "Well, Emilio," he said. "That may be the first honest thing you've told me all day. Now," he continued, "Perhaps we need to help T-Wright with this assignment." He turned to Sayles. "Ricky," he began. "Who else can work with T-Wright? Does he need more support -- maybe some instruction?"

"Do you mean hurt him or something?"

"No," Gray replied. "We don't need to hurt our own people. What I mean is, does he know how to persuade Harold; how to talk to him so Harold is less likely to make things difficult for him -- or us?"

"I think so," Sayles replied.

"Keep working on that angle, Ricky," Gray finally said. "Because I am becoming impatient with Harold Williams. Maybe the best we can hope for is to shut him up so he doesn't get in the way, rather than have to take him out." Gray noticed vigorous head nodding from Pepe Brantley and Tommy Burch, and turned to face them. "Comments, gentlemen?" he asked.

Brantley and Burch stiffened immediately. "Sorry, sir," said Brantley.

"Sorry for...?" Gray answered, amusement in his voice.

"Sorry, for, um, I mean..." Brantley paused and took a breath. "I think we need to find some way for Harold to decide it doesn't make any sense to work against us. I don't think he's ever going to work for us, Boss."

Gray gave a small smile. "Again, I think you are correct, Pepe. So our plan is to find a way to go around him."

"What about his parents, sir?" asked Cabral. "They're even tougher and they're always making trouble for us and our people."

"It's all that holier than thou shit they're always doing," Burch agreed. "They keep trying to make trouble for us, and I'm sick of it."

Gray raised his hand to silence Burch. "Patience, Tommy," he said. "At some time, the Williams' will be taken care of." The four lieutenants were silent again, and looked with puzzlement at their boss, who only smiled. "Everything in its time, gentlemen," Gray said. "I will develop a strategy for the Williams family that should quiet them. But you're right -- we need to tread lightly around them. They have far more influence in this city than I would like, and they also seem to have support from far too many police, and we haven't been able to quiet or neutralize them."

Cabral cleared his throat. "Getting to the cops isn't easy either, Boss."

"Agreed, Emilio," said Gray. "But even the police are vulnerable."

Gray smiled again. "As I said, gentlemen," he repeated. "All in its time."

Chapter Six

0700 hours saw Hart, Novak and other officers on the early shift facing Capt. Shoemaker and Lt. Samuel Perkins, Chief of Detectives for the 9th Precinct. As Hart sat down, she saw a police academy colleague, Susan Elliott, who was with O. C. Boyd for her final probationary rotation. Elliott didn't look to Hart to be very happy. After the pledge of allegiance, Capt. Shoemaker called the session to order.

"Alright people," Shoemaker said. "We have a lot to go over today, and the bad guys aren't going to wait for us." Shoemaker looked around, recognizing that he said the same thing almost every day -- yet no one seemed to mind. He continued, pointing to the screen at the front of the room. "Two major incidents occurred last night. "Armed robbery at the Quick Stop on Montgomery. Only eyewitness was the clerk, and he was too scared shitless to be of much help. According to the responding officers, the description was too generic to be of much help either, but it was…" he looked down and checked his notes… "a white male, probably middle twenties, with a very big semi-automatic pistol. The clerk described the pistol very well, perhaps because that's what he was focusing on."

Shoemaker flipped the pages of his notes. "Second major issue are BOLOs. Take a look at the three at your seats…." Shoemaker continued in the same vein, noting crimes that had occurred over the previous 24 hours, and indicating how he wanted the precinct to respond to them.

After reviewing several crimes and suspects to watch for, he called Lt. Samuel Perkins to the front. Perkins was a very tall Black man of about 44 who had been a Master at Arms in the Navy. He crossed to the podium and turned to face the officers. "Good morning, people," his voice boomed. "This is just another day in the neighborhood." The group chuckled lightly. "What I want to let you know about are a series of burglaries that started in Auburn and have extended throughout the city, and more recently in Saxon Hill."

Perkins could sense the changing mood of the group. O.C. Boyd's hand shot up.

"O.C.?" said Perkins.

"Just to be clear, Perk," began Boyd, "we're supposed to really work hard now that they've started hitting Saxon Hill, right?" The assembled officers laughed. Boyd had made his point.

"Not exactly, O.C. and you know that," said Perkins. "But if you're asking if the pressure just hit a new high -- yes." Perkins turned to face the entire group again. "I'm going to review what we know so far from the officer and detective reports. I'd like you all to be the eyes and ears out there, because the detectives believe that this is a very organized band, and someone's bound to have loose lips." Perkins looked on the podium for a clicker, found it, and turned to face the screen. He reviewed characteristics of the burglaries and the similarities that led the detectives to believe they were committed by the same group.

"Their hauls have been large enough and in such a short period of time that we're sure there are at least two of them, probably more."

Turning to her partner, Hart whispered, "That doesn't make any sense. Who works houses in such different places?"

As Hart finished, she looked up and noticed Perkins looking directly at her. "Something to add, Hart?" he asked.

Hart fought the urge to stand at attention, but managed, a "No, sir. Sorry sir." to Perkins' question.

Perkins momentarily turned his attention to Novak, who had raised his hand. "Yes, Novak," said the Lieutenant.

"Lieutenant, it seems really strange for anybody to burglarize homes in Lexington *and* Saxon Hill, don't you think? I mean, it doesn't seem like many people patronize both neighborhoods, if you know what I mean."

"We do, Danny," said Perkins. "On the other hand, the methods, professionalism, etc., suggest they're by the same people. But we are considering the possibility that they're not." Perkins' attention turned briefly to Hart, then to the rest of the officers. "Other thoughts about this?" Seeing none, Perkins said, "Thanks, Danny" and continued with his report.

The officers were dismissed at 0721, and both Hart and Novak rose from their seats. Hart faced Novak and said quickly. "Thanks, Danny."

"No problem, partner," said Novak. "But the lieutenant would have been happy to hear it from you."

"Perhaps," said Hart. "But I didn't want to push it."

As they turned to leave the muster room and go on patrol, Susan Elliott appeared in from of Hart. "Hey, Steve," said Elliott. "Everything going well?"

"Absolutely, Susan," Hart said. She glanced at Boyd who wasn't paying attention to her or Elliott. "Though I imagine you're questioning lots of things about yourself right now."

"I am," Elliott agreed, rolling her eyes. "And while I can handle it, I'm really looking forward to completing probation and getting my own cruiser."

"You and me both, sister," said Hart, adding, "but I think this is going to be a much better rotation for me, so I'm not complaining."

Elliott looked over to Novak and held out her hand. "Susan Elliott," she said.

Novak shook her hand. "Danny Novak," he said. "Stephanie is my first probationary officer."

Elliott smiled. "Does that mean you're going to be extra hard on her?"

"Maybe," Novak said. "We haven't figured out that part yet."

Just then, they heard the loud voice of O.C. Boyd. "Elliott, think you're ready to go now?" Boyd asked. "We have work to do."

Elliott look quickly to both Hart and Novak, saying "Just girl talk, Sgt. -- you know."

Both Hart and Novak smiled.

Boyd stepped up to the group looking at both Hart and Novak, adding, "Yeah, talking to Novak, definitely girl talk." he said. "Certainly not like talking to Stephie here." Hart managed not to react at all, but continued smiling.

"Time to go, Elliott," said Boyd, and both he and Elliott turned toward the door of the muster room.

As they left, Hart called out to her friend. "Eyes on the prize, sister," she said. "Eyes on the prize."

Chapter Seven

The woman in blue strode confidently to the reception desk of the precinct. As she approached, Kat Neely the receptionist, greeted her with a smile. "Hi, Sheryl," Neely said. "What brings you here?"

"Just heading to a site visit, and thought I'd stop by and see if Danny had gone out yet." She looked beyond the reception desk toward the squad room. "Is he still here?"

"Let me see," Neely said checking her display. "They finished muster about 10 minutes ago, so he and Hart should still be here." She looked up at Sheryl Novak. "Have you met Stephanie yet?"

"No, but Danny has talked about her a lot in the last couple of weeks; sounds like she's some kind of supercop."

"Well, not exactly," Neely said. "But she is pretty impressive; strong, confident, very tough." Neely paused. "I want to be just like her when I grow up."

Sheryl laughed. "Oh no, Kat," she said. "You stay just the way you are." Looking toward the squad room, she added, "Can I go on back?"

Neely waved her through. "The squad room is yours." And Sheryl Novak went through the double doors.

* * *

Hart and Novak were just preparing to go on patrol, when Hart heard a loud greeting at the entrance to the squad room.

"Sheryl!" exclaimed one officer. "Danny let you come down and see us again?"

"Not hardly, Mike," Sheryl Novak said. "More like I needed to come down and keep him in line." Sheryl turned to another officer and said, "Hey, Carson. How's that little one?"

Carson Poole gave Sheryl a small hug. "Doing well, Sheryl," Poole said. "Thanks for that book you sent. It's so much fun watching him play with all the pieces."

"Plus, the idea is that he'll grow into it," Sheryl replied. "Glad you like it, Carson."

As Sheryl was speaking, Danny approached her and waited for her to turn in his direction. Hart followed at a distance. She had been surprised by how well the officers seemed to know Sheryl Novak. Sheryl was a relatively small woman, perhaps 5' 3,"and seemed very energetic. Hart knew from Danny that Sheryl Novak was the head children's librarian for the library system, and she could easily see Sheryl Novak sitting on the floor interacting with eager young children.

"Hey Babe," Danny said, as he hugged his wife, "You checking up on me?"

Sheryl returned the hug and briefly made eye contact with Hart, then she returned her gaze to her husband. "Nope," Sheryl replied. "I have a site visit at the Lexington Branch this morning and thought I'd stop by on the way." Sheryl tilted her head toward Hart, adding, "You *are* going to introduce me to your new girlfriend, aren't you?"

Danny laughed as he turned to face Hart, saying, "Sheryl, this is Stephanie Hart, my probationary officer." Then he added, "Steve, you can obviously tell this is my wife, Sheryl."

Hart sized up Sheryl quickly, and decided to have fun, as she extended her hand. "How I can be sure you're not just another one of his girlfriends?"

"Uh-oh," said Sheryl. "You're sassy. Danny likes sassy, so now I really do have to watch my back." Looking quickly at Hart's outstretched hand, she added, "I'm a hugger, Stephanie," and she quickly embraced the taller woman. Hart, a little stunned, returned the hug with a bewildered look on her face. Sheryl broke the hug then stepped back, saying to her husband, "Got a few minutes before going on patrol?"

"I think so," he said. He looked toward the small galley. "And we have two new officers who can actually make coffee. I'll get some for all of us."

As he moved off, Sheryl Novak and Stephanie Hart sat at chairs set at the corner of the central table. Normally a somewhat reserved person, Hart felt genuine warmth from Sheryl Novak, and was immediately comfortable with her. Not surprisingly, it was Sheryl who started the conversation.

"Danny's said you're a shoe-in to glide through probation," Sheryl said. "He thinks you're really good."

Hart smiled, though was a bit embarrassed. "That's nice to know. Danny is like the man-about-town officer; everybody knows him and everybody likes him, and he seems really good at this job."

At hearing this, Sheryl smiled. "And he was really excited to have the chance to be an FTO for the first time." Sheryl leaned forward. "And he clearly thinks he hit a home run with you."

"I feel the same way," Hart replied. "And after my previous FTO, Danny is a welcome change."

Sheryl said quietly, "I know O. C, and while he's a good cop, I can see what you mean." Sheryl noticed Hart squinting a bit at her face, then returning her face to normal. "What," Sheryl asked. She used her hand to touch her face and hair. "Is there something on my face?"

"Sorry Sheryl," Hart reassured her. "I was just looking at your makeup. Is it Bare Naturals?"

"Yes!" Sheryl exclaimed. "How did... oh!" She placed her face against Hart's looking at Danny and calling to him. "Look! We're sisters, Honey!"

Hart laughed despite herself. Sheryl sat back in her chair and looked at Stephanie again. "Oh, we have some things to do, Stephanie, and if you haven't discovered the Eclipse Spa, I have to take you there. They have the best prices on Bare Naturals anywhere."

"I'd like that, Sheryl," said Hart. She paused, then added, "And, my friends call me 'Steve.'"

"I knew that," said Sheryl. "but thanks for letting me in. Oh, and before I forget, we're having a barbeque on Saturday that you just have to come to."

Hart took a breath, suppressing the desire to say "No," and instead said, "That sounds like fun, Sheryl. Thanks"

As Danny Novak returned to the table with three cups of coffee, Sheryl turned to Hart again. "And," she began," I'll let you know all the ways you can handle Danny."

Hart smiled again. "How can I say no?"

Chapter Eight

The doorbell rang just as Danny Novak was checking on the wood for his wood fired grill. Remembering that his wife was cutting up food in the kitchen, he answered the bell.

"I got it, Babe!" he said, as he headed toward the front door. Opening it, he was surprised to see Stephanie Hart standing there, wearing shorts and a white tank top that showed off her bronze skin. She wore her thick wavy her hair out and was carrying a bowl containing what looked like a dessert. Novak only stared for about 3 or 4 seconds before recovering.

"Hey, Steve," he said. "I almost didn't know you with your hair out -- which probably says more about me than about you."

"I understand, Danny," said Hart, as she entered the house. "Something tells me Sheryl didn't tell you I was coming over early to help out."

"Right," said Novak. "She didn't, but that's fine." He reached out to take the dessert. "We can always use a little help." Motioning with his head, he pointed toward the kitchen. "Follow me to the kitchen. Guess who just showed up, Sheryl?"

Sheryl looked up and smiled at Hart. "Hey Steve!" she said, and she reached out to hug Stephanie with just her arms, her hands still dirty from cutting up food. She stole a glance at Danny and evaluated his face. "Oh," she said. "I guess I didn't tell you Steve was coming by early."

Danny held up his hands, palms out. "Hey, it's not a problem for me, Sheryl," he said. "I kind of like Steve." He looked out toward the patio. "But ladies, you're going to have to excuse me. I have to head out to the man place and get ready to burn meat." With that, Danny left the kitchen to Sheryl and Steve.

Hart stepped back to assess the kitchen, and asked, "What can I do?"

"Well, if you can keep cutting up the veggies, I'm going to make the deviled eggs."

"Done," Hart said. She looked quickly for an apron, found one and put it on. Then she took up a knife, checked out the vegetables and began cutting. As she started, Sheryl continued their conversation.

"Thanks for coming early, Steve," Sheryl said. "We're going to be fine, but there's always one more thing, you know?"

Hart nodded. "I do -- and it's really no problem. I like this kinda stuff."

As they worked in companionable silence, Hart asked "So, how did you and Danny meet?"

"Well, that's kind of a long story, but..." she paused, smiling. "Well, the upshot is that we met when Danny was just finishing his probationary period, just trading in his blue shield for a silver one. Oddly enough, he came into the library for something. He was in uniform and I noticed that his badge was *really* shiny." She chuckled. "It was obviously new, so I checked him out."

"And apparently you liked what you saw?"

"I did, and still do," Sheryl said.

"But aren't you both from Port Angel? I guess I assumed you knew each other before hand."

"We are both locals, but from different sides of town. Danny likes to say that he's from the wrong side of the tracks, and while I can't say that I was from the *right* side of the tracks, I had it a whole lot easier than Danny did growing up."

"Danny's implied more than once that his upbringing wasn't the easiest."

"Well, I don't mean to say that his family isn't great," Sheryl said, "because they are, but it was rough growing up in Auburn then, and even now. He had to watch his back and had to make the decision to follow the right path." She looked up pensively. "His family gave him all the right tools, and he always said making the right choices was easy, but if you know the people who grew up when he did, you know a lot of them also had good parents who gave them the right stuff, and they made very different choices. Danny is in some ways pretty special -- and everybody knows it."

"I can see that about him, since we started working together." She smiled. "It's been an interesting few weeks."

"I'll bet," Sheryl said. Then she got quiet again. "There's ... something else I wanted to talk to you about, Steve."

Hart noticed the change in Sheryl's demeanor, and put down her knife. "What's up?"

Sheryl looked down before answering. "It's nothing really, but just…" She exhaled again, then looked Hart squarely in the eye, which caused Hart to straighten up. "Steve," Sheryl continued, "I need you to be strong. I need Danny to be with people he can depend on, and who will have his back. Do you know what I mean?"

Hart touched Sheryl's arm. "I do, Sheryl," she said. "And believe me when I say that I have it." She took a breath before continuing. "I've got a little experience in having my partner's back, especially in the MPs. It's a reflex now, and I'm going to make sure my partner is always covered."

Sheryl listened, reflected on what Hart said, then squeezed Hart's hand on her arm. "I know I'm probably being a bit dramatic, Steve, but it's important." She looked up at Hart again and seemed to relax. "Something else," added Sheryl. "Danny asked me to make sure you stick around for a while."

"Uhm…"

Sheryl continued. "Danny asked me to help you stay around because you're a good cop and *his* city needs more good cops."

Hart smiled. "That is my plan, Sheryl."

Chapter Nine

Preparations for the barbeque continued, and eventually, the Novak's other guests arrived. They were Jamila and Gary Stokes, along with Paula and Arnie Chase all longtime friends of Danny Novak. The only other unmarried person in attendance was Jim Freeman, an officer from Danny's police academy class who worked in the 7th Precinct. Before Freeman arrived, Sheryl stressed to Hart that Freeman was not invited to set her up with a date: he was actually engaged to be married, but his fiancée was out of town. However, Freeman was a former MP, and the Novaks felt that connection would make Hart feel even more comfortable with the group.

The Novak's needn't have worried. All the guests were friendly, and while they mingled over drinks, Hart found she had lots in common with them. Jamila Stokes had roots on the east coast as she did, and Arnie Chase practiced martial arts, and he further recommended a combined martial arts dojo he thought Hart should check out.

The conversations were low stress and pleasant, until Danny and Gary Stokes started talking about baseball, a passion for both of them. Stokes had played minor league ball for a short while after high school and before college, and both he and Danny were big fans of the local minor league team, the Port Angel Sparks. In fact, they spoke very little about major league baseball at all. While not a huge sports fan, Hart enjoyed the family atmosphere of minor league stadiums and she was perfectly happy to attend a game at the local stadium when Gary Stokes suggested it as the next outing of the group. That outing would also introduce Hart to Jim Freeman's fiancée.

It was something of a surprise that Hart and Freeman hadn't spoken much about the Army until the group had finished dessert and was relaxing on the patio with coffee. "Steve, Danny told me you were an MP for a bunch of years," Freeman said. "How have you found the transition?"

"It's been pretty good, though it's not exactly fun starting at the bottom again." She looked at Freeman again. "What was your final grade?"

"E-6," said Freeman. "I was in for 10 years before I resigned."

"Right," said Hart. "I was an E-7, so while I'm making more money now, 'bye-bye' to those nice on-post benefits."

Freeman laughed. "I hear you," he said. "That *did* make a difference. But I'm happy here -- it's a really nice place to live."

"Amen to that, brother," Arnie Chase agreed. "If you were to have asked me in college if I would ever live here, I would have said you were crazy." He turned to Paula. "But there's something about this place that draws you back in.

I agree," said Danny.

Arnie humphed. "Oh hell, Danny," he began, "How would you know? You've never been out of the damn city." Arnie shook his head. "Sometimes I think you ought to run for mayor or something."

"Please God, no," said Sheryl. "That's one thing we *don't* need to be thinking about."

Danny sat up straight in mock anger. "What? You don't think I'd make a good mayor?"

"You'd make a great mayor, Danny," Sheryl replied. "And I'd be an even better First Lady, but that's not the point. You should focus on just saving the people in the precinct, since you're already the young Daddy for everyone."

Hart laughed. "Oh, you've got his number, alright," she said. "Even some of the old-timers look up to Danny. It's kind of strange."

"Which reminds me," Freeman interjected. "You would have been a platoon sergeant, right?"

"Yep," said Hart.

"So probably everybody's 'Mom?'"

"Oh yeah," Hart agreed. "And that did seem to be the case for young and old troops alike." Hart and Freeman briefly reflected on their shared experiences, before Freeman looked up questioningly.

"I don't want this to be an MP 'old home week,' but I never asked you where you are stationed. I was mostly in Korea, a little bit in Iraq and for a short while in Germany," Freeman offered. "Stateside I was stationed at Hood and Meade."

"My travels aren't too far different from yours," Hart said. "Though I never went to Korea, I was at Hood about 6 years ago, as I remember." She leaned forward. "Maybe I left the Army because I just couldn't take the Texas summers."

"You got that right," said Freeman, laughing. "In fact it was sometime around then that I decided I wanted to get out. Though I have to say I really liked being an MP."

"Me too," said Hart. "Especially my time in Germany. The people were really nice and welcoming, and we got involved in Anspach during the tornado doing some relief and rescue work. That may have been when I first started to think about either the national guard or civilian police work -- or both," she reflected.

"You were in Anspach during the hurricane?" Freeman asked, suddenly more interested.

"Yes," said Hart. She was going to add more but Freeman continued.

"Then you must have been in the 17th, right?"

Hart was surprised Freeman knew her unit designation so easily. "Yes. Why? Were you there then as well?" She watched as Freeman's reaction changed from excitement to one approaching -- disgust?

"No," he began. "It's just that I have a former cousin who was in the 17th." Everyone was intrigued, but Danny spoke first.

"Jim, how do you have a 'former' cousin?" he asked.

Freeman took a breath before continuing. "Well, former because I don't have anything to do with him now." Seeing the interest of his friends, Freeman sought to change the subject quickly. "Look, the fact is that he refused to support a fellow MP when...." then he stopped. He looked up at Hart, and could see just enough in her face to know. Looking directly at her, Freeman continued. "The fact is my former cousin didn't support a fellow MP when that person really needed it. You have to know that your colleagues have your back, just the way we do as cops or firefighters for that matter. If my cousin couldn't support somebody in the toughest of situations, like this one, he is no cousin of mine." Freeman's voice was resolute, and Hart could sense his sincerity. Clearly, he *knew*.

"But enough about family," Freeman said. "Can't live with them, can't live without them." Turning to Paula Chase, he continued. "Which reminds me Paula, how is your sister doing in her doctoral program?"

Paula Chase began answering Freeman's questions, and with the attention on someone other than her, Hart relaxed again. She thought briefly about what she would need to tell Danny -- if anything -- if he asked about her time in Germany, but thought she would take care of that when it happened and not dwell on it. She didn't realize that Danny Novak had picked up on the quick exchange between Freeman and Hart and knew there were some important things about Stephanie Hart that he still needed to know.

Chapter Ten

Physical and self-defense training is required twice a year for Port Angel Police department officers. Novak and Hart were assigned to complete their training along with several other officers from the 9th. They arrived together in Novak's pride and joy vintage Chevy Nova, both wearing sweatpants. As they walked toward the secure entrance, Hart turned to Novak.

"Are we going to have Turner again?" she asked. "He's really a jerk to work with."

"Yes, and yes," Novak said. "He's the primary physical and self defense trainer for the department." Turning to Hart he added, "What -- is there bad blood between the two of you?"

"Not really, since the work we did at the academy wasn't too hard. In fact, it was only the basics, so as long as we all did what we were told to do, we were fine." Hart shivered. "He's just arrogant, and I'm not convinced he's as good as everybody thinks he is."

"Don't let him hear you say that."

"Oh no," Hart replied. "I'm not *that* stupid."

After scanning their IDs at the entrance, Novak and Hart entered to see several officers from the 9th waiting inside. Like Hart and Novak, they were wearing sweat suits, most with the PAPD logo. One of Danny's best friends, Angela Marin, was the first to greet the pair."

"Danny, Stephanie," Marin said. "Nice to have you join us."

"Hi, Gee," Novak said. He looked at the other two officers: Elaine Simpson, a 7 year veteran and Mick Canady who was about a year past probation. "What does joining mean?" Novak asked.

"We've been teamed up," said Marin. "I think it's us five and O.C." Upon hearing Boyd's name, both Canady and Hart shook their heads.

"Does this mean we can brain him and not get into trouble?" asked Canady.

"No such luck, Canuck," Simpson said. "Everything we do everywhere counts. Plus, I wouldn't worry about it; O.C. is fair in things like this for whatever reason."

"Is he here yet?" asked Novak.

"Well, I was the first of us here, and I haven't seen him yet," Simpson offered.

After this exchange, Novak introduced Hart to the other officers, most of whom she didn't know. Hart had spent a little time with Canady when she first started her probationary period, since he was an Iraq war veteran and actually knew of her while in the Army. While not a strong bond, it was a bond nonetheless. As they were talking, several other officers from both the 9th and other precincts came in, including Boyd. Boyd checked the grouping listing then turned to his fellow officers from the 9th.

"What have we here, people?" Boyd asked. "Are we gonna impress our favorite training instructor today?" Something in his tone surprised Hart.

"Is there something special behind those words, Sgt?" she asked.

"Nothing for you to worry about Hart," Boyd answered.

"Meaning?" asked Simpson.

"Meaning Simpson," continued Boyd, "That I think of him in exactly the same way that you all do." This surprised several of the officers.

"Again, O.C.," began Novak. "Meaning?"

Boyd leaned toward the other officers. "Well, if you must know, that arrogant son of a bitch got me in a headlock one time and I needed physical therapy for weeks afterwards." Hart could see that Boyd was genuinely angry. "There are lots of ways to teach, and I think he takes the whole 'sensei' thing too far." Boyd stood more erect again. "Now, can we just get through this, and go home?"

No one answered, but all of them agreed.

Ten minutes later, the group from the 9th was inside the training hall with two other groups, from the 4th and 7th precincts, groups varying in size from 6 to 8. The instructor, Alan Turner, was a burly man of about 45, wearing gi pants and a t shirt than emphasized his impressive physique. He strutted into the hall and gave perfunctory greetings to the senior officers there, including Boyd. Boyd returned the greeting, but anyone could see that his heart wasn't in it.

"We're going to refresh some of your skills today and teach you a few new ones for escape and for subduing suspects so we can ensure everyone's safety," Turner said. "You're already in groups, so pair off and let's review some of our current techniques.

Turner announced and demonstrated some of the basic techniques on "volunteers," then had the officers perform them. Hart noticed that Angela Marin, while competent, wasn't so confident with her techniques, and needed slight corrections to be more successful.

"Wait a minute, Angela," Hart said. "You should be keeping your arm bent more on this so you have more control."

After telling Hart that everybody called her "Gee," Marin listened to Hart, and tried the move with her arm more bent, but she turned her body the wrong way.

"Hold on, Gee," Hart said. "Remember that you don't want…."

"Excuse me, officer?" boomed the voice of Turner, directed at Hart. "I don't remember seeing you at the certification class last month."

"No, sir," Hart began. "I was j…."

"Right," Turner continued, "That is *Probationary Officer* Hart as I recall. You're not even a regular officer yet Hart, so let me take care of the instruction, alright?"

"Yes sir," Hart said. "Sorry, sir." And she immediately backed off. Her face showed no anger, just a blank expression, though Novak noticed that she was standing on the balls of her feet, which surprised him.

The training continued and Turner introduced newer takedown techniques that involved locking the elbow. Hart mastered the technique easily, as did many of the other officers, but again, Marin was having trouble, probably due to her size and body mechanics. Marin stopped working with Novak temporarily to watch Hart take down Canady.

"Stephanie," Marin said. "Could you do that one more time? I want to see it again."

"Sure," Hart said, "watch my dominant -- I mean -- right hand," and with that, she and Canady performed the move, with Canady advancing, and Hart holding his fist close to her body before executing the elbow lock move with a strong twist of her hips. Canady hit the mat quickly.

As he rose, Canady turned to Marin, saying with a laugh "And yes, she *does* have this move down, Gee."

"I didn't hurt you, did I?"

"Not at all," Canady said. "You just seem very confident and smooth with the move."

Hart laughed and put her hand on her hip. "Well, it helps to actually have hips and know how to use them." She turned to Marin. "And since you have them too, you can be really good at this, Gee."

Marin turned to face Novak and found herself face to face with Turner, who ignored Marin and looked directly at Hart. "Did our last discussion go over your head, Hart?" he asked.

Hart paused briefly before answering. "No, sir," she offered, then stayed silent.

Turner used his hand to gesture at the entire class. "If you feel you can teach this class better than I can, have at it."

"No, sir," Hart repeated, standing almost at attention.

Turner got a nasty smile on his face, and turning again to the entire group, said "Does anybody want to see an object lesson here?" Officers from the other precincts voiced their general assent, but all seem puzzled. Turner faced the group from the 9th. "Are you okay with having me kick the butt of your little probationary officer?"

"You know Alan," Boyd offered. "at 5'9" or whatever, Hart ain't exactly little." Some of the other officers laughed, but it was a tense laughter. When Boyd saw that Turner hadn't changed his stance, he continued, "No reason for this, Alan," he said. "I'll keep her in line for you."

Turner ignored Boyd, and moved toward the center of the room, waving for Hart to follow him. He waited, gestured again, and Hart turned briefly to her compatriots. Novak and Boyd both gave her shrugs as if to say "don't know what else you can do," so Hart removed her sweatshirt, revealing a dark t shirt and moved to the center mat.

Hart bowed to Turner by force of habit. Then, the two officers began circling each other before Turner lunged forward toward Hart's right leg. Hart avoided his grab and tried to grab his left arm, which left her left leg unguarded. Turner quickly grabbed at it, and while she avoided his grab, Hart was off balance, so when Turner took her left arm, he could easily sweep her to the ground. Hart landed safely, slapping out, then rose quickly and bowed to the instructor. Glancing left, she noticed what she thought were disappointed looks on the faces of her group from the 9th. Hart returned to the center mat, and readied herself for the next attack.

Turner lunged again toward Hart, and instead of a close encounter, Hart hopped to her right, and used her left leg to press Turner's knees down so be began to kneel. Hart quickly took Turner's outstretched arm, and keeping it straight and extended, pressed his head down for the point. After one or two seconds, she rose, backed off, then bowed again. Within a second, Turner advanced again, though this time, he concentrated on Hart's arms, since he knew it was unlikely she could match his upper body strength. However, Hart read his right arm as he was advancing, and she side stepped slightly, grabbed his right hand, and closed it into her stomach. Then she twisted her hips and locked Turner's elbow for the takedown. This was the same move she had been performing for Marin when Turner had baited her, and her easy success with the move wasn't lost on the other officers. Again, Hart rose after the point and bowed to Turner.

Turner was more wary for the next encounter with Hart, and decided to take his time. He hopped from side to side so he wouldn't telegraph his attack. Once, he tried to get Hart in a bear hug, but she escaped in time. Turner's second attack was his undoing. Hart had just escaped another attack and was very close to him so Turner tried to encircle her head with his right arm. Hart quickly grabbed his arm, pulled Turner close to her, then placed her hand on his chest and less than a second later, Turner found himself thrown to the ground. He looked up and saw Hart's face a foot above his.

"You know sir, you're really good, and I really don't want to do this again." Some of the officers near Hart and Turner laughed, and Hart leaned down again to Turner so no one could hear her but him.

"I think you ought to know, sir," Hart continued, "that the moves you've been teaching us today are similar to grappling and self-defense moves from Jiu Jitsu and Kenpo karate. I have a fourth degree black belt in Kenpo." She rose from Turner's chest, bowed again, then walked off the mat, allowing Turner to get up himself.

As she returned to her group, Novak said, "You're either really good or an incredibly fast learner."

Hart chuckled, and thought she saw approval on the faces of the officers from the 9th, even Boyd.

Chapter Eleven

Following their training, Hart and Novak went on patrol through both Auburn and Lexington. For lunch, they stopped at Heaven's Home so Novak could introduce Steve to Harold Williams. Harold greeted them as they entered the restaurant.

"Danny," he said, "Mom told me you came in a little while ago with your partner. Harold was a young man in his early twenties, Hart thought. And he favored both his parents in appearance, though he had his father's height.

Hart extended her hand. "Stephanie Hart."

"Harold Williams," Williams said, as he shook Hart's hand. "Mom told me that you're a probationary officer." He cocked his thumb at Novak. "Does that mean he's your boss?"

"You say it like it's a bad thing, Harold," Novak said. "I'll have you know I worked hard for this." His mock anger was funny even to him, and Novak burst out laughing. He turned again to Harold. "You look like you have somewhere to go."

"Yes, I'm one of the youth leaders at the church and we're taking some of the preteens down to the Black History Museum."

"Did you get tickets for the new Underground Railroad exhibit?" Novak asked, excited.

"Yep," Harold replied. "That's the main reason we're going. The kids have mostly already been to the museum, but the new exhibit is incredible."

"Man, it really is," said Novak. "Sheryl and I went a month or so ago with some friends, and we couldn't stop talking about it." He turned to Hart. "You've got to go too, Steve. It's definitely worth the time."

"Sounds good," Hart said. "I'll make sure I get there sometime soon. I've got some distant cousins on my mother's side in Canada whose ancestors escaped using the Underground Railroad. I'd really like to learn more about it."

"Awesome," Harold said. Then he checked the time, and said, "Hey, I really need to be going. The macaroni and cheese is really good today by the way. Danny, good to see you and nice to meet you, Stephanie." Harold went out the front door as his mother entered the dining room from the kitchen.

"Did Harold tell you about the macaroni and cheese?" Ruth asked. She was wiping her hands on her apron as she approached the officers, giving brief hugs to both.

"He did, Ms. Williams," Novak said. "Is there something special we should know about?"

Ruth Williams leaned closer to the officers, saying, "Well, I probably shouldn't tell you, and you can't tell *anyone* else," she admonished, "but we decided to use a little bacon grease in the recipe along with cheese that's a little lower in fat."

"Oh, God," Stephanie said, pressing her stomach. "Ms. Williams, you know I like fitting into my clothes."

"Hush, Child," Williams admonished. "Like I always say, anything in moderation. Set yourselves down and let me fix you both some plates."

While they sat and speculated about what Ruth Williams would bring them, Novak asked Hart about her performance on the training mat earlier that day.

"So Steve," Novak began. "You really cleaned Turner today. Are there any other skills I need to know about?"

Hart looked down at the table. "Don't remind me," she said. "I keep worrying that beating him like that is going to come back to haunt me sooner or later."

"I don't think so," Novak said. "O.C. was there and saw how it all went down. Turner would get in more trouble for challenging you the way he did than you would for kicking his ass. He brought it on himself."

"I hope you're right," Hart said. "I can envision lots of hassle from him, and I still worry about how our next training session will go." Novak thought he saw more to Hart's reaction than she let on, but he let it go, before shifting the discussion.

"So, how long have you been doing martial arts?"

Hart welcomed the change of subject. "About ten years, I guess. I started at my first duty station, and liked it enough that I scoped out all the Kenpo training halls wherever I was stationed, which took some work."

"So you used this stuff throughout the time you were in the Army?" he asked. "That must have come in handy."

Hart shrunk slightly into herself. "You have no... uh yes," she corrected herself. "Always good to have multiple ways to protect yourself when you have to take care of drunk soldiers." Hart smiled again..

"Plus," she added, "I was able to compete in a few tournaments, including the inter-service tournaments that are held all around the world." She was becoming genuinely excited now, and continued. "I've never won a tournament, but I've placed a few times, and got a silver about two years ago in Germany. And sometimes, military personnel would go off post in a group to help run local tournaments, kind of a public service thing. That was really fun." She looked again at her partner. "Martial arts has always been something that helped me connect with other people, and I started going to classes with other black belts here while in the academy."

As she finished speaking, Ruth Williams returned to their table with their plates, piled with moderate helpings of macaroni and cheese, baked flounder and green beans cooked with ham hocks. Williams also brought a basket of corn bread, and followed with two to-go boxes. Conversation ended at the table as Novak and Hart sampled their food and reveled in the wonderful flavor. They agreed with Ruth and Harold Williams about the macaroni and cheese: the bacon grease added a great flavor, and they didn't notice any negative change in flavor because of the lower fat cheese, so they felt they were "justified" in enjoying the brilliant addition of bacon grease.

Novak and Hart had a pleasant conversation with Ruth Williams as they paid their bills, then returned to their cruiser. Novak noticed that Hart had gotten quiet again after they finished their meal, and she moved to the driver's door without even asking or confirming with Novak who would be driving. Novak thought something might be up, so he let her be.

Hart made her vehicle check, then sat back in the driver's seat and reached for the microphone. She picked it up, then after consulting her watch, put in back in the clip. She turned to her partner.

"Side trip, Danny," she said, and Novak nodded.

Hart started the engine, and drove the cruiser to nearby Dolman Park and pulled in by the gazebo, where they often had lunch. She rose from her seat, and saying nothing, walked to the gazebo and sat on the railing. Novak followed her. He sat on the opposite railing and waited, trying not to look impatient. Hart took her time gathering her thoughts. Finally, she looked up at Novak.

"Thought I would let you in on a little something," she said.

Novak's eyebrows rose.

"And that," she continued, "would be the conversation at the barbecue with Jim Freeman." She exhaled slowly again, noticing Novak's reaction, then started again. She shook her head, realizing that Danny knew more than she thought he knew.

"Well, as you probably figured out," Hart began, "Jim was talking about me -- *I* was the MP who was assaulted and got thrown under the bus by some of my colleagues." Novak started to say something, but Steve waved him off.

"Yes, I *do* need to tell you this," she said, anticipating correctly what Novak was going to say.

"The story is pretty simple," Hart continued. "I was a platoon sergeant in Germany, and while we had a weekend pass, I was hanging with some other of the senior NCOs, when one of them put something in my drink. Well, he got me to a crash pad near the bar we were hanging at, and tried to rape me. Fortunately, I managed to wake up before he really got me, and I fought him off -- loudly enough that someone in an adjoining hotel room came to my rescue." Hart looked up again.

"Oddly enough, there were security cameras on the corner near the bar, and they clearly show that he practically had to carry me out of the bar. When you combine that with my blood test showing what he had given me, it was a slam dunk -- or at least it should have been.

Danny's face showed his confusion.

"The fact is, Danny, that a lot of people didn't want this to get out," Hart said.

"I went to the health center for medical attention and to file a report, when another NCO came to ty to get me to file the report as restricted, which essentially means confidential. That also means it wouldn't result in an investigation that could get my attacker in trouble." She looked squarely at Novak again. "Even in my mental state at that time, I knew I wasn't going to just talk to the Sexual Assault Response Coordinator -- I wanted justice. And that's when I really began to feel the pressure."

"Basically," she continued. "Some of the other NCOs and some of the rank and file MPs thought it would be disloyal to pursue a real court martial against the perpetrator, and they made that known after the official report was filed."

"Was that standard procedure?"

"There is some discretion that a victim can exercise in the beginning, and that's what the NCO who came to the health center wanted me to do -- to file it confidential." Novak could see Hart's lips tighten. "But I wouldn't do it."

"And so you shouldn't have," Novak said. "You were the victim; didn't that count for anything?"

"True, Danny, but it's not that easy in real life. Having your fellow MPs' back seems to apply only if you're the one assaulting somebody -- it doesn't apply so much if you're the victim."

"And you think Jim Freeman's cousin is one of the guys who threw you under the bus? Do you know who he was?"

"Don't know and don't care. Jim was right; I could never again depend on many of those guys, including whoever his cousin was."

"Didn't you get *any* support?"

"Yes. Absolutely." Hart said. "My platoon leader, company commander, regimental commander, and I would say most of my fellow MPs were solidly behind me, but the number of people who began to ignore me, or look the other way was astounding. Following the court martial, our regimental commander -- my colonel -- put the hammer down and disciplined several other MPs, and a lot of them left the Army as a result." Hart looked up at Novak.

"The colonel put his career on the line for me, as did my company commander, and I really appreciated them for it," Hart added. "Unfortunately, some of the higher ups weren't happy with my colonel over the whole debacle, and had him reassigned." Hart smiled for the first time. "Unfortunately for *them*, the colonel had a personal connection with a general who was above *his* commander, and he was eventually given a far better assignment than the first one, and he managed to bring my captain along with him -- as a major. They also watched out for my platoon leader, so he was okay, too."

She stood up. "The guy who attacked me was given a dishonorable. And," she continued, "I was offered a promotion and a reassignment to Army CID, something I had been coveting for a while."

Novak rose as well. "Which you didn't take?"

"No. As you can imagine, the whole incident soured me on the Army, but not on being a cop. It seemed to me that I should consider civilian law enforcement." Hart turned toward the cruiser. "As I told you before, I wanted a place near water, far from anywhere I'd ever lived, and somebody told me that Port Angel had a crackerjack police department."

"Still think that?"

"Pretty much," Hart said. "I mean, look at what happened today. It was a really small situation, but everybody from the 9th had my back -- even Boyd. That counts for a lot."

"The fact is Danny," she began, "I was looking for a big change in my life. I'm over 30, had one career that soured, but really wanted to do good things and help people. To me, coming to Port Angel was as much about running *toward* something new as moving *away* from my old life."

"And my guess is you don't share this with lots of people because it makes them feel sorry for you?"

"Not exactly," she said, screwing up her face slightly. "More that I don't want people to think I'm weak or need coddling. "I'm still a strong woman, you know."

"Oh hell, Steve," Novak laughed. "There isn't anybody who went to training today who doesn't know *that!*"

Hart shared in the laughter. "Well, I guess that's true, isn't it?" She paused before adding, "I mentioned all of this during my interviews so people would know what they were getting, but once I was accepted, I asked them to treat it as confidential, which they have."

She looked directly at Novak again. "But as my FTO, you needed to know it."

"But not O.C.?" Novak asked.

Hart shrugged. "Guess I didn't think about it with him." Then she burst out laughing again. "Yeah, I can just see how he might be if he knew all this stuff."

"Aw, O.C. isn't that bad," Novak began, "But I get your point. And it will stop with me."

"No," Hart said. "Always share things like this with Sheryl," Hart said. "She's really nice and if she and I are going to be friends, I wouldn't want to hide something like this from her, especially since it's bound to come up again; Jim Freeman probably knows a lot more than he let on."

"Agreed," said Novak. He looked directly at Hart again. "Steve, you know I'll always have your back, right?"

At that, Hart smiled again. "Yes, that I *do* know."

Chapter Twelve

Samuel Perkins, lieutenant of detectives for the 9th Precinct, was an early riser, and usually arrived at the office no later than 6:30 am. It was a surprise to him therefore that at shortly after 0730, he got a call from reception. He picked up the handset, distracted with looking at daily crime statistics.

"Perkins," he said, in a crisp tone.

"Reception, sir."

"Yes?" Perkins prompted.

"Well sir," the voice began again. "There is an Ernest Collins here to see you. May I send him up?"

Perkins looked at his watch again, somewhat confused that Ernest Collins would be visiting him so early in the morning, but he shrugged and answered.

"Certainly," he said. "Send him up." As Perkins hung up the phone, he thought it might be better to meet with Collins at his conference table rather than across the desk. As a wealthy developer for areas throughout the city and an influential community member, Collins wasn't accustomed to being on the wrong side of a desk. And besides that, Perkins and Collins had been friendly acquaintances for many years. Perkins opened his door to receive Collins when he arrived, and he didn't have long to wait, for Collins soon stood in the doorway.

A man of only average height, Collins always seemed much taller and impressive than his actual size would suggest. He was dressed impeccably, but not ostentatiously as always, Perkins reflected, which is the way truly wealthy people tended to dress.

Perkins smiled and extended his hand. "Deacon Collins, please come in."

"Good to see you, Samuel," Collins said as he shook hands. "I hope I'm not interrupting anything."

Perkins laughed. Certainly not yet, Ernest," he replied. "It's too early for most of my headaches to start, so you've come at a good time. May I offer you coffee?"

"No," Collins said. I'm just stopping by for a few minutes and don't want to put you out. Plus I've heard all the horror stories about coffee in police stations -- I prefer to pass."

Perkins smiled and gestured toward the chairs set at the corner of the conference table. "Why don't we sit down and you can tell me what's on your mind?" He waited for Collins to sit before he continued. "It must be something important for you to come here so early in the morning."

"Actually, Samuel, my mother was from the south, and she always told me 'if you're early, you're on time, and if you're in time, you're late,' so I tend to get an early start on the morning." Collins paused as if to gather his thoughts, though if prior experience said anything, Collins didn't need any time to gather his thoughts.

"Samuel," Collins began, "what I wanted to talk to you about is something that might actually be on your desk already." As he spoke, Collins tilted his head toward Perkins' desk. "There were a couple of incidents of drug violence last night in the Lexington district, not too far from Greater Mt. Zion AME, and the church is growing increasingly concerned about this activity so near our church. You can certainly understand that.

"I do, Ernest," Perkins began, carefully. "Do you think there is any connection to the church itself, meaning is there some sense that the church is being targeted with the violence?" Before Collins could answer, Perkins continued. "Because my experience is that drug violence doesn't really have any boundaries, even those imposed by rival drug gangs. It may just be that the church is in the 'wrong place at the wrong time,' if you know what I mean."

"I know that Samuel, and you're probably right," Collins said. "But you know that we've been working hard at Greater Mt. Zion to keep our kids as far from drugs as possible and honestly, it's been difficult. And I wonder if part of the problem might be that the young people in our church and in many parts of Lexington don't particularly trust the police presence in our community." Perkins reflected for a moment that Collins hadn't lived in Lexington for years, preferring the atmosphere of Diamond Head, a more affluent neighborhood of Port Angel, though Collins did maintain a professional presence in Lexington.

Collins put out his palm as if to placate Perkins, who hadn't yet reacted to his last statement. "It is a paradox, I know Samuel, that some of the people who want police to come when they call you, also tend resent to you when you answer their calls. Having said that, we have to find a way for the police to be seen as a positive, rather than a negative presence, and that's what I want to ask you about." Collins leaned forward. "Can you do that? Can you make sure the police truly become partners with us?"

Perkins had been nodding as Collins spoke -- perhaps owing to the latter's church background and position, but in truth, Perkins agreed with Collins, and had always been concerned about how deeply police were rooted in and seen as members of the community.

"I agree with you, Ernest," Perkins said. "And I am committed to doing all I can to make it happen." Perkins looked briefly skyward. "What I need to do is to speak with our captain, and some of our patrol supervisors," Perkins continued. "It's members of the patrol division that are truly the people most associated with police presence, for good or ill, and they're the ones who need to be reminded of their obligation to invest themselves in the community."

"Thank you, Samuel, and I appreciate what you're trying to do," said Collins. He sat back and shook his head. "You know, the young drug dealers are really just being seduced by the money from their higher ups in these drug gangs. And it makes the work of keeping our kids off drugs and the money that drugs can provide just that much harder."

As Collins spoke, Perkins had a thought. "You know Ernest," Perkins said. "One thing that does concern us is the rhetoric coming from the Rev. Price." Quickly holding his palm up in surrender, Perkins added, "Now I know that Rev. Price wants to do right for the church and the community, but every time you turn around, Price is slamming something we've done. That makes it hard to maintain the right kind of attitude among our officers. I wouldn't go so far as to call Price an impediment, but you know we might be in a much better place if he developed laryngitis for a couple of weeks."

Collins laughed at the image, which broke the small amount of tension that had developed during the conversation. Perkins continued.

"Ernest, I know Archie is a good man, and he wants the right things. In fact, I want the same things he does; he's just making it tougher than it needs to be."

"Well, I hate to admit it, Samuel." Collins replied. "But there are times when some on the Board of Deacons feel the same way you do." Collins shook his head. "But you know, he's a young man, trying to make a name for himself and take a leading role in the community, and I can't fault him for that. He's breathed new life into our church, and that was long overdue. I know he'll find his way in the community with the right mentoring." Collins leaned forward with a twinkle in his eye. "I'm committed to making that happen."

Perkins leaned in as well. "Ernest, let me make a deal with you: I promise to work even more on how our officers work with the community -- in ways that you might suggest -- if you'll work on having Rev. Price extend his hand in the same direction." As he spoke, Perkins noticed Collins slowly nodding his head. "Ernest, we're not talking about a great divide here. I know several officers who are very well situated and connected to Lexington and who truly 'get it.' We just need to get more officers on board, but that won't happen if they're being chastised for everything they do by somebody who I don't think 'gets it' on his side." Perkins wondered if he had been too strong, but Collins nodded again, more vigorously.

"You know, Samuel," Collins said, standing. "You're right." Perkins stood up as well, as Collins continued.

"And I guess, my friend, we both have a little work to do, don't we?" Collins smiled, and offered his hand.

"That we do," Perkins said, and shook Collins' hand.

"Take care, my friend," Collins said as he walked out the door.

Chapter Thirteen

At 0700, the following day, the squad gathered for muster and as they took their seats, both Novak and Hart sensed something different in the room -- a feeling that something had changed. Captain Shoemaker called the gathering to order, then turned over the muster to Lt. Perkins much earlier than usual. Lt. Perkins strode to the podium, looking grave. Hart wondered if something tragic had happened. Shortly, Perkins looked up and scanned the faces of the officers.

"Ladies and gentlemen," Perkins began. "I am coming to you this morning with some significant concerns about drug trafficking in our precinct and in all of Port Angel. And one of my concerns regarding this activity is the perception -- *perception*, mind you -- that our officers are more part of the problem than they are part of the solution."

Hart thought the other officers would explode in anger: she knew enough of them by now to know that they prided themselves on working well with the community. Instead, to her surprise, the room was silent, perhaps out of respect for Lt. Perkins who was very well regarded.

"I appreciate and truly believe," said Perkins, "that this is only a perception of people in the community, but we all know that perception is reality, and if people perceive that we are not engaged and not truly a part of the community, then that's the only reality they have. And while we could say that the community just doesn't 'get it' ...*yet*," he paused briefly again, "it really is our responsibility to make sure *we* 'get it' and that it shows throughout our community."

Perkins came from behind the podium and approached the officers. "I was made aware of this disconnect by speaking recently with Ernest Collins of Midtown Development, who is also a very involved citizen in our community." At the mention of Collins' name, Hart could hear the intake of breath and a slight rumbling of voices that suggested Collins wasn't too highly regarded within the 9th.

"Now I know that Mr. Collins hasn't always been a visible ally of our police force,…"

"Oh, really?" barked Boyd. "Perk, let's be honest; he's been on our asses for years, and now he's gonna be our best friend?"

"O.C.," Perkins replied, turning toward Boyd, "Collins *has* been less than an ally at times, but let me be honest and ask all of you, what have you done in the last couple of weeks to show members of the community that we're part of them rather than separate from them?" Perkins paced back and forth across the front of the room. "That's what Collins is talking about, and I think he's right." Perkins stopped before adding, "I think he's right, and I've already challenged myself to do better." Perkins looked up and caught the eyes of the captain. "Shoe?" he said, yielding the floor to the precinct commander.

Captain Shoemaker returned to the podium and addressed the officers. "Lt. Perkins is right, and he recognizes that while our detectives can try to connect with the community when they're involved in investigations, the people who can have the most impact on community engagement are you as patrol officers. Now, we have a number of community events coming up and we have officers contracted to provide security for all of them," Shoemaker said. "However, we are going to increase that number and have the department budget pay for additional coverage, so that more officers can attend the events and mingle with the participants. This is a low stress activity, and because of that, we believe our opportunity to connect with members of the community will be high."

"Pay for play?" a lone voice asked.

"One way to look at it," Shoemaker said. "Of course, it's also one way of investing in what we ought to be doing in the first place."

Hart and Novak glanced over and saw Boyd nodding his head slowly. Hart leaned over to Novak and whispered "Do you think Boyd supports this?"

"Probably," Novak said. "I mean, he has his own odd way of connecting with the community, you know --'always civil, seldom courteous,' but he always told me to be aware of and know the people in the community. He made a point of telling me that the cruiser can be an impediment to community even as it gets us to them faster."

The muster continued, with Boyd reviewing the most recent BOLOs and arrests. Hart took diligent notes on several of the BOLOs, and asked questions twice to clarify what she had heard. She was taken aback when Boyd changed his tone significantly.

"Something else, people," Boyd said. "We've been getting dribs and drabs of information about a drug turf battle that's brewing." Boyd turned toward the screen and called up several pictures, then began pointing to the pictures in turn. "You all know these three individuals, but for those of you who are newer, this man," Boyd pointed with a laser dot, "Is Louis Gray, otherwise known as "Cobra." He controls the largest part of the drug trade, and has a particular stronghold in the 9th." Boyd turned toward the officers. "And he has been a thorn in our sides for years now." Boyd turned back to the screen.

"The other two are Eldon Parker, and," he shifted the pointer, "Angelo Spino. They are the other two major drug traffickers in our city." Boyd returned to the podium. "For about the last couple of years, they have 'enjoyed' a certain peace because of the way they divided up the city. Everything east and north of central to Spino, Northwest and the western edge to Parker and the rest to Gray. But it's not a secret that Gray wants more, and he has been consolidating his power and becoming more brazen through little expansions into the Spino and Parker territories. Each little expansion is perhaps just a city block or two, and not worth much reaction from Spino or Parker, but eventually, something's got to give."

"Given that Gray is most solid in the 9th and 12th, we need to be ready if something explodes." Glancing briefly at Lt. Perkins and Capt. Shoemaker, Boyd added "And that's why what the Loot and Captain said is so important for us, and we are looking to you all to make this happen."

Boyd became more formal behind the podium, asking "Any questions?" Seeing none, Boyd continued, "The last announcement is that the next round of firearm qualifications has been moved up to today, which means," he consulted a document on the podium, "that the following officers should report at 1300 to the range." Boyd held up the document to focus better on the names. "Poole, Novak, Weiss, Marin and Simpson." Looking up, he added, "Dismissed."

As the officers rose from their seats, Hart turned to Novak.

"Do we just go off patrol at 1300, then?"

"Yep," Novak replied. "This is only twice a year, and we usually schedule it on days with lesser activity. Plus, they're likely to bring a couple of teams in early to cover for us if they have to." Looking at Hart, he added,

"Do you want to drive today?"

* * *

Hart and Novak walked down the stairs to the parking area to pick up their cruiser. As they were walking, Hart was distracted, which Novak picked up on.

"Steve?" he asked.

"Huh?" she said, before recovering. "Yeah, Danny, what is it?

"Not much," said Novak. "You just seemed to be somewhere else."

"Just wondering about what the lieutenant said," Hart answered, then she paused. "Actually, no. That wasn't what I was thinking about." She looked more directly at Novak. "What I was really wondering is who is this Collins guy and why did everybody have such a negative reaction to him? Is he some kind of troublemaker?"

"Not exactly, but...." His voice trailed off.

"But?"

"The fact is, Steve that he's one of the people from the neighborhood who really made good, and so good that he really thinks -- what is that phrase? Oh yeah, that 'his shit doesn't stink.'"

"So, not a good guy?"

"No, I don't mean that at all," Novak said. "He's actually a decent man, very involved in the community, and very influential."

"You know," Novak began. "Maybe it's my working class background, but I just wonder if Collins has too much influence in this community. I mean, he's from Lexington and always talks about how important Lexington is to him, but he thinks he's better than the rest of us who come from this neighborhood." Novak laughed. "You know, Steve," he said. Maybe I'm just jealous that he's a multimillionaire, and I'm just the cop from the neighborhood."

"I get the idea," Hart said, "he's too important to really be one of you anymore."

Novak laughed. "That's pretty much Ernest Collins in a nutshell for me."

Chapter Fourteen

Novak and Hart were the last to arrive at the range shortly before 1300. Novak left the vehicle quickly, saying,

"Can you finish up, here Steve?" Shuffling away before hearing a clear answer from Hart, he added over his shoulder, "I don't want to be late."

"Sure, Danny" Hart answered to Novak's back. Hart completed notifying central of their location, then closed up the cruiser before entering the firing range. She entered noticing Novak and other officers in for their compulsory firearms qualification, in addition to Sgt. Boyd, who was wearing ear protection and with his department issue weapon on the bench in front of him. Before advancing further, she picked up her own hearing protection and went to stand near Novak.

"Is Sgt. Boyd getting qualified, too?"

"I don't know, he hasn't usually qualified with me, but he might be." Novak turned back to Hart, leaving his weapon and magazines on the bench. "I do know he's a crack shot, and he loves to laud that over us."

"Umm," Hart said, again distracted. She walked over to Marin as the senior officer was getting ready. "Hey, Gee," Hart said.

"Hi, Steve," Marin replied. She noticed Hart's hearing protection, and added, "Yeah, good that you have those." She learned closer to Hart. "These guys like to shoot up shit like crazy and it gets louder than it ought to be."

"Boys and their toys, Gee," Hart replied. Marin laughed and continued her preparations. Hart was planning to stand back and watch the proceedings, and turned to chat with Simpson, when she felt a tap on her shoulder.

"Nice to see you, Hart," said Boyd. His eyes indicated a space to his left. "We have an empty bay. "Why don't you get your qualification out of the way early?"

"Naw, sir. Don't want to get in the way."

"Uh-huh," Boyd replied with a smirk. "Well, that's up to you, Hart, and you know, you don't even have to have the same score as everybody else." He picked up his hearing protection, adding "You don't have to do it now, I guess." Boyd turned back to his bench and continued checking his magazines.

Hart stayed for a few seconds, when Marin got her attention.

"Don't do it, Steve," Marin said, quietly. "You don't have to qualify again until you finish your probation. You never know what O.C. is up to."

"Got it, Gee," she said, but added "Though I wouldn't mind getting it out of the way, and I do have a new weapon, so I'm considering it."

"Up to you, Sis," Marin said.

"Plus, I guess I can let Boyd gloat some more. I mean, he has to get fed somehow, doesn't he?"

Both Hart and Marin laughed out loud, enough that it caught the attention of the rangemaster. He approached Hart, saying, "Officer, I'll need you to either get on the line or exit the firing area." His tone almost shocked Hart, though she remembered feeling the same at her last qualification, so she recovered quickly.

"Yes, sir," Hart said, and she turned to exit the range. Before she went five steps, the rangemaster called out to her again.

"Officer... Hart, correct?"

"Yes, sir."

The rangemaster turned and pointed to the last bay, saying, "Why don't you head into the last bay and get your qualification out of the way? I already have you scheduled for about two months from now, and this will make it easier for you." When Hart hesitated, he added, "Hey you've got to be here anyway -- might as well get something done at the same time."

Hart thought quickly, then walked to the supply area, where she took out two magazines for her weapon type, then entered the bay next to Boyd.

"Decided to take me up on my offer, Hart?" Boyd asked.

"I did, sergeant," Hart said. And something in her voice rebuffed any more conversation from Boyd. Hart checked her magazines, inserting both into her service weapon in succession and chambering rounds, before ejecting them and finally preparing her weapon for qualifying. She had been so engrossed in her work that she hadn't noticed the rangemaster standing behind her.

"Ready, Hart?" he asked.

Startled, Hart said, "Sorry, sir."

"No reason to apologize for doing this right, Hart." The rangemaster stepped back from her bay, and put on his hearing protection.

"All ready? he asked. Hearing positive responses from all of the officers, he continued,

"Hearing protection on!" He waited before his final instruction.

"One magazine at a time…Commence fire!"

The general din of the range would have been distracting to ordinary citizens, and while police officers seldom fire their weapons, they are far more accustomed to the incredibly loud report from their firearms. Within two minutes, the range was silent. The rangemaster scanned the officers, noticed that all had their weapons on their benches with their chambers open. Still, he went through the standard command.

"Cease fire!

"Make and show safe!" Once the rangemaster was sure that all officers had complied with this commands, he added,

"Firing line is cold!" All officers pressed the buttons on their bays to bring their targets up range to be scored by the rangemaster.

Boyd examined Hart's target out of the corner of his eye. "You may have qualified, Hart, but I wouldn't be too proud of that score.

Hart had been examining the grouping of shots, which was off to the left of the preferred zone, though it was very tight. She silently calculated how she would change her sights. To get Boyd off her back, she answered him. "Guess not, sir," she said. The rangemaster examined all the targets, giving officers feedback and letting officers know which of them needed to fire at third targets, since department policy required qualifying on two targets. When he got to Hart's target, the rangemaster said, "Nice grouping, officer," he began. "Can you adjust your sights okay?"

"Yes, sir," Hart said. She looked up at the rangemaster. "I'm thinking two and two?" The rangemaster looked at the grouping again, and answered,

"Yep. That should work."

"Okay, people, load!" Hart made adjustments to her sights, hoping that her calculations would be sufficient. While she hadn't let on, she was disappointed in herself that she hadn't beaten Boyd. She had checked out Boyd's grouping and it was very good and very close to center and the heart of the target. However, Hart had always known that she was best when handling situations coolly rather than in anger.

The rangemaster continued to survey the officers, and when he thought all were ready, he asked,

"Shooter's ready?" After hearing the officers indicate they were ready, the rangemaster continued.

"Commence fire!" This time, Hart waited perhaps five seconds as she breathed, then took careful aim and fired off her nine rounds in quick succession, in fact finishing before anyone else on the line. She removed her magazine, lowered her weapon to her bench, and stepped back from the firing line, awaiting further instructions. Finally, the rangemaster called,

"Cease fire!

"Make and show safe!" Followed soon by,

"Firing line is cold!" Hart and the other officers retrieved their targets and she was pleased to find that her grouping was even tighter and centered on the heart, about as perfect a score as she could have. She let out the breath she didn't realize she was holding, and relaxed. Boyd had noticed the grouping and was thankfully -- at least for Hart -- silent. The rangemaster went down the line, again making comments, and seemed pleased with the scores for the officers' second magazines. When he got to Boyd, he said,

"Nice, O.C.," He turned to his colleague. "Sorry we have to make you do this, my friend."

"Gotta do what you gotta do, Malcolm." The rangemaster went to Hart's target and stared. Hart wasn't even paying much attention, since she assumed she had completed her qualification. She waited patiently as the rangemaster examined her target.

"Nice grouping, Hart," the rangemaster said. "I don't know that I've ever seen a better grouping on this range. "Well done."

"Thank you, sir," Hart said, and she waited to be dismissed. The usual protocol was to wait until all officers had qualified, and she was interested in replacing her own magazines, when she heard Boyd's voice again.

"Bet you can't do that again, Hart," he said, and he turned back to his bay.

"Bet you can't either … sir." Her tone was even more defiant than she had intended, but at the time, she didn't particularly care.

"Ha!" Boyd replied. "It's *on*, Hart." The rangemaster completed his examinations and made ready for the final qualification round, surprised to see both Boyd and Hart still in their bays. He gave his commands and noticed that they each seemed more focused than usual.

At "Commence Fire," Hart and Boyd each took a few seconds to breathe, then emptied their magazines before unloading, then stepping back from the firing line.

At "Firing line is Cold!" Boyd and Hart each pressed their buttons, and brought their targets up. Boyd's grouping was even better than last time, yet when he looked at Hart's, her grouping seemed to be not much larger than an old silver dollar.

Hart just looked at the grouping, turned to Boyd and smiled.

"Thanks for your support, Sgt." Then she walked away.

Chapter Fifteen

While Hart and Novak were tempted to visit Heaven's Home every day, their wallets and common sense made them limit themselves to once or twice per week. On this warm August day, they were greeted warmly by Ruth Williams and served the meal she wanted them to have.

After lunch, both Ruth and Lester joined them at their table, and Hart could sense a very different mood on the Williams' part, so she reached across to take Ruth Williams' hands. The older woman was touched.

"Thank you Child," Ruth Williams said. "I knew you were special the moment I met you."

Her husband Lester was a slight man, clearly strong, but more wiry than bulky and with more etched features than his wife. Usually the quieter of the two, whenever Lester spoke, people listened.

Novak sensed the mood as well, and looked respectfully at Lester Williams. "Tell me what's on your mind, Mr. Williams," Novak said softly.

"I'm worried, Danny," Lester said after a pause. "I'm worried about my boy, I'm worried about this neighborhood." He looked up at Novak. "Hell, boy, I'm just worried about everything."

Novak knew that Lester Williams had endured a great deal in his life, and for him to be worried caused Novak some concern of his own. Novak noticed Hart looking at Ruth Williams' eyes, and he could see the concern in the older woman's eyes as well.

"Tell me what happened, Mr. Williams," Novak said.

"It's not any one thing, Danny," Lester said. "Well, actually it is one thing, but mostly, it's everything." Lester glanced at Hart then returned his gaze to Novak. "You know how some of the local drug dealers have been trying to recruit Harold to join them?"

"You know, I've known about that for a while," Novak replied. "But I never really understood it. I mean, why would they want Harold to join them knowing who he is? Wouldn't they be concerned that he wouldn't stick it out?"

"You'd think that," Ruth said. "But the fact is Danny, that Harold is one of the few young people who has always done the right thing." Lester and Novak both nodded as they heard this.

"Well, I -- we -- don't think Harold is ever going to sell drugs," Ruth continued, "but these people, these dealers you know, the big ones? They want someone like Harold who the kids look up to to join them. That would kind of make what they're doing okay."

Novak exhaled. "I guess I hear you, Ms. Williams, but it still doesn't make much sense to me." Shifting again to face Lester, Novak asked "Are you worried they're going to put even more pressure on Harold?"

"You know how these people can be, Danny," Lester said. "We can't tell Harold to give in but what is he going to do?"

"To say nothing," Ruth added, "of the fact that some of these young kids selling drugs are 18-19 years old and driving nice cars and throwing money around like water. It's not easy for Harold to see all that and keep working here at the restaurant and going to school part time. He wonders what the whole use of it is."

Novak was silent for a while and Lester Williams leaned closer to him to grasp Novak's hand. "A little too close to home isn't it, son?" he asked.

"It is," Novak said. He shook himself. "And I guess I didn't realize how close until just now." Looking up at the Williams', he said "And I guess I'm a little worried as well. And we have to do whatever we can to keep Harold from going down the wrong path or getting hurt in the process."

Novak reached for his notebook, and opening it, turned again to the Williams'. "Tell me anything you think that might be important: what people have talked to Harold, where it happened, what Harold said -- anything."

Hart took out her notebook too, in case Novak missed something. They found that the Williams' were as concerned about what they *didn't* know as what they *did* know. It seemed that Harold interacted with people in the neighborhood all the time at the restaurant, at college, and with his church. During an average day he might see doctors, teachers, street sweepers, custodians, contractors and drug dealers. Of course, only the drug dealers put pressure on Harold to do things he didn't want to do.

After a while, Hart finally felt comfortable enough to ask her own questions. "Mr. and Ms. Williams," she began. "Do you have any evidence -- let me rephrase that -- do you have anything specific such as people we should talk to or look into that might help us?" The Williams' seemed puzzled.

"Obviously," Hart continued, "what you're saying today concerns us because we all want Harold to stay strong and keep more kids off drugs. What I'm wondering is are there people we ought to be referring to the drug unit to help get the pressure off of Harold?"

"I really don't know," Lester said. He shook his head feeling helpless. "It's not like the police don't care; it's just that you can't do much with second and third hand information. And we also don't want to draw a target on Harold's back."

Novak noticed his friends in pain, added "Mr. Williams. Ms. Williams. I don't think we're just talking about Harold here. We also know that you've stood strong against drug dealing in this neighborhood for years now. You're two of the strongest voices against drugs and violence, and up to now that's discouraged drug dealers and traffickers from causing too much trouble around here because it just wasn't worth the hassle."

"Right," said Lester Williams.

"Well then, Novak continued. "What's different now? Why is there more pressure on Harold now than say a year or so ago, when we could all let some of this tension from drug dealers just roll off our backs?"

Ruth Williams sat back, pondering what Novak had said. "I don't know, Danny, and I never thought about it that way." She looked to her husband, then back to Novak. Continuing, she added, "But you're right, it does feel different now." Turning again to her husband, she asked "Is that how it feels to you too, Lester?"

Lester Williams only nodded his agreement.

"That's what I thought," Novak replied, more quiet than usual. "And to be honest, I don't know the reason any more than you do."

This was the first time Hart had seen Novak look so helpless. Knowing Danny, she thought, he'll come up with something.

"First," Novak began. "We can talk to Harold and see what he can share about this new pressure." Scanning the Williams' faces, he added, "I assume Harold is feeling a different kind of pressure too, right?"

"He's told us that more than once." Ruth Williams said.

"Okay, then," Novak said. "Stephanie and I will speak with him and get his ideas on things. Then maybe we'll have something more to work on." Danny started to close his notebook, but hesitated. "This may seem out of the blue," he began, "but has Harold been getting good support from other people at Greater Mt. Zion? I ask because Deacon Collins has asked for extra help from our precinct to help stamp out the drug trade."

"Oh, yes," Ruth Williams said, finally animated. "Rev. Price has made working with youth a priority for the church, and the activities he's started with our youth are doing a great job. That's why Harold has been working so hard at the church lately."

Novak considered asking another question, then decided not to. Checking the time, he asked, "When will Harold be back here?"

"Actually," Ruth Williams said. "He's going to be at the church for the rest of the afternoon; maybe you could catch him there."

"That sounds fine, Ms. Williams," Novak said. "Stephanie and I will head there this afternoon." Looking at both the Williams' he added,

"Please don't worry. We're all in this together."

Chapter Sixteen

Approaching the sanctuary door at Great Mt. Zion, Novak was ready
to try the door when Hart pointed to the yard to the right of the
church. There, they saw a group of teenage boys playing "shirts and
skins." The officers approached quietly and watched the boys play,
noting that several of them were impressive ball handlers.

"Is basketball another one of your talents?" Novak asked.

Hart turned to face him. "What?" she asked, then "Uh, no. I used to
play volleyball in high school, and played in the Army as well."

"'All Army' team, right?" Novak asked, a mischievous look in his
eyes.

Hart had been studying the basketball game, but finally answered,
"No. Second team."

Novak rolled his eyes and laughed, which surprised Hart.

"What's so funny?" she demanded.

"You." Novak said.

"What?"

Novak raised his palms in surrender. "Steve, it's just you." Seeing
the confusion on her face, he continued. "You have so many damn
talents, I was just jerkin' your chain."

"Okay," Hart said, with a slight smile.

Novak led the way to the fence outside the court so they could see
the action better. They watched the game, evaluating the skills of
the players and the generally positive mood of the game. Harold
was standing with his back to the officers, and seemed so engrossed
in the play that he hadn't noticed them. After about 5 minutes, the
action on the basketball court stopped, and the players went to the

sidelines for drinks and a break. Novak opened the gate and called to Harold. "Hey, Harold," he said. Hart smiled as they entered. Harold seemed comfortable to see the officers, but his general mood -- at least to Hart --seemed off.

"Hey, Danny," Harold responded, with a small smile. "You can't just be driving through the neighborhood." It was a statement, not a question.

"Well, no," Novak replied, "but this *is* part of the 9th, and I drive by the church often enough." He paused. "But I imagine you can guess that we just finished lunch and talking to your parents."

"Can we talk to you for a little bit, Harold?" Hart asked.

Harold pointed toward the side door of the church, leading the way. Once there, he asked, "Do you want to ask me questions or just want me to talk?"

"Your preference," Novak said. Neither officer took out a notebook, but Hart resolved to ask no questions and just listen so she could recall the conversation later.

What's been happening, Harold?" Novak asked. "Both in the neighborhood, and to you -- your parents are worried."

"I guess I'm a little worried too. I don't want them to get hurt."

"How about you?" Novak asked.

"Yeah, me too," Harold said. "But, they're older, you know...." "The fact is, there seems to be new pressure on drug deals and dealers in the neighborhood. It's been slow in coming, and maybe that's why I didn't notice it before. But it's here."

"Pressure?" Novak prompted.

"Right," said Harold. "It seems like some of the little boys - you know the guys who just sell a little weed or blow from maybe out of town, they're being pushed really hard -- hard enough that they're either joining up with somebody or leaving town."

"Joining anybody in particular?"

"Well, Cobra," Harold replied. "But that's probably since he's in charge around here, you know? There have been a couple of beatings." Harold looked around and leaned against the side of the building.

Novak saw how heavily things were weighing on Harold. "And these beating are worse than usual, am I right?" he asked.

"Yeah," Harold said. "It used to be that they would get a warning, and some pushing around, but the last couple of times, people have just had the shit kicked out of them. It's really crazy!"

"Harold," Novak asked. "Is that the kind of pressure you're getting?"

"No," Harold said. "With me it's the usual persuasion, and nobody has suggested that anything is going to happen to me, it's just that it's gotten so strong, you know?"

"Plus, " Harold continued, "They keep implying that changes are coming that are going to shake things up. They've never really threatened me, but the whole idea of change is what scares me." As he finished speaking, Harold seemed drained.

Novak glanced at Hart, wondering if she had any questions. She shook her head slightly. Novak thought a moment, then turned again to Harold. "This may seem like an odd question, Harold," Novak asked, "but besides not getting the shit kicked out of them, what is the attraction of these dealers going to work for Cobra rather than somebody else? Is his hold on them that strong?"

"No," Harold said. "Not at all. Cobra offers them a little bigger cut than some of the other dealers." Harold looked up. "Plus a couple of times, some of the dealers mom's needed something, you know, like medicine, and Cobra paid it for them. It's just the way Cobra approaches things. And then all the dealers walk around like they own a McDonald's or something," he said in disgust.

Novak's face showed his confusion.

"It's like this," Harold continued. "You know how everybody wants to be their own businessman, you know be their own boss? Well, the way Cobra operates is that everybody sees themselves as being their own boss, and the outside supplier to them is Cobra," Harold said. "As far these guys are concerned, they're businessmen, just like car detailers or insurance salesmen, not drug dealers, so they don't feel like they're doing anything wrong."

"You said Cobra offers them a better percentage than other dealers?"

"Yeah, but I don't know if it's really all that much more," Harold said. "Maybe it's just the idea that they get a bit more that they like so much."

"And," Novak replied, "that makes them even more loyal to Cobra as a result."

"Exactly."

"And your folks said some of these guys are showing off bling and other shit to impress the kids," Novak added.

"Right," Harold said. "And while these guys" he pointed to the court, "aren't falling for it yet, it may just be a matter of time before some of them start to slip."

"I get it, Harold," Novak said. "And you're probably right -- it's hard to stay straight when somebody else has all the toys." He looked up at Harold and squeezed the younger man's shoulders. "And Harold, I appreciate how tough this is for you. Thank you." Looking to Hart, Novak added, "Let's take some of this back to the precinct, Steve, and see what they can come up with." Before leaving the church, they turned again to Harold.

"Harold do you have any names we can look into, like who you got some of your information from?"

Harold hesitated. "Well, the main one is T-Wright, you know, Terry Wright?" he said, looking to Novak to see if he knew Wright. Novak didn't respond. "Terry and I went to school together" he clarified.

"No, I don't know him, but we can ask the narcotics detail -- they're bound to know him." Giving Harold's shoulder another squeeze, Novak added, "Thanks again, Harold." Turning to Hart, he said, "Let's go, Steve."

Hart nodded, gave a knowing smile to Harold, then joined Novak as he headed back to the cruiser.

Chapter Seventeen

Hart and Novak left the church, both silent as they continued on patrol. After a few blocks, Hart turned to Novak who was driving.

"What do you think?"

"I don't know, Steve," Novak said. "I believe everything Harold told us, yet beyond passing it on to the precinct or narcotics, I really don't know what to do with it." He glanced sideways briefly at Hart. "I also don't know this 'T-Wright' guy, and I probably should: this is my neighborhood after all."

"Right," said Hart. "Like you're the supercop who has to know everything and everybody on your beat."

Novak wasn't sure if Hart was serious so he frowned and looked at her again. She was smiling.

"Exactly!" she cried. "At some point, you need to give yourself a break. You can't know everybody and everything that goes on -- it just isn't possible. That's why we have to talk to people like Harold and his parents. It's what we do with the information that matters."

"Thank you, my master," Novak said as he waved his right hand in an elaborate bow. "When did you get so philosophical?"

"Eleven years of martial arts training, remember? Plus, it's actually the way I think." Then she added with a sigh, "Which can make it very difficult on dates."

"You know," Novak said, changing the subject. "Getting involved in this -- you know, connecting with Harold in this way is exactly what the lieutenant was talking about earlier."

"Let's head down to my old high school," Novak said.

"Do you go there often?"

"Maybe a couple of times a year. The school resource officer is a friend of mine."

"Like I've never heard *that* before," Hart said. "Well," she added. "Let's go."

Novak continued down Wyalusing, and was about to turn onto Alston, when Hart said, "Danny, I don't see any rear plates on that car." She pointed to her right.

"Which one?"

"That one," Hart said, pointing again.

Novak stopped the cruiser and turned his head to look at the car. "I don't either," he said. "Let's check it out." Novak checked the traffic, then turned the car around. They stopped and walked toward the car, pulling out their notebooks as they walked.

Novak went to the front of the car, examining it front and back as he walked. Hart examined the rear plates, then got on her belly to check under the car.

"Steve, what are you doing?" Novak asked. Hearing no response, Novak repeated, "Steve?

Hart got onto her hands and knees, and then stood up. "I was looking for an IED -- standard procedure."

"Nothing to be sorry about, Steve," he said. "It's actually a good idea. Turning to the windshield again, he looked for the VIN. "Let me call in the VIN." He gestured toward the cruiser with his head. "Can you get out the abandoned car sticker? They're in the glove compartment."

"Sure."

Hart walked back to the cruiser and noticed out of the corner of her eye two people down the street. The cruiser was partially hidden by trees, and Hart sensed that she needed to be hidden as well. She watched the two men and it looked like a drug deal.

While Hart crossed to the cruiser, Novak examined the car's VIN, and touched his microphone.

"Unit 224 to 9 Central."

"Central 9 to 224," the voice said. "What's up Danny?"

"Hey Kat," Novak said. "I have a VIN for you to run." As Novak talked to dispatch, he noticed Hart returning to the abandoned car, but not carrying stickers. Confused, he turned to Hart, his face showing his question.

"Looks like a drug deal, Danny," said Hart. "Call it in while I check it."

"Got it," said Novak. Hart took off walking toward the drug deal and soon began running as the men noticed her and took off. Novak was ready to call in the chase when the radio crackled again.

"Danny?"

"Possible drug deal, Kat. We're in pursuit!"

Chapter Eighteen

Novak hopped into the cruiser and took off after Hart. Unable to continue speaking to dispatch, he ignored any sounds on the radio as he tried to anticipate where the drug dealer and Hart might run. After turning one corner, one of the men seemed to disappear and Hart continued chasing the remaining suspect. And while she was far behind the runner, she seemed to be gaining as they ran.

"One more talent of Stephanie Hart," Novak thought as he watched her. *"She's even got a good sprinter's kick."* He shook his head. It appeared they were headed toward the high school, so he turned down Pine so he could catch up with them. For a short moment, he worried that he would be leaving Hart without backup and that she might be in danger. He laughed to himself as he thought that it's the drug dealer who would be in danger more than Stephanie Hart.

Novak made the left onto Hazel Ave., and followed straight toward the rear of the school. By the time he could see the school in the distance, he saw a figure running around the school. When Novak finally reached the school, he saw Hart standing by a rear fence, breathing heavily. Novak brought the car around the school with his lights flashing and pulled in by his partner. As he exited the cruiser, he heard,

"Son of a bitch!" coming from Hart's mouth. "Shit!" Hart kicked at the ground, and turned to see Novak. He was inclined to grin at her, but thought better of it when he saw her face. He walked over to her to see if she was okay.

"Steve?" Novak asked. "Are you okay?"

"Does it *look* like I'm okay?" she shouted. Hart knew she was out of line. So she held up a finger, and started her deep breathing. After about thirty seconds, she took another deep breath, and turned again to face Novak.

"Sorry, Danny," Hart began. She pointed toward the rear gate. "Lost my head because of the asshole."

"And where is the asshole now?"

"Well, *gone*," Hart replied, pointing again at the fence. "He had enough energy to vault the fence, and there was a car ready for him. How he arranged that is beyond me." Hart shook her head in annoyance and growled. "And they were just far enough away that I couldn't make anything off the license plate except that it was in-state. The car was a dark blue Chevy Malibu -- an '08 or '09, I think."

"Are you adding automotive expert to your list of skills, Steve?"

"What?"

"Nothing, Steve," Novak said. "Just playing with you. Turning back to the cruiser, he added, "We should probably call in the chase."

"Yeah," Hart said, her breathing finally under control. She keyed in her mike. "Unit 224 to 9 central." After a second, she heard,

"9 Central -- what's up, Stephanie?" The voice was crisp and business-like as always.

"Pursuit concluded," Hart began. "Suspect has fled the scene in late model dark blue Chevy Malibu. No license plate." Hart took out her notebook and waited.

"Reference is 025A for the date," the voice said.

Hart wrote it down in her notebook." "Thanks Kat," Hart said. "Film at 11 on this."

"Roger."

Looking at Hart, Novak said, "Let's walk around the school first, then we'll call Teddy."

"Teddy?" Hart asked.

"The school resource officer here at Park East," Novak said. Turning to Hart again, he added,

"Can you give a general description for the report?" Novak asked.

Hart made a gesture with her palm facing the ground and rocking her hand from side to side. "Not much of one," she said. "Most of it will be his clothing and general size, but even that's going to be pretty general."

"Can't be helped, Steve," Novak said. "You had to investigate what you saw, and you had to pursue. It's not your fault he was so far ahead of you."

"What do you mean?"

"I mean that you were gaining on him and in another 50 yards or so, you might have had him."

"Oh."

"Right," said Novak and smiling added, "Which means you used to run track as well, right?"

"Uh-huh," said Hart, still not seeing the amusement in Novak's eyes. "800 meters."

"Of *course* you did," Novak said and he led the way around the school.

Chapter Nineteen

Novak and Hart approached the front of Park East High School, with Hart wiping the back of her neck as they walked. Novak noticed her and laughed.

"So much for never breaking a sweat, huh?"

"Don't know where you heard that, brother," Hart replied. "Sweat is my friend."

"I hear you," Novak replied. "It's just that you hardly broke a sweat when you were fighting Turner on the mat last week."

"*That* wasn't hard," she said.

Novak keyed in his microphone. "Unit 224 to 9 Central."

"9 Central. Go ahead 224."

"We are entering Park East High School to confer with the School Resource Officer, Central," Novak said. "We'll let you know when we've completed consultations and return to patrol."

"Understood," said the voice.

"Also," Novak added, "Would you please contact Teddy for us so we can meet inside?"

"Way ahead of you, 224," said Neely. "He's in the school resource office. Do you know where that is?"

"I should, Central," he said. "I was sent there enough as a student; 224 out. With that, Novak and Hart entered Park East High School.

* * *

Once past the school vestibule, Novak and Hart entered the main office where they encountered the executive assistant. Hart noted her name plate which read "Denise Tanner Executive Assistant."

She barely had time to read the name before the woman burst from her desk to greet them -- or at least to greet Danny Novak.

"Danny! It's so good to see you!" She gave Novak a hug.

"Hello, Denise," Novak said warmly, as he returned the embrace. He stepped back and got a better look at his old friend. He quickly remembered himself, and turned to introduce Hart.

"Denise, this is my partner, Stephanie Hart. Stephanie, Denise Tanner, a classmate of mine."

"Nice to meet you Denise," Hart said.

"Nice to meet you as well, " said Tanner. She turned to face Novak again. "I didn't know you guys had partners now."

"Well, partner in reality, but her actual position is as a probationary officer. Stephanie is finishing her probationary period with me then she'll be a full member of the PAPD."

"Nice," Tanner replied with a smile. Focusing again on Novak she asked, "I suppose you want to see Teddy?"

"Yep. He already knows we're coming."

Tanner indicated the inner door to the corridor from the main office. "We generally see official firearms as enough authorization to head inside, so have at it."

"Thanks, Denise."

"Nice to meet you, Denise," said Hart as they exited the office.

They turned left to go to the main corridor, and Novak led the way past the hall of fame wall, adding as he did so, "No, I'm not on *that* wall, Steve." They walked past the Media Center then turned left down another corridor until they came to a cluster of offices on the left, one of which had "School Resource Officer, PAPD" on it and a handwritten sign saying "We ♥ Officer Somerville!" Hart and

Novak were about to knock on the closed door, when it opened and the tall imposing figure of Teddy Somerville came out, smiling at his colleagues.

"Dan," he said, griping Novak's hand.

"Good to see you, Teddy," he said, then tilting his head toward Hart, added "Have you met Stephanie Hart?"

Somerville extended his hand to Hart. "Haven't had the pleasure. Nice to meet you, Stephanie."

"Nice to meet you -- Teddy is it?"

"Yes, and short for Theophilus, so I really prefer Teddy. And I probably should tell you that while I don't know you, I heard about an awesome score on the qualifying range a little bit ago. That was you, right?"

"Guilty," Hart said.

Somerville back up a bit into his tiny office. "Shall we sit and talk here or is there something you want to see?"

"Let's sit and talk," Novak said. "Then we can decide what to do."

"Sounds good," Somerville said. Leading the way inside, he added, "It's not too large in here but we'll manage."

Somerville sat behind his desk, and Hart and Nova took the only remaining chairs facing him. Somerville immediately asked, "So, what's on your mind?"

"One of the usual things that would bring somebody here, Teddy," said Novak. "We were checking out an abandoned car and Stephanie saw what we're pretty sure was a drug deal going down. Stephanie chased one suspect to right behind the school where he vaulted the fence and escaped."

"Vaulted?" Somerville, asked his eyes widening. He shook his head and took out his notebook, then seeing Hart's opened in her lap, put it back.

"What can you tell me about this guy, Stephanie? Anything we can use to identify him?"

"Not too much, I'm afraid, Teddy," Hart said. "Here's the best description I can give for him -- he was probably no closer to me than 50 yards when he vaulted the fence."

Somerville took the proffered notebook, and read the brief description. "Average height, solid blue pants and hoodie, Red Kufi, red rimmed sunglasses. Short hair, medium complexion. Excellent runner."

"Excellent runner?"

"He was damn fast Teddy," Hart explained, "and he still had the energy to get over that fence in about a second and a half. I don't think I could have done that after sprinting for over half a mile, and I train for this stuff."

"Understood," Somerville said. He sat back in his chair, thinking. "I have to tell you," he began, "that doesn't sound like anybody who's here now. Somebody who can run like that even if he wasn't on the track team? That's the kind of thing people would talk about, you know?" His eyes glanced over at the telephone on his desk. He reached for it saying, "I'm going to call up the Assistant Principal: he may have some thoughts to share with us." Somerville picked up the phone and dialed an internal number.

He sat back slightly when the phone was answered.

"Hey, Bill. This is Teddy Somerville." He looked up briefly at Novak and Hart. "Say, I've got a couple of PAPD Officers here and we want to run a description by you. Can we come down now?" Somerville listened for a bit, then said, "Thanks, Bill. See you in five." Somerville hung up the phone, and looked to Hart and Novak. "Bill Lewis is the Assistant Principal who's been here the longest, maybe ten years. While I've been in and out for a while, he has a better memory of the students than I do, so I thought he could help us."

"That'll work," said Novak. "Lead the way."

* * *

At an office suite next to the main office, Hart, Novak and Somerville met Bill Lewis standing outside his office speaking with a student. He finished his conversation shortly after the officers arrived, and ushered them into his office. After introductions, Somerville took out Hart's notebook and described the situation that had brought Novak and Hart to Park East.

"Danny is an alumnus of Park East," Somerville added.

"Nice to know, Officer Novak," Lewis said.

"Danny, please."

"Anyway, Bill," continued Somerville, "here's the description they have of a guy who Officer Hart here chased around the school until he vaulted the fence and took off in a car." Somerville read the description slowly to give Lewis a chance to think; given the look on the Assistant Principal's face, he was listening quite intently. After hearing the details, Lewis turned to Hart.

"Obviously this guy was really far in front of you for a while, Officer Hart, but do you have any idea of how old he might be?"

"Not really," Hart replied, "but he was really sure on his feet, so if I was a betting woman, I would say late teens to early 20s, but that's totally subjective."

"I understand," Lewis continued, "I can share some information on people who are known to be close to the drug trade, but I can tell you right now, none of them are ever in school, and I check the numbers and attendance every day -- They're not here, nor do they match the description." He looked up again at Hart. "Did you get any kind of look at the other person in the drug deal?"

"No," Hart replied. "At that time, they were really far away from me, and once the first guy peeled, I focused on the one I thought was the seller," she said. The other guy was gone practically before I could even give chase."

"Got it," Lewis said. "Teddy and I can get that info together now if you want to wait." He looked up at Somerville, adding, "I'm thinking about Jamal, Eldon Hess and Poola, Teddy."

"I figured," said Somerville.

"Well," continued Lewis, "Maybe it will do some good with Danny and Stephanie on their trail -- we certainly haven't had much luck."

"Amen, brother," said Somerville.

Chapter Twenty

Novak and Hart left the school and returned to the abandoned car. Finding it gone, they continued on patrol, focusing more on regular patrol duties than on the chase around Park East. Somerville and Lewis had given them a copy of the names of current high school students who were suspected of being involved in the drug trade, and planned to give that to detectives at the 9th once they completed their shift. Hart was driving toward Dolman Park where they intended to have lunch, when Novak received a call on his cell.

"Hello?" he said. Hart couldn't hear the other side of the conversation, but noticed Novak tense up slightly.

"Okay," Novak said "We can do that." Novak looked out the window at their current location, and added "We'll be at Dolman Park in about 10 minutes. Why don't we meet there?" Novak nodded as he listened, then finished with,

"Got it, and we have some other information about some students for you as well. Yep. See you then." While his tone was neutral, Novak ended the call with a stabbing gesture.

Hart glanced at him. "Something tells me that wasn't a pleasant phone call," she said. "If so, don't take it out on the phone." She noticed that Novak didn't appreciate her attempt at humor.

"You're probably right, but I've never liked phones that much anyway," Novak replied. Turning to Hart, he added, "Actually, that was Thomas Fair on the phone."

"The detective, right?"

"Yep" said Novak. "And he wants to talk to us about our time at Park East."

"Meaning we did something wrong?" asked Hart.

"Well, Fair certainly thinks so." Novak shook his head, then spoke again. "No, that's not exactly right. "Actually, Fair is one of the better detectives when it comes to working with uniforms, but I still have the sense we're going to get our hands slapped today. My guess? He'll probably have a problem with our giving chase or not calling them earlier, or some other shit." He turned and smiled at Hart. "I'm not going to worry about it, Steve; he isn't our boss, after all."

"Well," began Hart, "that's a very comforting thought, Danny. Thanks."

As Hart pulled the cruiser into a parking slot close to the gazebo, Novak turned to her and asked, "Have you ever met Fair, Steve?"

"No," Hart replied. "I know the name, and may have seen him before, but I can't put the name with the face."

Novak laughed. "Well, as I said, he's one of the nicer detectives, but he does do things by the book, which I guess is really okay. He certainly won't take any negatives up the line unless he things something is really egregious, and this wasn't. Anyway, let's just call it in and wait."

Novak left the cruiser as Hart called in their location and that they were standing by to speak with a detective. She had just joined Novak at the gazebo when an unmarked police car drove up and a tall man in a suit walked out. The man stretched, reached into the car and retrieved a small notebook, then approached the gazebo. He had a comfortable gait, Hart noticed. Novak didn't rise when he approach, but in other ways seemed receptive.

Motioning toward a side rail, Novak said "Take a load off, Thomas." Before sitting, Fair approached Hart.

"Thomas Fair," he said, extending his hand.

"Stephanie Hart, " Hart said. "Pleased to meet you, Detective."

Fair smiled and leaned on the side railings.

"Where's Shore, Thomas?" asked Novak, referring to Fair's partner.

"Finishing some reports at Central," Fair replied. "I really hate that shit, and she's so much better at it anyway." The small talk apparently over, Fair turned to Hart. "So Hart, you were the track star earlier?"

"Looks like it," Hart said. "That wasn't what we set out to do, by the way. The original job was to call in an abandoned car; the race was just the gravy."

Fair chuckled at this in spite of himself. "My understanding is that you don't have much of a description to give us." The tone in his voice had become ever so slightly accusatory."

"I think that's about right, Detective," Hart said, not taking the bait. "What I've got is what I've got." With that, she took out her notebook to show to Fair. Novak noticed the unusual color of the paper and that it wasn't standard issue. Hart paged through several sheets, then tore some out of the book to both Fair's and Novak' surprise. Noticing their reaction, Hart laughed.

"Relax guys," she said. "They're no-carbon pages, so I still have a complete record within the book." Turning to Fair she continued. "This way you can have everything I wrote without having to re-write it yourself." She gave the sheets to Fair, who looked them over slowly. From Novak's vantage point, it looked like there were a lot more words on the pages than he thought they contained while at the high school. Fair continued to read, but finally looked up.

"You know," he said, "taking on that drug dealer alone with only cruiser backup wasn't the smartest thing to do, Hart." Hart only nodded, so Fair continued. "Please avoid doing that in the future so we don't lose somebody who -- unlike Novak here," he gestured with his thumb - "can provide me with some really decent notes." He gave Hart a small smile then turned to Novak.

"Does she always produce notes as complete as these?"

"Of course," Novak replied. "All my probationary officers do that."

Fair was silent for a while, before asking, "You said you had some information for me about some drug dealing students?"

Novak handed Fair the information he had received from Somerville and Lewis, which Fair also examined carefully. He looked at each profile in turn, then pointing, said "I think this one here -- Hess? He sounds like someone who's affiliated with Cobra. I just can't remember if he has another name, but we'll check it out. Thanks, folks," Fair said, rising. "Now you can get back to business." Fair shook their hands, ambled back to his cruiser, then backed out and was gone before Hart spoke.

"That wasn't so bad," she said.

"No," Novak agreed. "It wasn't. And while it may not have been the best decision to give chase so quickly, I don't know what else they expected us to do, so don't worry about it."

"Does that mean you'll be called on it?"

"I doubt it," Novak said. "Fair actually is 'fair,' so if he seems to be okay with it after all, it won't go anywhere else." He turned to Hart again, glancing at her lap. "A no-carbon notebook?"

"It was standard procedure in my MP company."

Novak shook his head again. "You never cease to amaze me," he said finally.

"I thought I was supposed to."

Chapter Twenty One

The team from Great Mt. Zion was holding its own in the pick up game against the Melrose Avenue Bullets. Harold felt that getting the guys away from the familiar environment of the church to test their mettle against another, more experienced team was a good strategy for them. Harold was pleased: his team kept their heads after a series of steals, kept to their zones, and had gotten more aggressive under the boards as they warmed up. And he sensed they were feeling good about themselves as well. Harold had given them valuable feedback during halftime, and he had also conferred with the other coach for his comments so he could share them with his team after the game." As he watched the final few minutes of the game, Harold looked beyond the court to a white SUV parked at the curb. Harold frowned as he saw it, then returned his attention to the game, but he was concerned and a bit annoyed at the sight.

A foul was called against one of his players, and while the teams lined up under the basket, Harold glanced again at the SUV and saw what he was dreading -- a long time friend and drug dealer leaning against the SUV. Harold sighed and brought his attention back to the game, but his heart wasn't in it, and once the game was over a minute or two later, he gratefully shook the hands of the opposing players and coaches. The host team had agreed to supply ice cream to both teams when they completed the game, so Harold excused himself briefly, and approached the SUV.

Harold walked with confidence, though not particularly willingly. As he approached, the other man spoke.

"What up, Harold?"

"I'm good, T-Wright," Harold responded. "You're a little out of your turf, aren't you?"

"I could say the same about you, Harold," Wright said. Wright seem to even talk with a swagger.

"I'm just a college student and youth basketball coach, Terry -- I don't *have* a turf."

"You could have *and* have a lot more of what you probably want, too," said Wright.

"Do we have to do this every time we talk, Terry?" Harold said. "You know I don't do this." Looking straight at Wright, he added, "You don't have to either, man."

Wright made a dismissive gesture. "Save it, Harold." he snarled. "What I got goin' is taking care of me, taking care of my Moms," he turned to touched his SUV. "And givin' me this sweet ride." Wright smiled a very wide smile at his friend. "You could have it too, Harold, and it ain't that hard."

"You can save it, Terry," Harold countered. "You know I don't roll that way." Leaning forward slightly, Harold added. "You don't need to mess with my guys either, Terry. They don't need the cars, the money…they just don't need it, alright?"

"Can't say that, Harold, but" Wright glanced briefly at the boys eating ice cream. "I don't need to hassle them; they'll be looking for me soon enough."

No threat was implied, but Harold felt closed in anyway. Harold sighed, then remembered his original question.

"You *are* out of your turf, Terry," he asked. "What's up with that?"

"Things change, Harold," Wright said with a shrug. "Lines can change, you know."

"You can get hurt too, Terry," Harold said. "Watch out, alright?"

"You don't need to worry about me, Harold," Wright said. "I got this."

Harold turned toward the basketball courts, saying, "That's what I'm afraid of."

Chapter Twenty Two

Muster began sharply at 0700, with the usual discussion of recent crimes, gang activity and suspects to look out for. The meeting was routine until Sgt. O.C. Boyd turned to the topic of the increasing drug trade in the precinct.

"Folks, this is getting out of hand," Boyd began. "The loot told us how important our connection to the community was and this is really important, particularly now that we are seeing more and more people dealing throughout the precinct." Boyd removed his reading glasses and stepped away from the podium. "Let's just bat this around for a while, people. What have you been hearing or seeing?

The squad was silent until Novak raised his hand.

"Danny?" Boyd. "What do you have?"

"I have a couple of things, O.C.," Novak said. "First, Stephanie and I spoke with somebody a couple of days ago about some changes in the boundaries for the big traffickers."

"What do you mean, Danny?" asked Patrick Weiss. While not usually so responsive, Weiss was clearly interested.

"What we discovered," said Novak, "is about some of the boundaries between the three big traffickers, you know, the Patrick, Spino and Cobra groups." Picking up a marker, Novak drew a crude map of Port Angel.

"If you look at this incredibly accurate map of our fair city..," Novak said, with a snicker. "Anyway," Novak continued, "We know there are three major traffickers in the city, and the lines, look a little like this for the Spino, Patrick and Cobra groups." Novak drew lines that divided the city, which approximated the lines of the trafficker's turfs and how they intersected in or near the 9th precinct. Turning back to his fellow officers, Novak continued. "Obviously, there is some area that no one seems to own, and these guys seem to operate pretty comfortably without a lot of conflicts."

Novak returned to his table, but stood and continued to face the squad. "What is happening according to this source, is that Cobra's people -- actually Cobra himself, this person thinks -- is accelerating his push into the other territories. It looks like Cobra's becoming a lot more aggressive, and we're just about in the middle of it."

"Who is this source, Danny?" asked Boyd.

"Harold Williams."

"Good enough for me," Boyd said.

Hart rose to face the squad as well. "What we also heard from Harold, is that there is even more pressure from Cobra on those few independent dealers to leave the area. Harold said that people who would usually be ignored or warned off are now getting the shit kicked out of them."

"Have we heard anything from other precincts, about the other traffickers?" Angela Marin asked. "Are they doing the same land grab that Cobra is making?" Marin looked around the room to the silent officers. "Anybody?"

"We may have to ask some other people about that, Gee," said Boyd, picking up his clipboard. "I'll make some calls today." He turned again to Novak. "Which reminds me Danny, what was the second thing you were going to talk about?"

"Oh," said Novak. "Hart and I chased a dealer on Monday around Park East who ended up near the high school." Novak shrugged. "It may not be a big thing, but according to Teddy Somerville, some of the trafficking near the school has been picking up as well. He gave us info on a few students he thinks might be involved."

"Did you say 'chased,' Danny?" asked Boyd.

"Well, it seemed like the right thing to do, O.C.," Novak began.

"Not arguing with you on that, Danny -- just curious," said Boyd. "Everything passed on to the detectives?"

"Yep," said Novak. "Gave it to Fair yesterday."

"Okay," said Boyd. "You think we ought to get Fair and Shore here to bat it around some more?"

"Sure," said Novak.

"I can make copies of my notes from yesterday if you want, Sgt." said Hart.

"That would be good, Hart," Boyd said. Facing the entire group, he added, "Maybe we can start to make a dent in this."

Chapter Twenty Three

The uniformed officers left the room as muster concluded. Hart and Novak gathered their gear and prepared to go on patrol, when Hart received a text on her cell phone. She took out her phone, checked the text and smiled.

"What's up?" Novak asked.

"Just got a text from my best new girlfriend," Hart replied. "We're going to get massages on Saturday."

"Really?" Novak asked. "Hell, she never takes me for massages."

"She told me you don't even like massages, Danny."

"Not the point, Steve." Novak turned to leave the muster room and ran into the standing figure of David Moody, one of the precinct's detectives. Right behind him was his partner, Siem Porter.

"Detectives," Novak said. "What brings you here this fine morning?"

Moody waited before responding. "Novak," he said. "Siem and me --we're just doing our jobs." Something in his mood bothered Hart and she approached Novak to back him up.

"And?"

"Well, part of our job is to investigate things, you know what *detectives* are supposed to do."

"Fascinating," said Novak. "You want to get to the point, Moody?"

"The point," Porter answered instead, "Is that you're not making it any easier for us to do our jobs by not doing *yours*."

"Uh huh," Novak answered. "And just how did we do that, Siem?"

"A little respect, Novak," Porter said. "And cut the shit. Did it ever occur to you that chasing suspects all over the place and investigating things that aren't really your job, might get in the way?"

"Nope," Novak replied as he crossed his arms, "Maybe you ought to tell me about that."

Porter advanced toward Novak, who held his ground. Hart moved closer as well.

Moody snarled at her. "And you, some God damned probationary officer, just thought you would chase a suspect without permission? Do you ever want to get rid of that blue 'babycop' shield, Hart?

Hart held up her hands in mock fright. "Ooh," she said. "Please don't hurt me, Mr. Detective!"

Despite the tension, Novak laughed. Looking squarely at Moody, Novak said, "You obviously haven't met Hart before have you, Moody?"

"Look, Novak," Porter said, as he stepped closer, "we're just trying to do our job, and part of that is to work on the drug trade here. We just need you guys to help us and not get in the way."

"No problem there, Siem," Novak said, after a pause. "All you have to do is ask for our help, you know."

"Alright, Novak," Porter said. "Why don't we just take it from there?"

Moody still seemed annoyed, and turned to Hart, holding out his hand.

"I need you to give me your notes, Hart," he said brusquely.

"No."

"*No?*" replied Moody.

Hart raised her palms in surrender. "Hey, I already gave them to Detective Fair, and the only copies I have left are in my permanent notebook. So, no." Developing a milder tone, she added, "But I'd be happy to make you a copy; I'm on my way to copy or scan them now. Or, you can ask Detective Fair to share his notes with you: your choice."

"Look Hart, we don't have time…"

"Dave," Novak said quietly. "Fair asked us for information and Hart's notes and she gave them to him. It was a righteous move, and Fair isn't hard to deal with. And like Hart said, she'll gladly send you a copy as soon as she gets to a computer or a copier."

"We got it, Dave," interjected Porter. Turning to his partner, he added, "Let's catch up with Fair and Shore and see what they got." Moody paused, then turned to accompany his partner, when Novak stopped them.

"Wait a minute, guys," Novak said. Glancing briefly at Hart, he added, "We probably ought to share some of the information we got from a man in the precinct. You might know the Heaven's Home restaurant in Lexington. Well, the son of the owners is named Harold and…."

"Will this be in your notes, Hart?" Moody asked.

"Some of it, Detective, though the notes …." Hart began,

"Fine," Moody said dismissively. "We'll take it from here."

"Dave, we just want to give you the information -- we don't intend to do anything with it."

"First smart thing you said today, Novak," Moody countered. "Like I said, we'll take from here." Turning to his partner, he said, "Let's go, Siem." And the detectives turned down the hallway to the bullpen. Novak rolled his eyes as they left. He turned to Hart and noticed that two other officers had overheard the exchange.

"Still as arrogant as ever," Novak said.

"And that's a *surprise* to you?" replied Carson Poole with a snicker.

Novak shrugged, then turned back to Hart. "First negative encounter with our detectives, huh, Steve?"

"Eh," Hart replied, checking her watch. "They're not as scary as they think they are." Moving toward the door, she continued, "Can we make those copies and go on patrol now?"

Chapter Twenty Four

Terry Wright waited outside Gray's office nervously. He had only met the big boss a few times, and had never before been the focus of the conversation. Wright liked working for Cobra: the work wasn't took hard, the money was good and it didn't take much out of him. But he also knew that the drug trade wasn't something he could or would want to do forever. Could Harold Williams be right -- that it just wasn't worth it at all? Wright could hear some rumbling within the office, right before the door finally opened. Emilio Cabral came out.

"Come on in, T-Wright," Cabral said. Cabral stepped back from the door to let Wright in. Wright walked in slowly, not wanting to do anything out of turn.

"Sit down, Terry," Gray said, as he gestured with his hands. "We're just going to have a talk."

"Yes, sir." Wright said, sitting down carefully. He waited and tried to sit as casually as possible.

"Would you like something, Terry," Gray asked. Maybe some water?"

"No, sir. I just want… uh.. no sir.

"Don't be nervous, Terry," Gray said. "We're just having a conversation."

"Yes sir."

"Very well, said Gray. "Emilio here has told me that you spoke again with Harold Williams. Is that right?"

"Yes, sir."

"And?"

"He don't want to join us, sir," Wright replied, shaking his head. "I mean, I asked him and I already told him what he can get if joins up, but he doesn't get it, you know?"

Gray continued to look at him, and Wright shrank a little bit more into himself.

"What else did he say?" asked Cabral.

"Well," Wright began. "He asked me to leave his guys alone, you know, the guys on his basketball team?"

"Well *that's* not gonna happen," Cabral said.

A glance from Gray silenced him. "Alright, Terry," Gray continued. "What do *you* think we ought to do?"

Wright eyes widened. "About Harold?" he asked, incredulous.

Gray only nodded.

"Me?" Wright continued, shaking his head. "Well, sir, I mean.. I really...."

"Terry, you're not in trouble," Gray said, though his tone left some doubt in Wright's mind.

"No?"

"No," Gray replied. "I just want your opinion -- on what we ought to do about Harold Williams."

"Well he *is* my friend, sir, I" Wright paused. "wouldn't really want to have to hurt him or anything."

"Neither would I, Terry," Gray replied.

"But we want Harold on our side or at least not in our way," Cabral said. "You can understand that, can't you, T-Wright?"

"Sure, Griffin," Wright replied. "I get what you're sayin'. I just don't know what else I can do to help you, you know?" Wright tried hard not to fidget, which almost guaranteed that he squirmed in his seat."

Cabral glanced briefly to Gray, seeking some kind of signal. A very slight nod was all he needed.

"The problem, Terry," Cabral began," is that for things to work out the way we want, we have to make sure Harold is out of the way one way or the other." Cabral said this slowly so it would sink in. "Mr. Gray has to take the long view of his business, and we can't have things messing up our plans." Cabral leaned even closer to Wright. "Do you see what I'm sayin' here, Terry?"

"Sure Griffin," Wright replied, even more nervous. "I mean, what are you gonna do to Harold?" At this, Wright turned his head toward Gray. One look at Gray's eyes and Wright didn't ask any more questions.

"I think you're getting the idea now, Terry," said Gray. He smiled at Wright adding, "Thank you for your time. You can go now."

Wright shot up from his seat. "Yes, sir, Mr. Gray," he said. Wright added, "Thank you, sir" as he made his way to the door. Wright left, and Cabral closed the door behind him. Then he turned his attention back to Gray.

"What do we do with Terry, sir?"

"Nothing," Gray said. "Terry is loyal and while he is afraid for Harold, he is more afraid for himself."

"Yeah," Cabral said with a laugh. "I thought he was gonna shit his pants."

Gray looked angrily at Cabral. "He doesn't *matter*, Emilio. *Focus*," said Gray. "What we need to work on is either getting Harold out of the way or taking away any power or influence he has."

"Not take any real action against him?"

"That's what we have to decide, Emilio," Gray replied. "But my instinct is that killing Harold would backfire. Somehow taking away his influence, discrediting him in the eyes of the police and the community would be better plus it wouldn't lead to other problems we don't need."

"How do we do that?" Cabral asked.

"Simple," Gray said almost casually. "We simply have to put him in situations where people see a different side of him, or plant evidence of drug involvement on him so people stop following him." Gray smiled. "It's simple, really."

"And you think we can do that?" Cabral asked.

"You should know by now, Emilio," Gray began. "That there is very little I can't do when I put my mind to it." Gray leaned back in his chair before continuing.

"Bring in the rest of the boys so we can get started on this," Gray said. "We have work to do."

Chapter Twenty Five

The sound of a pen scratching on paper was all that could be heard from the pastor's office at Greater Mt. Zion AME Church. Rev. Archie Price preferred the feel of pen and paper to a computer when writing his sermons, though he was quite computer literate with everything else in his life. Younger than his predecessor, Price was always cognizant of his vision for the future for both himself and his church. Once he had his bible verses and the theme for his sermons, he generally found the words flowed easily, but his sermons still took time and solitude to complete.

He was a bit annoyed, therefore, to hear the knock at the door to his study.

"Come in," Price said. The door opened, and Deacon Ernest Collins entered with a smile. Collins approached the desk with his customary confident stride. Price rose to greet his visitor.

"Good afternoon, Deacon Collins -- Ernest," Price said as he extended his hand.

"Good to see you, Rev. Price," Collins countered. He glanced briefly to the desk and noted the paper. "Hard at work on the sermon, Archie?"

"It *is* that time, Ernest." He smiled and came from behind the desk, moving toward the overstuffed chairs. "Let's sit," he said.

"I don't want to interrupt you," Collins said.

"I can get back into it, Ernest," he said. "What can I do for you?"

Collins began after gathering his thoughts. "I am concerned Archie, about what I see as the wrong kind of increased police presence in the neighborhood connected to the drug trade. You know as I do that the police don't always understand that people in our community are people, and not just statistics." He sighed, and continued. "I want people to be helped and want the community to be whole, but what really concerns me is this sense that somehow we're going to be living in a police state."

"I agree with you," Price said. "But Ernest, we have to understand that we focus more on the souls of our people than just the flesh." Noting the tightening in Collins' hands, Price quickly continued. "As a congregation we can work to influence what happens in our community, which is what we've been trying to do since long before I arrived at Greater Mt. Zion."

"Yes, yes," Collins said, dismissively. "But that doesn't take away our responsibility to protect the Lexington and Auburn neighborhoods from drug dealers and overzealous police."

"I agree," countered Price. "We *do* have that responsibility, but we are not the only players in this." He sought to reduce the tension by speaking more quietly and slowly. "The decision to take or sell drugs is still one that people have to make one at a time. We spend much of our time working with youth here to help more of them make the right decisions."

"And you think that's been working?" The challenge in Collins' voice was clear.

Price sighed, but tried to maintain his smile. "I do, yet it is something we have to address every single day. Ernest, I'm not a big fan of the police in this city, either. I think they've generally abandoned Lexington and Auburn and other neighborhoods, for that matter. And when they want to make a splash by making big arrests they come back in and round up everybody, including people who've never done anything wrong." Price could hear his own tension rising again, and paused. "So yes, I know they often don't get it or care to get it."

"There must be more we can or should do, Archie."

"Perhaps, Ernest, though I must tell you that I don't think this church should become involved politically, and that's what this sounds like to me."

Here Collins smiled. "That isn't exactly what I was thinking about Archie," Collins replied. "What I've been thinking about instead is simply using our pulpit to promote the kind of community we want." Collins leaned forward. "And that may also help us in giving Lexington the kind of police presence we really want -- you know, police who care about us, maybe because they are really a part of us." Collins stayed silent then. He knew that Price didn't like him very much. Pastors and deacons often clash on issues of the spirit, while trustees of the church clash with pastors on issues of finance. However, Collins also knew that Price was smart and committed to the betterment of the community. And Collins hoped that would be enough.

Leaning forward himself, Price asked, "So what is it you have in mind, Ernest?"

"I spoke to one of my friends, Archie," Collins said, "Lt. Samuel Perkins at the 9th precinct a while ago, just to ask that the police spend time with us as people rather than as just police. He seemed to get it, and is trying to make that happen. I don't think it's too much to ask that we see police in our neighborhoods when we have big church events, basketball games and the like and not just when they're arresting us, you see?"

"I do, Ernest," Price agreed. "And I think there is a way we can promote this; a way we can make that happen even as we continue to fight against the drug trade, but it may be tough."

Collins laughed. "Well, you always told us you were a tough non-nonsense preacher."

"Well, I guess I did at that," Pricce said. Rising, he continued. "Let me work on that."

Chapter Twenty Six

Gray and his lieutenants sat together in his office after Terry Wright left.

On the table in front of them was a street map of Port Angel. Gray examined the map silently for a while, before turning to Cabral.

"Emilio," Gray began. "How do you think we should do this?"

Cabral was quiet for a while. "Cobra, I think we should just know where they're going to be and strike them."

"We know that Emilio," Gray snapped. "What I am asking you is how we ought to do that." The other lieutenants chuckled, until Gray silenced them with a glance.

"Let me make this clear to all of you," Gray said, very deliberately. "We need to make this strike carefully and without error."

Sheepishly, Ricky Sayles asked "I don't know how you want to do this, sir. I mean, you always say you don't want to kill people unless you have to, and I don't know how else we can get what we want." Sayles looked down, hoping he wouldn't provoke an angry response from Gray."

"Well, I would rather you ask than do the wrong thing, Ricky," Gray said. "Well done." Gray rubbed his eyes, then continued.

"What we are trying to do is to secure our territory and show the independent dealers that working for us is the only way they can truly be successful. At the same time, we need to show them that working for anyone but us can be dangerous to their health." Turning to his lieutenants again, he added, "Now, can anyone tell me how we might do this?"

"Well," Cabral said. "I have two of our people ready to strike when I tell them to." Turning to his colleagues, he added, "How many do you guys have?"

"I have three," said Sayles.

"Me too," Pepe Brantley said.

Tommy Burch was counting on his fingers. "I have three who are really good, and another one who can pull it off, but he's a little scared -- he's never used a gun before and doesn't want to kill anybody."

Gray bristled. "I did not say we were going to kill anyone, Tommy," Gray said. "Did you tell him that?"

"Sure, Boss," Burch countered. "But -- I don't know, maybe he just thought I was lying to him."

"Building trust with your people is very important, Tommy," Gray said softly. "They must always know what you expect and what you mean." The disapproval in Gray's voice was clear, but he did not belabor it.

"Eleven people will probably be sufficient," Gray said. "Now, let's look at the map so we can determine where our strikes need to take place."

The group leaned over the map, and the lieutenants began marking the corners with the greatest amount of activity for the independent drug dealers. They determined that they could cover five corners -- perhaps six -- with the people they had already identified. If the lieutenants themselves participated, they could cover the sixth corner easily.

Gray turned to Burch. "Tommy, let us assume you will use your dependable three. If you want to use the fourth, I want you to be there with him to back him up."

"Yes, sir," Burch said. "I can do that."

Brantley's eyebrows creased as Burch was speaking.

"Yes, Pepe?" asked Gray.

"Boss, I don't know how many of us you want out there," Brantley offered. Seeing no reaction from Gray, Brantley continued. "I mean, how much do you want *us* out there?" A light bulb went on in Cabral's head.

"I get it, Boss," Cabral said. "The more we're out, the more they can get to you." Cabral nodded as he spoke. "Yeah, that does make sense," Cabral wondered out loud. "Do you think maybe five corners would be enough?" Cabral asked. "Five good strikes that we know we can count on is better than five and one half assed one that might or might not work, you know?"

"A valuable question, Emilio," Gray said finally. "That is what we should determine." He turned to the map again. "If we were to strike only five corners, which should they be?"

The group discussed several potential strike areas, and talked about some of the independent dealers they wanted to target. Based on where the dealers usually operated and made the most sales, they settled on the five corners: Diamond at 17th; Uber and Lowe; Berks and Moore; 21st and Pell, and Canal and 12th. These corners were close enough to the strongest areas of the independents, and also bordered on the territories of the other two major drug traffickers.

"Now," Gray said. "We need to be sure that we pick a time when we have the most action on each of these corners; what do we know about that?"

"What action are you looking for, Boss?" Burch asked. "Like, action with dealing, or action with lots of people around to see what's up?

"That's a good point, Boss," said Cabral. "The timing is going to be important, now that I think about it."

Gray sat back in his chair and sighed. "That is not a difficult question at all, gentlemen," he said. "We are not here to hurt innocents. We are making an attempt to clean up the trade and push the independents out as part of our long term plan." He took a deep breath and continued. "So, our objective is to disrupt the trade without hurting innocents, is that clear?" To a chorus of "Yes, sirs," Gray said,

"Good. Now we can make a final decision and put this plan into effect."

Chapter Twenty Seven

The corner of Diamond and 17th Streets is a relatively quiet corner within the Lexington district. It is home to a large number of people, given that several public housing units were located close by. In addition, people commuting to or from work often passed by the corner as it is one block from a major bus line. These two factors contributed to it becoming a significant corner for the drug trade. Located four blocks from the Spino territory, three from Parker, and seven from Gray's stronghold, it was an area in which the smaller drug dealers worked and managed the trade.

Sitting in a car a block away, Emilio Cabral sat in a car with three of his dealers, waiting and watching the action. While Cabral was calm and contemplative, the younger men in the car were anything but.

"How are we going to do this, Griffin?" asked Boo, an eighteen year old Black youth with a shaved head. "I want to be ready, man."

Cabral turned his head slowly, silently wishing he had brought someone less trigger-happy with him.

"Boo, you need to just chill," Cabral said. "What we want is to get people to leave and not buy anything else from these dealers." Cabral added. "But we don't need to kill anybody, got it?"

Boo nodded vigorously. "Yeah, I got it Griffin," Boo countered. "I just want to do it right, you know?"

Cabral turned around in his seat to look at the two other man/ boys in his car, Jimmy J. and Kody. "You got this, right?" he asked.

Both of them nodded, with Jimmy J. adding, "Just point me to it, Griffin."

"It's got to be quick and we can't have any mistakes," Cabral said after a brief pause. "Cobra is not gonna like any bystanders being hit." The demeanor of the other three in the car changed visibly.

Cabral was annoyed. "What the fuck is it now?" he said angrily. "Can you do this or not?"

"Yeah, Griffin, yeah," Kody replied. "It's just that it ain't so easy to shoot at a guy and not hit nobody, you know?" Kody shrugged. "I mean, I can't be sure we're not gonna hit somebody."

Cabral turned in his chair again, and his tone was quiet and menacing. "You do that, and you may be next, Kody," he said. "Cobra doesn't want anybody hurt who isn't a dealer. It's better to shoot your own damn self than somebody who isn't a dealer."

Kody shrank into himself. "Shoulda picked somebody else," he said, under his breath.

Cabral heard the young man, and said equally quietly, "Should have at that." Cabral took a deep breath and looked down at his phone checking the time. After a moment, he placed a call.

Cabral heard "Yo?" from the phone.

"'Sup' Ricky?" Cabral asked Sayles, who was stationed with his people at the corner of Berks and Moore, almost into Spino territory.

"We good here, Griffin," Sayles said. "Except...."

"Except?" Cabral prompted.

Cabral could hear Sayles sigh. "Except people getting scared they're gonna fuck things up."

Sayles could hear the exhale from Cabral. "Same shit here, Ricky," Cabral said finally. "Is this shit as hard as they're makin' it out to be?"

"No, it's not," Sayles said with an edge to his voice. "How hard is it to shoot into the air, maybe push 'em around some and fly?" The distaste was evident in his voice. "Who the fuck did we bring to this party?"

"You got that right," Cabral said, then added as he surveyed his people, "But I think they can do it." Turning his attention back to the street and the corner of Diamond and 17th, Cabral asked, "What kind of action you got there right now?"

"It's slow," Sayles began. "I mean, that little guy -- what's his name -- Pookie? He's here, but not much happenin'. I think maybe another 15 minutes."

"You called anybody else?" Cabral asked.

"No, you want me to?" Sayles replied. "I can call Tommy."

"No," Cabral said. "I'll call Tommy, because he needs to hear from me; you call Pepe." Cabral took his phone from his ear and examined the time again. "Tell you what, Ricky," he said, "you call Pepe and see if he thinks he can make it happen at 6:30 and then get back to me. I'm gonna do the same with Tommy."

"Okay," Sayles said.

Cabral hung up, then quickly called Tommy Burch. Burch was seeing normal activity at his corner as well. Cabral told him to keep his people in line and be ready for a call, but to plan on 6:30, which Burch confirmed.

As Cabral ended his call to Burch, he checked his corner again. He saw a few people walking past the corner and one dealer talking with customers and others. Cabral turned in his seat. "Kody, you said there's two dealers who work this corner, right?" Cabral asked.

"Yeah, Griffin," replied Kody. "Usually it's Benny and Scratch; Benny only sells weed." Kody said it as though Benny was a lesser being. "Scratch has been selling rock for a while, and someone told me he has gotten ahold of some smack, too."

Cabral pointed through the window. "So where is Scratch?" he asked. "You said he's here around 6:00 at night, right?"

"Yeah," Kody said. "I checked it out for I think three of the last five days, so it should be okay." Kody looked out the window as well and was slowly losing confidence as time marched on. "We just gotta be patient is all, Griffin," he said.

Cabral looked out the window, saying "You better hope you're right." Thinking again, he took out his phone and hit speed dial.

"You have news, Emilio?" came the voice of Gray.

"No, sir," replied Cabral. "Not yet. We're just getting the timing organized. Ricky and I talked to Pepe and Tommy so we can get them organized. We think the strike will be at 6:30."

"That will do, Emilio," Gray replied. "Do you have the proper control on your people?" It was the question that Cabral had dreaded hearing. Figuratively crossing his fingers, Cabral said "Yes. I think so. We emphasized it with our people and they know what has to happen and how."

"Then we have nothing to worry about, do we?" asked Gray.

After a brief shiver, Cabral answered, "No sir."

"Good," said Gray. "Call me when you are finished." And Gray ended the call.

Cabral looked up and noticed that a second man had joined Benny at the corner." Turning to Kody and pointing to the corner, Cabral asked "Scratch?"

Kody leaned forward in his seat, and, seeing Scratch at the corner, said "Yeah."

"Good, " Cabral said. "We should be ready soon. Jimmy and Kody, we're going to drop you off at the middle of the block on 17th, and then Boo and me will pull up right onto the corner. All you have to do is walk normally right up to the corner. By the time you get there, we'll have them blocked in by the car, you got it?

"Sure," and "Yeah," were the replies.

"Good," Cabral continued "Remember shots into the ground or in the air, and if either Benny or Scratch get to you, rough 'em up and make some noise -- don't hit anybody ese, but make sure they're scared." As he finished speaking, Cabral's phone rang."

"We got everybody ready, Griffin," came Sayles' voice.

"Good," Cabral said. "Then we're go at 6:30 which is in" he checked his phone again -- "two minutes."

"Got it," said Sayles. "I'm out."

Cabral started the engine, then turned for the last time to his companions.

"Let's do this."

Chapter Twenty Eight

Harold Williams drove the twelve passenger van from the church carefully down Canal toward the baseball stadium. Harold and the pastor felt that field trips like this were a good incentive to keep members of the church basketball team members engaged with the church and community in the right ways. They also hoped it would keep them from spending too much time on the streets. As Harold drove into the parking lot, two of the drug dealers who had been attacked during the strike ran from Canal and 12th to the stadium, arriving at about the same time.

Harold opened the door to the van, and turned around to be tackled by Stack, a short stocky dealer who had escaped his beating when a bystander at Canal and 12th called the police. Harold picked himself off the ground, crying,

"Hey, man!" What are you doing?" Harold brushed himself off as Stack arose.

"What the f…," said Stack. "Oh, hey Harold man, umm…."

"What are you doing Stack?" said Harol. Then Williams noted the bruises just beginning to form on Stack's face. "Whoa, Stack, what happened to you?"

Stack brushed himself off and kept looking from side to side, hoping to spot his buddy Luke from Canal and 12th. But before he saw Luke, he saw two uniformed officers moving quickly toward him and the van.

"Shit, I gotta go, man," Stack said as he turned to leave.

"Wait," Williams said. "What happened to you, man?"

In answer, Stack turned to take off down the parking lot, just as he heard,

"Stop right there, Stack!" from one of the officers. Stack froze, with his hands raised, and slumped. The officer turned then to Harold and said, "You, too. Get over there with your friend!"

"*Me?*" Harold asked, stunned.

The officer turned Harold around to face the van. "You see anybody else here, asshole?"

Harold could hear Stack cursing under his breath. "Shit, man," he said to no one in particular.

"Hey, man," said Stack to the officers. "Hey, he don't know anything, he's...."

"Shut the fuck up!" the officer countered. Not knowing what else to do, Harold got quiet and followed Stack's lead. He looked over his shoulder into the van and hoped his players would contact someone from the church to take care of them since Harold couldn't, and both he and Stack were led into patrol cars and whisked away.

* * *

The drive back from the Evolution spa seemed leisurely to Hart and Sheryl Novak. After facials, massages, manicures and pedicures, they were truly relaxed and content. Sheryl pointed out other landmarks and shopping areas to Stephanie as they drive. While she had lived in Port Angel for over a year, Hart still didn't know her way around certain parts of the city. She reflected on how she had perhaps been too focused on career and not enough on herself through the police academy and her probationary period. She turned to Sheryl Novak.

"Sheryl," she began. "This was wonderful. Thank you for the day and helping me feel about the best I have for a long time."

"Happy to do it, Steve," Sheryl said. "I know how hard it can be to move to a new area, especially to Port Angel."

"Why is here so different?"

"Well, maybe not so different," Sheryl said. "I guess since I moved during high school it was harder than it was in previous moves."

"But your Dad wasn't military, was he?"

"Nope," said Sheryl. "But he was trying to move up in his company, and they sent him to quite a few places while I was growing up." Sheryl gave a satisfied sigh. "And we finally ended up in Port Angel." She laughed. "Then my mother put her foot down and said we're not moving anywhere else." She turned to her friend. "And my Dad figured if she wasn't happy, then she would make sure *he* wasn't happy, either. So...."

"I get the picture," Hart said. "But, you do like it here, right?"

"Now, I do. Absolutely. I truly can't imagine living anywhere else. Danny is the one who could never really leave Port Angel, and I can't imagine being without him."

The two friends were silent for a moment, until Hart, still curious asked, "Danny is really different, isn't he?"

"Different?"

"What I mean by different," Hart began, "Is that he is that rare person who everybody likes, who seems to know everybody, everything about them and how they tick." Hart paused to collect her thoughts and phrase her next statement carefully. "Plus, even as positive as he is, he seems to have this undercurrent of sadness about him. I mean, it's not obvious, because he is usually pretty upbeat. But as I've gotten to know him, he seems to be making up for something, and feeling like he's never quite measured up."

Sheryl's eyes grew moist as she listened to Hart. "Wow," she said. "You know, Steve, you've gotten a better read on Danny in a month than some of the other officers or our friends have after years of knowing him." Sheryl kept driving and it seemed to Hart that Sheryl wanted to be anywhere other than in the car. After a few minutes, Sheryl made a right turn into a parking lot and turned off the engine.

She turned to Hart and with a smile said, "time for tea." And she got out of the car, leading Hart across to a small tea and coffee shop.

After ordering and picking up their drinks, Sheryl led Hart to a table near the idle fireplace. She played with her tea for a while before finally facing her friend. "Danny wasn't exactly a hellion when he was younger, but he ran with a crowd that was on the edge of trouble -- you know, the guys who aren't usually in trouble, but just ten minutes later or one bad decision more and they would have been the habitual troublemakers. They just managed to fly under the radar."

Hart nodded, though she didn't know if Sheryl noticed her nod or not, as her eyes seemed far away.

"And as you can imagine knowing how smart Danny is, his parents and teachers were always telling him how he just wasn't living up to his potential -- the usual parent/ teacher stuff. The thing is," continued Sheryl, "they were right, and Danny knew they were right, but that didn't keep him from having his fun."

Sheryl sat back in her chair. "Well, one day the trouble got out of hand. Danny and four friends were cutting school to hang out and came across another kid who hadn't been in school for a while, so they decided to hang with him. As Danny tells it, the kid kept excusing himself to make calls and disappear around the corner, and Danny and his friends didn't know what was going on, but began to suspect that something was up."

Sheryl turned to face Hart again. "The guys with Danny were basically decent kids, and they didn't want to be involved in drug dealing, which is what this other kid was doing." Sheryl got a chill. "Well, one time the kid came back to the group, and out came a car trying to take him out. Well, they did take him out *and* one of Danny's best friends. Hart could noticed Sheryl tearing up, and she took her friend's hand.

"Cut down right in front of his friends and they all had to watch." Sheryl breathed again. "That changed Danny and his friends, Steve. In fact, the other three guys all left town as soon as they graduated and right now are as far from Port Angel as they can be. Danny is the only one who stayed, but as you said, he may never be satisfied that he is doing enough because of what happened to him and his friends that day." Sheryl looked into Hart's eyes.

"But that's what drives him and he's never going to stop trying to keep kids on the right path." Sheryl stopped and look down at her tea.

Shortly, Hart asked "Why are you telling me this, Sheryl? I mean, I'm happy to know more about Danny and what makes him tick, but I wasn't looking to get into his head or anything."

"Because you needed to know," Sheryl replied. "Since he was commissioned, Danny has talked about lots of other officers, and many are his friends, but he talks differently about you, and that's not just because you're his first probationary officer, Steve. I think he may trust you as much or more than anybody else, and he has genuine friends in the precinct. Since they know this story, or at least a version of it, you needed to know it, too." She chuckled. "And Danny probably wasn't going to tell you."

Sheryl looked at her coffee.

"And I think we ought to head back to the house so we can get ourselves relaxed again." She smiled and rose from her seat.

* * *

As they arrived at the Novak home, Sheryl and Hart were all smiles, once again relaxed and happy. Ignoring the front door, they parked Sheryl's car in the driveway and went outside to the patio, assuming Danny would be out there enjoying the sun. Not seeing him there, they entered the patio doors and saw Danny sitting in the family room.

"Hey, Honey," Sheryl cried. "Did you miss us?"

"Hi," Danny said, as he rose from his seat. His manner and inflection brought both women up short. Before they could say anything, Danny looked at Hart and laughed. "You look nice with your hair out, Steve," he said. "Is your hair naturally wavy like that?" Hart nodded, then stood giving him a look that said "what's going on?" As Novak turned his attention to his wife, he saw the same look on her face. Shaking his head, he indicated the TV with his hand.

"Coordinated strikes against some drug dealers in Lexington, Steve," he said. His face showed the strain. "It looks like we may have the beginning of a real drug war on our hands."

Chapter Twenty Nine

Novak and Hart entered the squad room to meet briefly with Mike Canady, who had called Novak earlier. While not in uniform, they has been asked to stop by the precinct for a briefing about the strike. Hart could see Novak's jaw tighten as he listened to Canady.

"This sounds like it was very organized, Canuck," Novak said.

"We think so too, Danny," Canady said. "We also have something of a lead -- one of Cobra's mid-level dealers; we brought him in along with the other three, but the others were the attackers."

"Which one is from Cobra?" Hart asked.

Canady checked his list. "A Melvin Wells; they call him 'Pebbles' I think."

"I know him," Novak said. "And yes, he is one of Cobra's posse." He shook his head sadly. "A real piece of work, and a little trigger happy." He turned to Canady again. "Which reminds me, is there a body count?"

"That's the surprise, Danny," Canady said. "There was a minor gunshot wound -- really just a flesh wound -- but that was it. The strange thing is that witnesses at all of the scenes reported multiple gun shots. Who is that bad a shot?"

"Someone who isn't trying to hurt anybody," said Hart.

"Meaning?" asked Canady.

"Meaning," Hart replied, "That someone was sending a message."

"I think Steve's right, Canuck," Novak said. "This is Cobra widening his claim, which is exactly what we heard about less than a week ago."

"And you think that's good intel?"

"I do," said Novak. "It came from more than one source," then added, "we already passed it on to Porter and Moody, so they can confirm it."

"Thanks for that, Danny," Canady said, scribbling into his notebook. Looking up he added, "I'll let you know anything else I get, too. I need to get back."

"Appreciate the scoop, Mike. Thanks," said Novak. Canady returned to the holding area, and before Novak and Hart could exit the squad room, they heard a familiar voice.

"Novak! Hart!" called Samuel Perkins.

"Yes, sir," said both officers.

"In my office!"

Novak and Hart nodded their heads and followed Lt. Perkins to his office. Perkins' stride was a little faster and more deliberate than usual, Novak thought. Perkins opened his office door and motioned for Novak and Hart to enter, and when they did, they saw the somber faces of Ruth and Lester Williams. Novak stopped walking and looked at the Williams', wondering what brought them to the precinct. Their faces told him something was very wrong.

Going directly to them, Novak dropped to one knee. "What's wrong?"

Ruth Williams began to tear up and Lester patted her hand. "It's Harold, Danny," Lester said. Novak's face fell.

"No, no, Danny," Lester Williams said. "He's not hurt." Lester looked up at Perkins. "But my boy should *not* be in jail like a common criminal.

"Harold is in *jail*?"

Perkins nodded, saying, "Officially, brought in for questioning, but yes, he is in an interview room now."

Novak rose and faced Perkins. "Well, can we get him *out* of the interview room?"

"We will, Danny," Perkins said. "But as I was telling Ruth and Lester here, we'll release him as soon as we have the chance to interview him. It shouldn't take long."

Danny took a deep breath, trying to check his tone. "Can we make that really fast, sir? And just who is interviewing him?"

"Porter," Perkins said. "He's going to speak to Harold once he finishes with one of the drug dealers."

Novak glanced at Hart, who moved her hand slightly to stop Novak from speaking. She turned to Perkins.

"Sir," Hart asked. "Just why is Harold in custody?"

"Because he was with one of the drug dealers --actually two of them -- when they were picked up at Sparks Stadium."

"He was taking his basketball team to the game today!" Novak cried.

"That's what we told him!" Ruth Williams shouted.

"I know that, Danny -- Ruth and Lester," Perkins said. "And I also know that Harold knows two of the drug dealers. We just want to talk to him in case he knows something we need to know."

Novak took another deep breath and stroked his hair, frustrated.

"Lieutenant," Hart began, "We also spoke to Harold a week ago and passed some info from him along to the detectives." She paused, then added carefully, "We know that Harold isn't involved in this. Can we do anything to get him home to his family?"

Perkins relaxed as he sensed Hart's tone, and turning to the Williams', said,

"We'll get him out of here as quickly as possible. Deacon Collins and I spoke and I'll make sure of it."

Neither Ruth nor Lester Williams answered Perkins. Novak and Hart sat down in chairs near the Williams' to wait for Harold.

Chapter Thirty

A knock on his office door woke Gray from a quiet rest. He lifted his head saying,

"Come in." The door opened, and Cabral, Burch and Sayles came in accompanied by Melvin "Pebbles" Wells, the lone dealer from Cobra's organization arrested after the strike. Gray smiled slightly as the man entered, looking uneasy. Gray rose to show the man he was welcome.

"Sit down, Melvin," Gray said, indicating a chair. Cabral, Burch and Sayles sat as well, but they remained on the edges of their chairs.

Gray faced Wells and smiled. "I understand you've had a difficult night," he said.

"N - no, sir," Wells replied. "I mean, it wasn't so bad." He was desperately trying to be cool, and failing.

Gray's eyes pierced the young man. "What did you tell the police before your lawyer arrived?" The question was casual, but the meaning was anything but.

"Nothin', sir," Wells said. "I told them I didn't know what they was talking about and that I wanted to see a lawyer."

Gray faced his lieutenants. "Which of you did he call?"

"He called my old burner, sir," Sayles said. "I already got rid of it."

Gray smiled and relaxed, then turned his attention back to Wells. "And what did they ask you? Tell me as many questions as you can remember." Gray sat back in his chair and folded his hands on his lap.

"Well," Wells replied, licking his lips, "they asked me what I was doing at the corner, you know, and…"

"Wait a moment," said Gray. "How did you answer that?"

"At first I didn't say nothin' sir, like I said. I mean what I did after every question was to look to the lawyer and he would tell me if I could answer or not. When I answered about the corner I said I was just walking past the corner, and didn't say nothing else."

"Very well. Proceed."

Wells licked his lips again. "Well, then they asked what I was doing walking around there, and why I messed up the guys at the corner." He looked up. "Then I said I was just walkin' and that I didn't hit nobody, you know?"

"Did they ask you anything else?"

"No, sir. Just stuff like that. Like what was I doin' there, why did I hit those guys, who was I working for, do I deal drugs, stuff like that. I just kept telling them I didn't do nothing wrong and said as little as I could."

"Sounds like you gave him the right training, Tommy."

"Yes sir," Burch said, flatly, but inside he was beaming.

Gray brought the attention back to himself. "Any more questions for Melvin?" he asked his lieutenants. The three men looked first at each other then at Gray. Then, they shook their heads, with Cabral saying "No, sir."

Gray turned again to Wells. "Good job, Melvin, he said. "Head on back home and wait to hear from Tommy; then you can go back to work."

Wells took this as a dismissal, and rose, but before he turned away, asked,

"Sir, I got people who need stuff, you know?"

Wells asked quietly so as not to rile Gray, but Gray took the question in stride. "That's a good attitude toward your customers, Melvin." Glancing briefly at Burch, he continued, "Tommy will make sure they get supplied for the next few days then get you back out there."

"Thank you, sir," Wells said, more relaxed. "I can go now?"

"Yes," Gray said, sitting up in his chair. "Just go home and watch TV or something. Take a couple of days; Tommy will call you."

With that, Wells completed his turn toward the door. He opened the door quietly and exited, closing the door without a sound. When the door was fully closed, Gray spoke again.

"Assessment? How do you think the operation went?" Gray asked, then he turned to Cabral. "Emilio?"

"Pretty well, Boss, "Cabral said. "No bystanders were hurt at all, and there was only one gun shot that hit anybody, and that was really nothin' -- the dealer it happened to went home in a couple of hours." Cabral chucked. "I know that little shit, and I don't think he's going to want to deal with anybody ever again."

"One small step," Gray said. "Anything else?"

"Yes," Cabral said. "One more thing: Harold Williams was taken in too."

"Why?" Gray said, frowning.

"The way I heard it," began Cabral, "he was at the stadium when a couple of the independents were running away from the cops, and they took him in along with the dealers."

"The police can't possibly believe that he had anything to do with the operation." Gray said. "He's one of the 'golden boys' of the neighborhood."

"He is, Boss," said Sayles. "It don't make no sense to me, except that he was in the wrong place at the wrong time."

"The question will be," Gray began, "if this will soften the Williams family or just harden their resolve." He noticed Cabral react.

"Emilio?"

"I don't think it's going to help us, Boss," Cabral said. "They're a tough bunch."

"I tend to agree, Emilio" he said. "But it does seem odd that they wouldn't release him as soon as they got to the station. Where is he, the 9th?"

"Yes, sir," said Cabral.

"How long did they keep him there?" Gray asked.

Cabral turned to Burch, who answered, "He was still there when Pebbles left -- I had him walk two blocks before I picked him up, and Pebbles told me Harold was still inside when he left."

Gray leaned back in his chair again. "That doesn't make sense given what you've told me about Harold in the past."

"Oh, and Boss," Burch added.

"Yes?"

"Harold's parents were there too, and they were really pissed. Plus, they called in a bunch of off-duty cops today, so the place looked real busy."

"Well, it looks as though we made an impact, gentlemen." Gray said with a smile.

"Yeah, Boss," added Burch, "Plus Pebbles told me that when he was leaving, he heard a lot of loud talking between Harold's parents and a couple of cops, that Novak dude from Auburn and his lady cop plus that big lieutenant."

"Novak, I know" Gray said, thinking. "He's a pretty tough cop. Who is this lady cop you're talking about?"

"I seen her," said Sayles. "She's tall, dark hair, probably mixed; looks pretty tough herself."

"Tough enough to worry about?"

The lieutenants looked at each other, not knowing how they should respond. Cabral broke the silence. "Hard to say, Boss," he answered carefully. "Somebody told me she was in the Army -- an MP I think -- and kinda no nonsense." Cabral shrugged. "She looks like she can handle herself."

Gray's face tightened. "An MP?" he said, as much to himself as to the men. "That doesn't impress me; nothing about them impresses me." Turning his attention to his men again, Gray added,

"Might be as much fun taking out a former MP as the other meddlesome police in this city."

Chapter Thirty One

Separate tiny observation spaces are located between the interview rooms at the 9th precinct, as they are at all Port Angel Police Department precincts. Novak and Hart were seated in an observation room watching the interview of Harold Williams by Detectives Moody and Porter. As Novak and Hart listened to the questions and answers, Hart could see the growing tightness in Novak's face and hands as he leaned forward, then leaned back in disgust at the way the questions were being asked. Given that the room was soundproof, Novak needn't have been so quiet, so Hart said,

"We don't have to like it, Danny. We just have to get Harold through this."

"I know! I know," Novak said. "It's just frustrating to see those two treating Harold like he's something he's not. And he doesn't even have a lawyer!"

"Danny," Hart replied. "We couldn't tell him to do it, and those two" -- she indicated Moody and Porter with her head -- "weren't going to go the extra mile so Harold would be encouraged to ask for one." Hart could feel her own tension rising along with Novak's, and she took a few deep breaths to re-center herself. "We'll get him through this, Danny," she continued. "And since Harold hasn't really done anything wrong, we'll get him home to his family soon."

"I know, Steve," replied Novak. "I just get a little weary with injustice, and with cowboy detectives."

"I hear you, partner," said Hart with a smile. She paused before adding, "You ever think about becoming a detective?"

"Me?" Novak shrugged. "I guess I've thought about it, but somehow I've just never pursued it." Cocking his head at the one-way glass, he added. "Of course, I couldn't do any worse than those two idiots." Novak stopped, then said, "Actually, that's not fair.

Moody and Porter aren't bad people, nor are they bad detectives, however arrogant the may be. I ju...."

"Just think they're barking up the wrong tree with Harold?"

"Oh, absolutely. That's it. And you know, I don't like putting Ruth and Lester through this either."

Novak and Hart overhead Siem Porter's next question.

"When did you go from the corner of Berks and Moore to Sparks Stadium?"

"I told before," said Harold, "I wasn't on that corner or even driving by it. We took Scott St. to 10th, then turned down Canal to the stadium." Harold sounded both tired and frustrated.

"That's what," Novak began, "the third time they've asked that question?"

"Fourth, by my count."

"This is ridiculous, Steve," said Novak. "Is this what they teach in detective school? If so, we need to apply as soon as you have the required time on the job."

"I know," said Hart. "You know, the one thing we were always told in the Army when we would investigate something, is to listen carefully and critically." Pointing toward the interview room, she added, "That's one thing they don't seem to have a clue about, and I guess that's what bugs me the most."

"Yeah," said Novak. "That's a good way to say it, and I agree -- they aren't listening to either what Harold is saying *or* the way he's saying it." He stood up again, frustration rising. "And I don't want them to back him into a corner so he makes a mistake!"

They listened to more statements from the adjoining room.

"Look, Harold," Moody began. "This whole thing was a very coordinated strike against some of these drug dealers, and the one guy we have in custody who is a known dealer isn't smart enough to pull this off."

"Exactly," Porter agreed. "There had to be somebody a hell of a lot smarter organizing it -- and there you were." Novak and Hart saw Harold's demeanor change. The normally quiet young man hardened.

"I don't know what you're talking about, Detective," Harold said slowly and deliberately. "And I'm not going to speak to you anymore. If there is something else you need to know, you can contact my lawyer." Harold sat up even straighter. "And he's going to have a lot of fun sorting through all the questions you've asked me while letting the real drug dealers and traffickers watch and laugh."

"Yes!" Novak said from the other room. Looking at Hart, he added, "Do you think they're going to take the risk of him bringing in a lawyer, or just back off with the 'don't leave town' spiel?"

Hart shrugged, then they heard,

"You need to keep yourself available, Mr. Williams," Siem Porter said. "We may have more questions for you." Both Hart and Novak could heard the chairs scraping across the floor in the interview room. They opened their door, and saw Moody and Porter striding down the hall. Novak suppressed the urge to confront them and turned instead to Hart.

"You know what I want to do, right?" Novak asked.

"Oh, *yeah*," Hart said. She smiled, hoping to break the tension.

Harold exited the interview room, turning toward Novak and Hart. As he looked in Novak's face, Harold could see the strain and knew that Novak was probably as annoyed as he was.

"Danny," Harold said.

"Hey, Harold," Novak said. "Sorry you had to put up with that."

"Happens too often, Dan."

"That I know, man," Novak agreed. The three of them heard voices coming from the direction of the bullpen, then heard the strong steps of Ruth and Lester Williams.

"We got tired of waiting," Lester said. He moved to embrace Harolds. "You okay, son?"

"How can he be okay, Lester?" Ruth cried. "They had him in jail!" She turned to Novak. "What kind of people do you work with, Danny?"

"People who need somebody to teach them how to be good cops, Ms. Williams," Hart replied. "We're going to work on them, don't worry about that."

Ruth suddenly burst into tears, then found herself embarrassed that she couldn't hold it together. "Damn it!" she said. "I said I wasn't going to do this!"

"Hell," her husband replied. "I'm surprised you could hold it together this long." He turned to Novak and his eyes weren't forgiving. "This is wrong, Danny," he said. "You know it is." Standing more erect he added, "And you have to do something about it."

"I don't know what that is yet, Mr. Williams," Novak said. "But I will."

Standing next to her partner, Hart added, "No. *We* will."

Chapter Thirty Two

The Williams family started to leave the precinct, while Novak and Hart turned toward the bullpen to confront Moody and Porter. Something in the way Novak held his body concerned Ruth Williams, who called to him.

"Danny," she said.

"Yes, Ms. Williams," said Novak.

Ruth approached Danny and placed her hand on his shoulder. "We don't want you to take on everybody's problems, Danny," Ruth Williams said. "Don't go in there and make it bad for yourself, you hear?"

"I know that, Ms. Williams," Novak said. "But there are some things we need to change around here."

"I know that, Danny," Ruth said. She chuckled, adding, "But we need you here not just today but tomorrow and the day after; we can't afford to have you self-destruct."

"You're right, Ms. Williams," Novak said. "And I get it. I promise to keep my cool."

Hart stepped up. "I have his back, Ms. Williams," she said. You don't have to worry about him."

Ruth Williams smiled and dropped her hand from Danny's shoulder. She gave him a kiss on the cheek, then joined her husband and son walking silently down the hallway.

As they left, Novak turned again to Hart. "It's not going to be as easy keeping my cool with Moody and Porter," Novak said.

"Do we have to do it now? said Hart. "There's something to be said about cooling off first."

"True," Novak said. "But I don't want them to get away before I can talk to them." He made a move toward the bullpen, but Hart took his arm.

"And just what are you going to ask them?" she asked. "We already heard every question they asked *and* every answer they received, and to be honest, they didn't learn anything that we didn't already know."

"True."

"Plus," Hart continued, "We already gave them information before these attacks that I'm guessing they still haven't followed up on yet."

"Damn it!" Novak said shaking his head. "So in the meantime, it's just another cluster-fuck; like we didn't already know that?"

"Yes," said Hart. "But that doesn't mean that some other detectives can't make a dent in this whole thing."

"Your point, Steve?"

"The point," Hart began, "is to keep us focused on what's really important, which may not be giving Moody and Porter a piece of our minds." She got quiet and closer to Novak. "You know, it would probably be wasted on those guys, anyway."

"Also true," Novak agreed. He sighed as he turned and started walking toward the front of the precinct. When they neared the office of Lt. Perkins, the lieutenant emerged from his office and beckoned them in.

"Hey you two," Perkins called. "Come on in." Novak and Hart looked at each other before shrugging almost in unison and entering the lieutenant's office.

As senior officer, Novak spoke first. "What can we do for you, lieutenant?"

"Sit down, folks," Perkins said. He sat down heavily behind his desk.

Hart and Novak were silent waiting for Perkins to speak. Eventually, he looked at his two officers. "What do you think?" Perkins began, then added, "Both of you."

Novak and Hart looked at each other, then Novak spoke. "First, I think Moody and Porter wasted a lot of time interviewing Harold Williams, and…."

"Agreed," Perkins said. "And you should also know that if they hadn't interviewed him at all, *somebody else* was going to have a problem with that."

"You're right as usual, lieutenant," said Novak.

"And don't you forget that either," Perkins said, chuckling. He sat up again, "But, tell me what you think we ought to do now."

"Sir," Hart began. "We gave Moody and Porter," Hart paused. "Sorry, *Detectives* Moody and Porter lots of information about movements of the Cobra drug trafficking group and if they had payed attention to it, then they could have asked what Harold knew about that, or what he could help them with."

"But they didn't do that," countered Novak. "Instead, they tried to connect Harold to something he has no connection with at all." Novak shook his head. "So what they did was go over stuff that was irrelevant and completely ignored something that Harold might have helped them with."

"And," Hart added, "Do you really think Harold's going to be eager to help them now?"

"I agree," Perkins he said. "But he'll talk to you -- both of you."

Seeing Novak's and Hart's reactions, Perkins raised his hands. "Now, I don't mean you have to interview him again. From what you're told me, you've already done that."

"We *have*." said Hart.

"I know that," Perkins said. "Look, I know how Moody and Porter come off to you and to lots of other people. And there are times when they make me crazy too, and I'm their boss." Perkins leaned forward again. "The fact is, they're very smart cops, and they've learned things through tough investigation that other cops wouldn't have." Perkins smiled again.

"But that doesn't mean," he continued, "that they're perfect or don't have blind spots."

"And you think we can somehow get them off the dime?" Novak asked. He looked at Hart with a sarcastic grin. "Yeah, that's gonna work."

"I'm with Danny, lieutenant," Hart said. "I don't know what you expect us to do that the detectives can't."

"Well, Hart," Perkins began. "I've been in this department long enough to know that every cop can contribute something, especially when they have the kind of community connections that Danny here has." Perkins stood up. "What we have to do is to start using what you" -- here he looked at Novak -- "have to offer to get the job done." Perkins turned his gaze to Hart.

"And you don't get off without a job too, Hart."

"Umm, Sir, I…"

"Oh please, Hart," Perkins said. "Like we haven't seen you practically walk on water and turn it into wine during the last couple of months." Turning to both officers, he continued. "We need both of you to continue spending time with Harold, and make sure anything he shares with you gets to the detectives *and* to me. There may be ways I can connect the dots that they can't. I do have the same credentials, you know."

Hart and Novak were silent until Hart turned to Perkins and asked, "I don't suppose we could think about this first, sir?"

"Given what's at stake, Hart," said Perkins. "What do *you* think?"

Chapter Thirty Three

Hart and Novak left the precinct, still in civilian clothes, and wondering what they should do next. Novak started his engine and put the car in gear, then he stopped, put the car in park and shut off the engine. Rather than ask what was going on, Hart stayed silent.

"This is -- I don't know, Steve," Novak said.

"I know," Hart said. Then, she perked up and said, "Dolman Park, Jeeves."

"Huh?"

"I said Dolman Park," she repeated. "Let's go there and talk or just walk around, I don't know." She gave Novak a impish look. "You could use it and so could I."

Novak started the car and put it in gear, saying "Yeah, you're right. Let's head there."

Turning away from the precinct, Novak drove quickly to Dolman Park and parked near the gazebo. He got out of the car while Hart stayed inside. Novak turned to her with questioning eyes. Hart had her phone to her ear, saying "Calling Sheryl," she said. "Wives worry, you know."

Novak nodded and headed to the gazebo. A few minutes later, Hart joined him.

After a deep sigh, Hart asked, "Okay, where are we?"

"Damned if I know," said Novak. "I was just a concerned cop a couple of hours ago; now I've got to head off two cowboy detectives, satisfy and appease three long-time friends, and make our lieutenant happy."

"So, just a regular day in the neighborhood, right?"

Novak smiled, but his heart wasn't in it. "When did you become such a cheerleader?" he asked.

Hart rolled her eyes. "Honestly," she began, "I've never been a big fan of cheerleaders." She crossed her arms. "I was just trying to relieve some of the tension here -- I'll let girls with a lot bigger boobs and hips take care of the cheerleading."

"I'll let that comment just die where it is, thank you very much," Novak replied. He leaned back onto the railing of the gazebo. "There's just so much, Steve," he said quietly.

"So much?"

"What, you want me to lie down on a couch?"

"Nope," said Hart. "Just tell me what you want to tell me."

Novak looked away, then returned Hart's gaze. "I don't know how much you know about me as a teenager, because I don't talk about it much." As he said that, Hart couldn't help an involuntary reaction which Novak noticed right way. He broke out laughing.

"What?"

"Nothing, Steve," Novak said, "Except that I can see that you and Sheryl are close enough now that she told you a lot about me, am I right?"

"I guess I'm that transparent?"

"Not really," Novak replied. "I just had a feeling." He sighed again. "I just remember how tough some of the cops were to my friends when I was growing up -- seldom to me since I was one of the few white kids. But it was tough for my friends, lots of whom were Black, Latino or mixed. Eventually, I got treated badly too, just by association.

"Sounds familiar," she replied. "And it certainly happened to both me and my brother." She looked away briefly. "When you're one of the mixed kids, you can only fit in with certain people, and seldom with the people you want to fit in with." She looked to Novak. "Hey, I don't mean to say that I really had it rough, because I didn't. After all, being a girl can help a lot. Plus I was always pretty tough -- people just didn't want to mess with me. My brother had it harder than me, which is probably why he left home as soon as he could." Hart was silent again.

"And you're thinking this is what's happening to Harold?" she asked finally.

"No," Novak replied. "I *know* it's what's happening to Harold, and I know it happens every day in this city. I just remembered how it felt to be on the receiving end of that, especially when someone who is really good like Harold gets treated this way. And just remembering it hit me in the gut."

"And?"

Novak chuckled again. "You're really good at this," he said.

"Eh," Hart replied, shrugging her shoulders.

"Well anyway," Novak continued, "I also just remembered how tough it makes it for all of us when detectives like Moody and Porter and the uniforms who are just like them get in the way. You know it doesn't take many Moody's out there before the people we're supposed to be helping just close us off."

"And," Hart added. "It's tough being one of the few who people always trust. I get it Danny," Hart said. "But you can't make the police good all by yourself."

"I know, I know," Novak said. "Sometimes I just feel all alone in this."

"Look around, Danny," Hart said, hand on her hips. "I'm still standing here, when I would much rather be sipping tea on your patio with Sheryl." Novak started to respond, but Hart waved him off. "And there are plenty of cops in the 9th who get it, Danny. I mean are you saying that Gee and Carson, for just two, aren't doing the right things?"

"No, you're right, Steve," Novak conceded. He shook his head sadly. "But it's still so much to do, and for some reason some of our fellow cops just don't understand that."

"I guess we'll just have to be a little stronger or a little louder, that's all."

"Did you do that in the Army, Steve -- not wanting to bring up bad memories."

"No," said Hart. "Most of my memories of the Army are good ones Danny, and yes, I liked to see myself as one of those MPs who could do the job and not get backlash because of the way I treated the soldiers I worked with. But even that took an everyday commitment, plus I knew some of my fellow MPs just relished the badge and the sidearm and not what the job was all about, and that was to keep soldiers at their best so they could fulfill the mission; it's not to slap them around just because we could."

"Which sounds a little like some of our fellow officers here, though to be honest, they're in the minority aren't they?"

"Now you got it, Danny," Hart said, smiling.

Novak was silent again then stood up, stretching. "Maybe you were right, Steve."

"I usually am, but about what this time?" Hart asked.

"About us becoming detectives," Novak said. "Maybe we could change some more things if we were."

"Maybe," said Hart. Standing up and brushing off her slacks, she added, "Can we go back to your house so I can have my tea now?"

Chapter Thirty Four

Gray sat back in his chair, mulling over his plan. He had dismissed his lieutenants, including Cabral, so that he could have the solitude to make a phone call. He checked the time, selected a cell phone from the four on his desk, and dialed a private number. As the phone rang, he rose from his seat and paced near the window.

"Good evening, my friend," Gray said. "I hope this is a good time." Gray smiled as he spoke, and the emotion was communicated through the phone as well.

Gray nodded as he listened to his partner. "Of course it is," Gray said. "We were very careful in our operation. In fact, only one of my people was taken into custody, and he was released a mere hours later."

Looking at his desk surface, Gray's eyebrows furrowed as he listened. He added a few comments and "goods" along the way, but mostly, he listened.

"My people believe many of the independents are having second thoughts about staying independent, which is exactly what we were hoping for," Gray added.

Gray listened further, shaking his head in mild annoyance. *Didn't we address all of these questions days or weeks ago?*

"Of course," Gray continued, "As we know, working on Harold Williams to neutralize his influence and that of his parents is a priority. We were fortunate that he was taken into custody, since it might drive a wedge between them and the police."

Gray turned away from the window, and rubbed his temples. It was so annoying, he thought, to have nervous partners who have never really worked a day in their lives.

"Of course. We will have a stronger strike the next time, but as I told you and my people, we do not want to kill innocents -- collateral damage is to be expected but not embraced."

As he listened, Gray began to relax.

"Exactly," he said in reply to a long statement from the phone. "The framework for this is important, so if you will just do your part, all will go smoothly."

He tried to end the call, but listened instead to one more concern.

"Yes," Gray said. "Yes. I understand." Relaxing even more and preparing to hang up, he said, "You worry too much, my friend. Stick to the plan." Then, the ended the call.

Chapter Thirty Five

Ruth Williams looked up and saw Harold pouring a cup of coffee. She placed a bookmark in the ledger she had been working on and approached her son.

"You ready to head to the game son?"

"Yes," said Harold. I'm just about to leave. Don't want to be late."

Ruth reached up to Harold and kissed his cheek. "Bye," she said. Be careful out there."

* * *

Harold Williams and his assistant coach steered their church van through the main gate of the Port Angel Sparks baseball stadium. They had received tickets for the game from the Chamber of Commerce and the boys were all excited to be at the stadium. The team arrived in plenty of time for his team to secure autographs from some of the baseball players and get to their seats to watch the warmup.

Harold parked the van, then turned around to face his team.

"You already got your tickets, right?" he said to the boys. With a chorus of "Yes, Coach," and "Sure," Harold released them from the van. Then, the entire group walked toward the group sales gate. Showing their tickets and being properly screened, the team was almost completely through the gate when Harold turned and looked about half a block away, noticing Terry Wright huddling with a small group of other youth. Turning to his assistant coach, he said, "I'll meet you all inside. I already have my ticket," he said, patting his pocket.

"Something up?" the assistant coach asked.

"No, it's okay, Harold said. "I'll just see you inside, okay?"

"Okay, Harold," the man said as he walked away, frowning.

Harold patted his pocket again to ensure he had the ticket, then walked the short distance to Wright.

"What up, Harold?" Wright said with a grin.

"I'm good, T," said Harold. He looked around at some of the other youth, and sighed. "You have to do this now, T?"

Wright raised his hands in surrender and smiled. "Got bills to pay, Harold."

"Did it ever occur to you to get a job?"

Both he and Wright could hear murmuring within the group surrounding them.

"You don't get it, Harold," Wright said. "This *is* my job." Wright pulled out a pack of bills from his pocket. "And the pay's real good," he added. "You got to get in on this, Harold."

"Sure," Harold replied. "Sell some rock, get my head blown off -- sounds like a nice life."

"Hey, it's not like that," Wright countered.

"No," Harold said. It's just like that if you would just look at it with your eyes and not your wallet."

Wright glanced back at his group with a smirk, then turned back to Harold. Before he could speak, Harold continued. "You don't need to be selling to my guys, T," Harold said. "I asked you that before, right?"

"Look, Harold," said Wright, "If they ask, I'm gonna sell." Wright stepped back again. "Like I said," he continued, smiling widely, "I'm a businessman." His other friends laughed.

Harold advanced and towered over Wright. "You have plenty of people you can sell to, Terry; you don't need my guys."

Wright stood his ground. "Can't stop me."

For the first time, Harold laughed. "You ain't that much, T," he said. "You think you're all that, but you're not."

Wright stared at Harold, responding to the taunting voices in the crowd. "You ain't much, either, Harold," Wright said. "Little Momma's boy." While Harold's eye's flashed at that, he didn't attack Wright, but just as he relaxed again, Wright struck by pushing Harold in the chest. Harold countered by hitting Wright with a strong jab to the chest. Wright retaliated, and from then on, neither Wright, Harold, nor the other youths noticed that security guards at the stadium had observed Harold and Wright posturing. They had called the police who were on their way.

Another group which had noticed the tense conversation were two mid-level dealers from Cobra's organization in addition to Ricky Sayles.

Sayles turned around in the car to speak with his people. "This is a good time, yo," he said. "Go over and get in that for a couple of minutes, then we can fire some, you got it?"

"Okay, Ricky," his men said. They left the car, crossed the street and added to the melee by attacking some of the bystanders.

The fight expanded, but had gone on for only a minute or so when a siren could be heard in the background. Sayles heard it, and called to his people.

"Hey! Yo, Jo-Jo! Cash!" Sayles cried. "Hit it!" Right after Sayles spoke, shots rang out and the entire group began to scatter, while Sayles' two men returned to the car and were able to flee the scene before the police arrived. Some of the young men were able to leave the scene, but Harold, Wright and several others were stopped by drawn sidearms and a police dog. All were ordered onto the ground, but one of the young men was already there, and he wouldn't get up again.

Chapter Thirty Six

There may have been an element of order outside the stadium, but it looked like pandemonium. Police officers, rescue workers, and medical personnel went about their business efficiently, and with a morbid sense of cooperation. The last police vehicle to arrive was driven by Danny Novak, who along with his partner had barely had time to put on his full uniform. Stephanie Hart, who was seldom seen in anything other than a tight French braid, wore instead a plain ponytail, and her face was as grim as her partner's.

Novak parked half a block away so he wouldn't block egress for any of the other police or rescue vehicles. As he left the cruiser, he turned to Hart. "This is a fucking mess, Steve."

"No arguments from me, Danny," Hart said. They stopped to survey who was present and what was going on before they saw Capt. Andrew Shoemaker directing the action. Shoemaker was consulting with Detectives Moody and Porter, who seemed very frazzled. Sgt. O.C. Boyd was also there along with Don Brown, another senior officer.

"Wow," Novak said. "They really brought out the heavyweights for this one, Steve."

Hart and Novak could hear lots of noise and commotion, centering on Moody and Porter and tried to find rhyme or reason to it. They waited for a while before approaching Don Brown. Hart enjoyed her probationary period with him.

"Hey, Brownie," she said.

Don Brown, all six plus feet of him ambled over and smiled. "Good to see you, Hart," he said. Looking around resignedly, he added, "Though I wish it was under better circumstances." He turned to Novak, saying, "Good to see you, Danny."

"Thanks, Brownie," Novak said. "Do you have a clue what's going on here? The report we saw didn't say too much."

Brown pointed to the people on the ground. "The short story is that there was a group of kids hanging around on that corner, including one of our known drug dealers." He turned to Novak again. "Do you remember Terry Wright?"

"Yeah," Novak said. "Everybody calls him T-Wright."

"That's him," said Brown.

"The one we heard about right, Danny?" Hart asked.

"Yep."

"Anyway," Brown continued. "He got challenged into a scuffle and at some point, the fight went from two people to the whole group. Then somebody took out a gun and started firing; two people were hit, one dead."

"Do we know the kid who was killed?" asked Hart.

"No," Brown answered. "Really, once they got here, Moody and Porter just took over." He leaned toward Novak and Hart to avoid speaking too loudly. "I'm not sure they've told the Captain much since he arrived."

"I hear you," said Novak. "I guess we're all used to that."

Just then, the three officers heard even more noise, and noticed some people from the neighborhood coming out and taunting the police.

"Something tells me we ought to be out there taking care of the crowd," said Brown.

Novak and Hart agreed, and moved to get between the citizens and the police. After about fifteen minutes, they turned to see Captain Andrew Shoemaker.

"Novak, Hart," Shoemaker said, confused. "Did you get called in?"

"No, sir." Novak said. "We heard the call and decided we could make ourselves useful."

"Spoken like a true cop, Danny."

"Do you have any idea what actually happened, Captain? I mean, we don't usually have this kind of action around here."

"I know, Danny," said Shoemaker. "Though it may well be an escalation of the previous strike." Shoemaker paused and frowned for a few seconds. "Danny, don't you have a personal connection to the Williams family?"

"Ruth and Lester," Novak began, concerned. "Yes. Is something wrong with them?"

"No, not with them." Shoemaker replied. "It's actually their son."

"Are we still on Harold, Captain?" Novak asked, already tense. "I would think that Moody and Porter have realized by now that he's just not that kind of kid."

"Then obviously, you don't know," Shoemaker said.

"Know what?"

"Witnesses said that Harold started the whole thing today," said Shoemaker. "He's under arrest."

Novak flashed a look at Hart, then suppressed the urge to react. Instead, he took a few breaths, and faced his captain again.

"This is from witnesses?"

"Yes," Shoemaker said. "According to the people we've already talked to, the whole thing only started after Harold approached them."

"What was Harold even *doing* here?" Novak asked, then a light bulb went off in this head. "Wait, his basketball team, right?"

"That's what we think," said Shoemaker. The captain turned briefly to the action, then said to Novak. "Look, Danny. I appreciate your help with the crowd. I think it's all died down now."

"Where are Moody and Porter?"

"They left about ten minutes ago," Shoemaker replied as he turned to go. "I've got to get over there and coordinate with rescue."

Novak answered "Okay, sir," even as Shoemaker began walking away.

Novak faced his partner. "I don't believe this," Novak said. "It's like being in the *Twilight Zone*."

"And I don't think it's over, Danny." Hart looked around and saw O.C. Boyd standing to the side and consulting with a rescue worker. "Sgt. Boyd is over there."

Novak followed Hart's gaze to Boyd and quickly went to join him.

"O.C." Novak said.

"Novak. Hart," Boyd said, turning his attention to each officer in turn.

"This is a mess, O.C.," Novak said. "Can you make anything out of it?"

Boyd said. "The way I get it, Harold Williams went over to confront a drug dealer who is actually a friend of his. They had words and got into a fight." Boyd paused. "Most of the witnesses said that Williams threw the first punch, but that the other guy pushed Williams first. Personally, I don't think anybody here did the shooting; no gun here that I can find."

As Boyd paused, there seemed to be something else he wanted to say.

"Is there something else, Sgt.?" Hart asked.

"Well," Boyd began, "Our favorite 9th precinct detectives have decided that Harold orchestrated the whole thing *including* the gun shots.

"That's crazy!" Novak cried. "O.C., do you really believe that shit?"

Pointing to his head, Boyd asked, "Novak, do I have 'stupid' tattooed on my forehead?" Then he walked away.

Chapter Thirty Seven

The distance between the baseball stadium and the 9th precinct station house seemed incredibly short the way Danny Novak was driving. He broke protocol by using his lights, then finally turned them off two blocks from the precinct. Few words were spoken between he and Hart, given that the one thing Hart said to Novak provoke an annoyed response. Hart thought she'd simply wait it out.

As the cruiser stopped, Novak opened his door, saying,

"Get it logged, Steve," Novak said. "I want to see what the hell is going on."

"No."

"*No?*"

"No," Hart repeated. "You're not going to go in there and do or say something stupid without me in there with you." She looked at Novak again, more softly. "Danny, shutting it down the right way takes less than two minutes. She patted the cruiser's dashboard. "Sit. I'll take care of it."

Novak's lips pressed tightly together, but he said "Fine." And sat down.

They entered the precinct, with Novak's mood clear to all who saw him given the pace and strength of his stride. Kat Neely had been called in to work because of the high volume of calls to the precinct. She smiled at Novak, then quickly realized something was wrong.

"Hey, Danny," she said, with little enthusiasm.

Novak actually smiled at her, forcing himself to be cordial to the one person who had nothing to do with the fiasco that was today's event.

"Kat," Novak said. "Are Detectives Moody and Porter in the bullpen?"

"I'm not sure," Neely said. "They went by here, so they might be in the bull…"

"Shit!" they heard, coming from behind them. Novak, Neely and Hart turned to see David Moody looking both angry and nervous.

"What's the story *detective*?" Novak asked..

"Novak, we're still working on this," Moody said quickly. "Why don't you…."

"Moody!" Novak cried. "You're not speaking to some rookie here. The question was simple: what's going on? And where is Harold Williams?"

"Look, Novak," Moody said, getting into Novak's face, "I don't owe you an explanation or anything else, so just back off and get your ass back on patrol."

"You're not my boss, Moody," Novak countered. Another voice stopped the forward motions of both Novak and Moody.

"Jesus, Novak!" Siem Porter said. "Back off! We're just doing our job!"

"And Harold Williams?" Novak asked.

"He's been arrested as an accessory, and we think we might be able to get him for manslaughter," Porter replied.

"Have you two lost your minds?" Novak said. "You take a good kid into custody and let the other assholes go?"

"Hey, it's *your* job to keep the order and ours to clean it up," Moody screamed. "Did it ever occur to you that *you* might be the real problem?"

"*What*?" Hart said. "You *can't* be serious." Hart got between Novak and Moody.

"Clearly," Novak said with surprising calm, "you don't know much about this community at all, since you don't seem to know any of the people here or know what's going on, even though we've *tried* to tell you." Novak shook his head. "You two just proved that you're clueless." While still tense, Novak's shoulders had relaxed a bit, and a quick glance to Hart told her that he was under control.

"The truth is," Novak continued. "You two are a big part of the problem."

Moody hadn't calmed down much at all, and advanced again toward Novak. Hart shifted her weight to face Moody and glared at him. Moody's advance stopped and he turned in anger toward Hart, but before he could see or do anything else, the reception area reverberated with a loud shout from the corner office.

"Moody! Hart! And all the rest of you," shouted Captain Andrew Shoemaker. "In my office now!"

Chapter Thirty Eight

As the officers entered Shoemaker's office, Shoemaker simply stared at them. They stood waiting for instruction until they saw the tilt of the captain's head indicating that they should sit. Lt. Perkins was already leaning against Shoemaker's desk, also waiting and also angry.

Shoemaker took a deep breath and looked at each of the officers in turn.

"I'm sensing problems in this precinct that I don't want." Shoemaker began, his mouth hardly moving. "Does somebody want to tell me what the hell is going on here?" The officers looked at each other for a time, before Moody spoke.

"Cap," he began, "We're just trying to do the job here, you know?" Moody licked his lips. "We just don't need people getting in the way."

Shoemaker looked at Novak for reaction, and seeing none, instead looked to Hart.

"Officer Hart," he said. "I hope you understand your role as a probationary officer in this department. We know you've done good work so far, but the idea of probationary is just that."

"Yes, sir," Hart replied. She made an effort not to sound defensive, and maintained an open posture in her seat.

"Perk?" Capt. Shoemaker said, turning to his colleague.

Lt. Perkins stood up from the desk, his imposing figure made taller by the fact that the officers were seated. He looked primarily at Novak and Hart.

"Being a detective is a very difficult job, Officer Novak," he said. He pointedly ignored Hart. "This is made all the more difficult when uniformed officers don't do what they need to do and work at cross purposes to us."

"And giving detectives important information more than once is working *against* you?" Novak replied.

"This is your time to *listen*, Danny," Shoemaker said. "The lieutenant has a point; you and Hart need to listen to it."

Novak sat back in his seat and turned his attention very deliberately to Lt. Perkins.

"What is working at cross purposes," Perkins continued, "is causing conflicts with fellow officers, and making public declarations about the innocence or guilt of suspects." Perkins leaned down farther. "And that's simply unacceptable." While Perkins said it to Novak and Hart, Moody and Porter were taken aback as well.

"Now," Perkins continued. "You apparently have some things to say." Scanning the faces of all four officers, Perkins said, "Why don't we hear it now?"

Novak took a deep breath. "Harold told Hart and I that he had been seeing several independent drug dealers in and around Auburn and that they were getting scared."

"Why was that?" Shoemaker asked.

"As Harold explained it," Novak said, "in the past, guys would get pushed a little and shoved out of the way when a bigger drug dealer was around. But now, the pushes have become more violent, and it's really got some of the little guys nervous."

"And besides that," Hart added, "Harold's been getting even more pressure than ever to join up with the dealers, especially from T-Wright."

"In essence," Novak continued, "Harold was telling us about this escalation and Cobra's land grab a couple of weeks ago, and he even gave us the names of some dealers who were involved."

"And you passed this on to the detectives?" Shoemaker asked, turning his gaze to Moody and Porter.

"Yes, sir" Novak said. "Both Moody and Porter and some information to Fair and Shore."

"What did you two do with that information?" Shoemaker asked Moody and Porter

Moody and Porter looked at each other, then down at their hands. Finally, Porter raised his head.

"Well, Cap," he began, "we haven't had a whole lot of time to look into everything." Feeling more confident, he continued. "Plus, we're general detectives -- we're not supposed to go too far into narcotics."

"That's true," Shoemaker said. "So what did narcotics say?" Moody and Porter were silent. "Gentlemen?" Shoemaker repeated. Perkins glared at Moody and Porter.

"Perk, we've been working on leads for all our cases," Porter said finally. "We didn't exactly give anything to narcotics yet." Perkins and Shoemaker glanced at each other. Shoemaker finally turned his attention to all four officers.

"I'm going to avoid using the term 'cluster fuck,'" Shoemaker said. Then, looking at Hart, his eyes widened in embarrassment. But Hart's face was impassive, so he continued. "You two," he said, looking at Moody and Porter, "need to pass on relevant information to narcotics division, and work with them on what each of you will do in the investigation -- unless you've forgotten how to do that."

"Shoe," Moody blurted. "These two aren't helping us." Pointing at Novak and Hart, he added. "They're adding fuel to the fire in Lexington so everybody is against the cops now *especially* that damn preacher. How are we supposed to talk to anybody if other cops are making it harder for us?"

"Oh, really," Novak said. "There was already fuel on the fire because you two -- *especially* you two -- don't get it." Novak pointed at Lt. Perkins. "The lieutenant told us to connect with the community so we can get the job done, and you've done just the opposite."

Moody stood up again and faced Novak squarely. "Damn it, Novak, just whose side are you on?" Novak stood up in response, but before he could say anything, Hart shot up and beat him to it.

"There's only *one* side here, detective," Hart said. She paused as she noticed the angry breathing of Novak and Moody. More slowly and quietly, she added, "Or does what I was told in the academy about 'one department, one community' not apply here?"

"Ha! So what, Novak," Moody snickered. "You got to have Stephie back you up now? I thought you were better than that."

Hart smiled and looked at Novak. "You were right, Danny," she said. "They are stuck in the third grade."

The detectives puffed up their chests and prepared to unleash another volley, when Hart's face changed from mocking them to a cold stare.

"All of you, stop and remember you *are* on the same team," Shoemaker said, "and nobody better make any snide remarks questioning that." Turning to Novak and Hart, he added, "you are the eyes and ears on the street, but you are *not* the investigators. You need to pass on whatever you hear to the detectives without conducting your own investigations *or* whipping up community sentiment." Hart tightened her lips to keep from talking. The captain noticed this and after about two seconds, shifted his gaze to the detectives.

"We are not going to railroad anybody because it is convenient," Shoemaker said. "Lt. Perkins and I expect full investigations and at the very least chasing down the leads given you by any patrol officer. You two need to talk to the victim's family and that damn preacher so they know we aren't ignoring them." Before Moody and Porter could say anything else, he added, "this is not window dressing -- there's bound to be something we can learn from them so long as we approach them like partners rather than suspects." He looked at the detectives again. "You are probably going to have to eat crow for a while and listen to people saying you're only asking questions because you were forced to: take it and probe respectfully and thoroughly."

Turning to Hart and Novak, Shoemaker added, "and you two need to encourage people in the community to talk freely and completely with the detectives so we can get to the bottom of this." Surveying the four disgruntled people in his office, he returned to his chair and added, "is that clear?"

"Sir. Yes, sir!" Hart replied. Shoemaker stared at her, and she sheepishly shrunk back adding, "Sorry, sir. Army force of habit."

The captain rolled his eyes before saying, "you four can all get out of my office, now." The four officers left the office, and carefully closed the door. Moody looked to Hart, snickered and said, "Sir. Yes, sir?"

"Shit, it seemed right at the time."

All four of the officers chuckled, before the Moody asked, "Alright. Look, do we have everything from you two now?"

"I think so," Novak replied. He touched his belt and added, "we have you both on speed dial if we have anything else."

"Understood," Porter said. "We're going to head out." He started to leave before turning back and adding, "Hey, let us know any new reactions you get...." as his voice trailed off.

Chapter Thirty Nine

Emanuel Johnson, Age 15, died on August 26th in Port Angel. A student athlete, "Manny" is remembered as a great friend, helper and leader among his peers. He is survived by his mother, Pearl, and sister Estela. Celebration of life will be held at Greater….

Rev. Archie Price sat in his office, pondering which bible verses he would choose to conduct the funeral of Manny Johnson. Price had conducted an untold number of funerals in his career, though few were as difficult as those of children. And make no mistake about it, Manny Johnson was a child. *No one should die at 15*, Price thought. He was actually surprised how deeply this death was impacting him. How can he do more to combat this? He was also torn between his concern about Manny Johnson's death and the imprudent arrest of Harold Williams for the murder. Price could feel his face tightening as he thought about Harold Williams, perhaps the kindest and most committed young man he knew, and one who was trying to keep himself and others on the right path. Putting him in jail was just one more confirmation of how badly the police treated the people of his neighborhood. Though Harold had been released on bail, Price was still angry about it. He was trying to turn his attention back to his work when he heard a knock at his door. He wasn't expecting anyone, but rose anyway.

"Come in," Price said.

Deacon Ernest Collins entered, looking grave.

"Reverend," Collins said as he advanced.

"Good morning, Deacon," Price said. Price indicated the seat in front of his desk rather than his overstuffed chairs, then waited for Collins to sit.

Collins quickly scanned the desk, and indicating the obituary with his eyes, said "Are you as incensed about that as I am?"

"Incensed. And incredibly sad," Price said. "I have a whole range of feelings about this right now."

Collins pressed his lips together. "I'm staying at incensed. And I'm at a loss to know what we can do, but something needs to happen here, Reverend."

"I agree, Deacon," Price said cautiously. But before he could continue, Collins spoke again.

"And aren't you angry -- angry enough to do something?" Price could feel his anger rising, and acknowledged to himself that he had been holding some of his righteous anger back.

"Yes," he began. "I am angry about the situation, Deacon. But I have to do more than scream and shout about it." Moderating his tone, he added "My reaction can't only be anger, it has to be looking for ways to heal the congregation -- that's my job."

"You're right, Reverend," Collins agreed. "I guess I'm just concerned that we can do more as a congregation than we are doing."

"And what do you think we *should* be doing?"

Collins held up his hands. "That's surely your job as our pastor, Reverend," Collins said. "It just seems to me that with this kind of violence and with 15 year olds being killed, we can't afford to be quiet. And I'm also angry - no make that furious - that the police arrested someone like Harold Williams instead of going after the real criminals, the drugs dealers and others."

"Which still begs the question of the role the church should have," said Price his shoulders slumping. "I have to tell you, Deacon," he said. "Taking on that role is not going to be easy. And it's going to draw a lot of attention to our church, perhaps attention that our board of deacons would not want."

Collins listened quietly, noticing the energy that the preacher had developed during their conversation. Carefully, he asked,

"Given this, Reverend, are you okay with leading this effort, with taking this on?" Before Price could respond, he continued. "We're talking about both the violence and drug trade that you're already doing, and taking on the police even more."

"There is important work to be done here, Deacon," Price said. "What I guess I should be asking you is are you willing to take this up with the board of deacons?"

"You do what you believe you have to do as a pastor, Reverend," said Collins. "I will work with the board." Collins smiled again, then rose. "I can see you have important work to do, so I'll let you get to it." Price extended his hand. Collins took it and shook it heartily.

"You take care, now, you hear?" Collins said.

"You too," said Price.

Collins squeezed Price's hand again, then left the office. Price sat down again, rubbed his eyes, then turned back to his work.

Chapter Forty

The contrast in the Williams home was chilling. Danny Novak was accustomed to the brightness and warmth of Ruth and Lester's home, and not at all comfortable with the sadness he saw now. The Williams' had known Manny Johnson all his life, and knew his family as well. Ruth, ever the host, offered Novak and Hart tea and coffee, which they accepted. After sipping their coffee and engaging in small talk, Novak spoke.

"Ms. Williams," he began. "I am so sorry about this loss. From everything people have told me, Manny was a good boy, the kind of boy his parents were proud of." As Novak spoke, he could see Ruth's eyes glistening.

"He was that, Danny," Ruth Williams said. She smiled slightly. "Harold did tell me that he -- Manny -- was being tempted by some of those drug dealers." Ruth rubbed the back of her neck. "I think he was just dazzled by all the money, but was too scared to start selling."

"So, he just wanted to be close to the money and bling but not earn it himself?" Hart asked.

"Just like any other young boy who gets blinded by gold," Ruth said. "No," she added. "I really think he was too scared to deal drugs which is just fine with me and his family."

"What I still haven't figured out was why Manny was there; near the stadium I mean," Novak asked. "Doesn't he live in Auburn?"

"Harold said he didn't know that either," Lester Williams replied. "That may have been one of the reasons Harold went over to Terry Wright that day, to keep people like Manny away from the drug trade."

"But we don't really know that, Lester," Ruth said. Frustrated, she rose from her seat, and went to the window. "The fact is," she continued, "We don't know why Manny went there, we don't really know what happened," slowing, she added, "and it really doesn't matter." Ruth's words were met with a long silence.

Looking around the house, Hart asked "Where is Harold today?"

"He's staying in the house today," Ruth said. "After getting out of jail, he asked to be left alone for a while, and frankly, I don't blame him."

Novak and Hart could see the anger in Ruth's stance and in her inflection, and as she sat down again, Lester took her hand. Seeing this, Hart left her seat and went to kneel next to Ruth Williams. Hart took Ruth's hand.

"We're very sorry, Ms. Williams," Hart said. "The more we hear about Manny and the more we see how this whole situation has hurt people, the sadder we get."

Ruth Williams looked down at Hart, the tough female cop who never seemed to get rattled, and smiled. Squeezing Hart's hand, she said,

"We know, Child." Sneaking a glance at Novak, Ruth added, "We know the kind of people you are and know you always try to do right by us. Don't ever doubt that."

Novak sat forward and met Ruth Williams' eyes. "Stephanie and I were talking about the memorial for Manny. And" he paused, glancing at Hart. "We'd like to attend the memorial and funeral for him; not because it's our job, but because this is a terrible loss for our community, and we're a part of that." Ruth and Lester glanced at each other, then looked back at Novak, waiting for him to continue.

"The problem," Novak continued. "Is that we don't want our presence to be a distraction to either the memorial or the family." The room was silent for a while.

"Have you spoken with Manny's family?" asked Lester quietly.

"We went to see them earlier today," Hart answered. "It was a little difficult speaking with them but Danny and I felt that they were doing as well as they could."

"Which isn't too well, I'm sure," said Lester.

"True," said Novak, sadly.

"I see," said Lester, gravely. He breathed a heavy sigh, and looked to his wife for support. "I think you both ought to come. People know you Danny, and they know how straight you are."

"Which doesn't mean some people won't be angry," Ruth added quickly. She looked down briefly, then, "I didn't want you to come not knowing that."

"I think we can handle that," Hart said after a pause. "But thank you for the heads up, Ms. Williams."

"And we want to be with you in this," Novak added.

Ruth Williams squeezed her husband's hand again, saying. "You come to the services. And don't you hide while you're there."

Chapter Forty One

"Rejoice Ye Pure in Heart!

Rejoice Give Thanks and Sing!"

So began the processional at Great Mt Zion AME Church for the "Celebration of Triumph" for Emmanuel Johnson, Age 15. The church was full, with a long line of cars outside sporting funeral flags for the procession to the cemetery, and several police escorts waiting as well. The occupants of one cruiser, however, were not waiting outside. Officer Danny Novak and Probationary Officer Stephanie Hart were seated toward the rear of the sanctuary in uniform. Right before the processional, Novak and Hart saw Capt. Shoemaker and Lt. Perkins enter the church as well. Perkins greeted several other congregants, and introduced Shoemaker to a few. He and Shoemaker made their way toward the rear of the sanctuary, giving silent greetings to Hart and Novak on the way.

Novak found himself generally comfortable, given that he had attended church services and other events in this church several times, but this felt different. Looking at this partner, he saw that Hart, who was usually quite confident and strong, was nervous and ill at ease. Novak touched her leg, and she jumped.

"Sorry," Novak whispered. "Didn't mean to scare you." Looking at her again, he asked "What's going on, Steve?"

"Just feeling a little uncomfortable, is all," Hart said. She turned to Novak and gave a small smile. "Just a bad vibe, you know?"

"I know," Novak agreed. "I'm just trying to focus on Manny's family." He directed his eyes toward the front. "Did you say anything to them when we walked by them? I didn't notice."

"No," Hart said. "I just said a few words -- not really much. I got the impression they were fine with us being here."

"Oh, I agree," said Novak. "Going over to their house yesterday is probably what made the difference." Novak's voice grew sad. "They seem like a really nice family."

"You don't ever get over having your child die, Danny," Hart said, after a pause.

"I've heard that," Novak agreed. He turned to face Hart again, his eyes down. "People tell me it can last forever and tear families apart, too."

"Um hmm," Hart agreed.

The associate pastor stood in front of the congregation, and raised his arms, directing the congregation to stand. He bowed his head, causing everyone else to lower theirs as well as he began to pray.

"Let us pray," he began. "This is the day that the Lord has made; Let us rejoice and be glad in it." The prayer continued, and both Novak and Hart could see visible reactions of the Manny Johnson's family, even from the rear of the sanctuary.

After the prayer, the service continued with two scripture readings, and two songs by the choir, and two by the congregation. After the reading from the New Testament, the pastor moved to the pulpit. He surveyed the congregation with a somber face and breathed in and out a few times as he centered himself. Finally, he raised his head, and spoke.

"Let us pray. Heavenly Father, we come to you in prayer and thanksgiving; we come to you in sorrow and pain. Be with the family of young Emmanuel; be with his mother and father and younger sister, suffering with his loss; be with his friends who have to come face to face with loss; be with the family of all those hurt by drugs and violence in the city who deserve more and may not know your love and comfort. Be with the family of those falsely accused so they can also be made whole again…" To this, both Novak and Hart sat up in their seats and frowned, distracted enough that they missed part of the prayer, and only heard "…in Jesus name, we pray, Amen."

Novak and Hart looked at each other and sighed. The pastor had completed the prayer, and looked again at the congregation.

"This is a challenging time, and of course our hearts to go the Johnson family," the pastor said. "We knew Manny here at Greater Mt. Zion, and our sanctuary is full because of the love we have for you and for Manny." The pastor stopped and his face grew more serious.

"Now," he continued, "There are those among us who purport to protect and serve. When you ask why they chose to come into the house of the Lord on this day, they may tell you to it was to show that they care." He paused. "I have to tell you, brothers and sisters, that the time to show you care is really before a tragedy like this happens, and not afterwards."

"But our God is a Living God, a Loving God who can forgive, but also a God who asks us to do our part, our part to love one another; our part to care, our part to make our community whole and free of crime, free of drugs, and free of harassment." At this, there were murmurings and some even turned their heads to look at Novak and Hart. The officers were frozen in their seats and wondering what was really going on at Greater Mt Zion. The pastor continued, with some seated behind him, among them members of the board of deacons, looking uncomfortable.

"We have to ask ourselves, are we doing our part? Are we doing enough? Are we challenging others to do their part?" The pastor looked directly at Novak and Hart.

"We should know that sorry or we can't is too little too late when our children are dying. That's not the kind of community Jesus was creating when he showed us the way." The pastor paused for effect, then said,

"Let us pray." Novak and Hart were too stunned to close their eyes during the prayer, nor did they hear much of it. They wished they could have, for as they looked up during the prayer, they each saw ten or twelve pairs of eyes on them assessing them. Hart sighed again, feeling uncomfortable and very much unwelcome.

The service was concluded, and those wishing to travel to the cemetery were told where to go. Hart and Novak used that time to prepare for escort duty. As they walked to their cruiser, Ruth and Lester Williams hailed them. Hart and Novak walked over the join the Williams'.

"Hello, Ms. Williams," Novak said. Hart only gave Ruth Williams a smile. As always, Ruth Williams took command.

"Let's come over here and sit," Ruth said, pointing to a bench. "We're going to be one of the last cars in the procession, and you're coming up the rear, so you have time. Novak only nodded.

"Good," Ruth said. "Then let's sit." The officers followed Ruth to the bench, trading glances with Lester who only shrugged.

When they arrived, Ruth sat and patted the seat next to her, looking at Hart. Hart sat down and took Ruth's hand.

"How are you doing, Ms. Williams?" she asked.

"That's what I was supposed to be asking you, Child!" Ruth said. "I'm not the one in there who the pastor was talking about."

"It is what it is," Hart said quietly.

"Why do I think that doesn't really tell us how you feel?"

Hart hesitated before responding, then decided which way she wanted to go. "This might be the hardest day I've had since I joined this department," she said. "And I've had some tough ones, like being part of the team that had to visit families and tell them that their sons or daughters had died. You know I've taken those calls from field commanders, and made those calls to families along with my commanders, and I've seen people die before, and attended their memorials." Hart sat back and pulled her hands to her. "This was very different."

Ruth, Lester and Novak were silent, waiting for Hart to continue. Her eyes met each of them, then she sighed again.

"This was very different," she repeated. "And different enough that I really wonder if I have what it takes to be a street cop -- either here or anywhere else." She cleared her throat. "And that just gives me a lot to think about." Hart gathered her strength, and added, "Which I'm certainly not going to be able to do today, so...."

Ruth took her hand again. "I thought that might be it," she said. Then she smiled. "And you don't have anything to worry about, Stephanie."

"Ms. Williams is right, Steve," Novak said finally. "The fact that you feel this way is how I know that this is exactly what you should be doing."

"I know it's different, Steve," Novak continued. "And I bet if I went into the MPs I would find it really different and tougher than this. But I just know that you are made for this, probably more than any other probationary officer I've ever known or worked with." Novak smiled again, and added "So, that's why you have to stay right here." Leaning forward he said. "Plus, if you were to leave, Sheryl would be *really* upset."

To this Hart smiled, and looked to Lester for support.

"Don't look at *me*, Stephanie," he said. "If I were you, I'd do whatever Ruth and Danny say."

To this, Hart broke into her first genuine smile of the day and laughed.

Chapter Forty Two

The news crews had already gathered in the social hall of the church and were awaiting the arrival of Rev. Archie Price. Price was in his study, going over his notes and preparing for the press conference. Deacon Ernest Collins had assured him that taking this more activist stance would be supported by the board of deacons, and while he was still a bit concerned about this development, he was just as confident that taking a strong stand with the was the right thing to go. At the knock to his study door, he refocused on the present, saying, "Come in."

"Deacon Ernest Collins opened the door. He approached Price, smiling. "I think all the news outlets you contacted are here, Reverend," Collins said. "Are you ready?"

Price stood up. "I believe so, Deacon." Smiling himself, he added, "Why don't we go to the social hall and get started?" Price and Collins walked down the hallway to the stairs, then down one flight to the social hall, which had been set up with theater style chairs facing a podium on the floor. Price walked to the podium and stood behind it, quiet and formal. The podium had five microphones already placed on it. He closed his eyes to say a silent prayer, then after a minute, he raised his eyes and looked at the reporters. As he did so, several cameras clicked on and additional microphones were raised.

"Ladies and Gentlemen," Price began. "I would like to welcome you to Greater MT. Zion AME Church. We are pleased that you have come to visit with us today, because we believe we have important things to say about the Lexington and Auburn communities." Price paused again, surveying the group of about 20 people. He saw two TV personalities from network affiliates, and two or three of the faces from the other reporters looked familiar, perhaps from their pictures in Port Angel's *Times Herald*.

"Violence in our city is an epidemic, and one major cause of that is the drug trade, which is sucking the life out of our community, and causing violence, death and dependency among our young people.

Greater Mt. Zion AME Church is doing what it can to stem this tide, by increasing our youth oriented programming, by getting more young people involved in the right kinds of activities and teaching them values that would make them happy, moral and successful adults.

"Greater Mt. Zion cannot do this alone, and we try to engage other community partners, people and organizations who care about our youth. These partners include the Rotary Club of Lexington, several businesses in our community such as Heaven's Home Restaurant, Bill's Bike Shop and the Corner Gym, and all of those efforts are making a difference in stemming the tide of the increasing drug trade. But we cannot do this alone, and I am concerned, *we* are concerned that an important partner is simply not at the table.

Price paused again, and seemed to grow even more serious were that possible. "There are several members of the Port Angel Police Department who understand our community and engage positively with us," Price said. "But there are many more who have made themselves firmly a part of the problem and not part of the solution. These may be detectives or patrol officers, but in any case, we cannot it seems, expect our police force to protect all of us uniformly." As Price spoke, he could not see the faces of those behind him, and many of the members of the board of deacons seemed somewhat uncomfortable with Price's tone, though many might have agreed with his sentiments.

"A mere week ago, Emmanuel, Johnson, a 15 year old member of this congregation, was brutally gunned down not far from Sparks Stadium. Our police force responded right away to that, but my question is where were they *before* this happened? Where were they when they received information from a community member about rising tensions among drug traffickers? And that's what we continue to ask ourselves. Where is our police force when we need them and not when they want to lock us up? We don't have the answer to that question, yet we are calling for that answer today from our Commissioner of Police and from our government officials. And," he added, "so far, they have all chosen to be silent."

Price changed to a softer tone. "Shortly after Manny Johnson was killed, the police in their infinite desire to lock us up rather than partner with us, arrested one of the finest young men in our community and charged him with the crime, rather than to look beyond the obvious." Price placed both hands on the podium, his hands in fists. "This is not the police force we want, nor the policing we deserve," he said. "So this is a challenge to our police force. If you care about Lexington and Auburn as much as you care about other areas of our city, it's time to show it; time to come to us, rather than us coming to you. For the sake of our community, we hope that you do." Price paused, then stepped back from the podium and caught his breath -- not realizing that his emotion had gotten the better of him. After a few seconds, he relaxed. Facing the reporters, he added, "I'm happy to entertain questions now if you have them," he said. When the hands were raised, he chose one from a TV reporter.

"Rev. Price," the woman began, "Sara Stiles from Port Angel Action News." Not waiting for acknowledgement, she continued. "You have made several statements criticizing the police for their arrest, and we understand that was of a Mr. Harold Williams. What evidence do you have that he was, in fact, falsely arrested, and are you suggesting that Mr. Williams sue the Port Angel police for false arrest?"

Price put up his hands in surrender. "First, I won't comment on what the Williams family should or should not do, though I can tell you that Harold Williams gave the police information over a week ago about rising tensions among drug dealers, and no one from the department followed up on it. It seems to me that they were simply looking for low hanging fruit and the first arrest they could make easily: why, I don't know." Price turned his attention away from Stiles and toward another reporter, and nodded to the man.

"Rev. Price, what would you have the police do differently from what they're doing now?"

Price smiled and looked at his watch, saying "How much time do you have?" The reporters and members of the board of deacons all laughed, lowering some of the tension. Price continued talking about what he felt would be a far better police force in Port Angel, answering several questions until the press conference concluded about 30 minutes after it started.

* * *

In the squad room, several officers and detectives from the 9th Precinct and both Lt. Perkins and Capt. Shoemaker watched the press conference with a mixture of disgust and sadness. Once the press conference was over, Lt. Perkins walked to the large screen TV and turned it off, saying,

"I guess he's drawn his line in the sand."

"The question is, Perk," said O.C. Boyd. "What do we do with it?

Perkins nodded gravely. "That is the question of the hour, O.C." Perkins replied.

Charter Forty Three

Gray looked out at his lieutenants as they waited for Pepe Brantley for arrive. Gray turned to Cabral.

"What did you last hear from Pepe, Emilio?" Gray asked.

"He's on the way, sir," Cabral said, quickly. "He wanted to be sure to hear what the TV people were saying after the press conference."

Gray nodded. "Good," he said. "That's what I was hoping." Gray checked the time, and impatient as ever, asked, "What else did you hear from people at the funeral?"

Sayles and Burch looked at each other.

"What do you mean?" Sayles asked.

"Simple Ricky," Cabral said. "Like did people talk about being scared because of the strike, shit like that."

"Yeah, I get it," Sayles said after thinking. He turned again to Gray. "Yes, sir. Some of the people were kind of scared? I mean, they were scared, but then kind of mad because of what the preacher said, you know?" Sayles' voice trailed off.

"Yes," Gray replied. "I know what you mean, Ricky."

"Boss," Cabral interrupted. "I was a little surprised by what that preacher said at the funeral and at the press conference. He was really taking the cops on."

Gray made a dismissive gesture. "True, Emilio," he said. But let's wait until Pepe arrives so we know exactly what happened at the press conference, since it won't be broadcast for a while."

"Yes, sir," said Cabral. The group was silent, until Pepe Brantley arrived a few minutes later. Brantley knocked on the door and was admitted to Gray's office. He took his seat quickly, and looked up at Gray.

"Welcome, Pepe," said Gray. "What do you have to tell us about the press conference?"

Brantley licked his lips before answering. "Well, uh, sir, the preacher really went after the cops, you know? I mean, he was even worse than he was at the funeral; he really hammered 'em."

Gray looked to Cabral. "As you thought, Emilio," he said. "And certainly something of a surprise." Seeing the confusion on the faces of his lieutenants, Gray continued. "We usually assume that the church, especially Greater Mt. Zion will be working *with* the police rather than against them." Gray nodded as if agreeing with himself. Sitting back he added, "This is an interesting turn of events."

"Could this make it easier for us?" Cabral asked. "I mean, if the church and cops don't talk to each other, that might make it easier for us, right?"

"That's certainly possible, Emilio," Gray answered. "Anything that keeps people out of our way is something to be desired." Turning to Brantley, he asked. "Were you able to hear any police reaction to the press conference, Pepe?"

Brantley twisted his mouth, thinking. "I didn't see any of 'em around the church, and I didn't want to get too close," Brantley said. "But I heard one of the TV people say that she was on the phone with one of the big cops and he was so pissed that he didn't want to talk to her."

"Do you know the name of this 'big cop,' Pepe?" Gray asked.

Brantley lowered his head. "No, sir." he said. "Like I said, I didn't want to get too close."

Gray nodded and raised his right hand. "You did the right thing, Pepe," Gray said. "We do not want our plans interrupted by curious media people."

"Any new orders for us?" Cabral asked, maintaining his position as Gray's most senior lieutenant.

"A good question, Emilio," Gray asked. "And in fact, we may need to accelerate our action."

"Why," Sayles asked, sitting up. "We got the church and police fighting, why do we have to go faster?"

"More to it than that, Ricky," Cabral said. "Just because they're fighting each other doesn't mean they aren't going to fight us, too." Then as he looked at Gray, he added, "At least that's the way I see it, sir."

Gray gave a small smile. "Well thought out, Emilio," Gray said, "and I think accurate." Turning to the entire group, he continued. "The church doesn't matter to me, but there is likely to be a much stronger police presence around for a while, which could make our work more difficult. As a result, we will want to strike quickly so that the independents don't have the chance to recover."

Sounding almost like a general, Gray added, "we will need to strike soon and with enough force that no one will be able to resist us. Gentlemen, you must be sure that all your people are ready, armed and know exactly what they have to do. And before we can make this strike, we will need to move to the new base at the edge of Auburn and abandon this one. We need to be ready to do that in the next two days."

"The new place is ready for us?" Cabral asked.

"It is," Gray replied.

The group was quiet for a while, as the mood grew more somber. They knew what it meant to change their location and how serious the situation had become.

Sayles looked more and more uncomfortable with the silence. Turning first to Gray, then Cabral, then finally back to Gray, he asked, "How hard are we gonna hit them, sir?"

Gray spoke slowly and deliberately. "We are securing our future, Ricky," he said. "We need to make sure this strike gives us what we want." Gray leaned forward again to admonish his lieutenants. "Do I have to remind you about not hurting innocents?"

The eyes of Cabral, Sayles, Brantley and Burch widened then returned to normal size. Every head moved from side to side.

Gray sat back in his chair. "Good," he said. "Other than that, I don't give a damn who gets hurt."

Chapter Forty Four

Capt. Andrew Shoemaker asked several officers to remain after morning muster, including Novak, Hart, Moody & Porter. As the other officers were leaving the muster room, Hart turned to Novak.

"Could we be in trouble again?" she asked.

"Unlikely," said Novak. "We haven't done anything we weren't supposed to do over the last couple of days." He smiled at his partner, teasing her. "Steve, you've just got to learn to roll with it."

Hart's stare at Novak told him what she thought of his suggestion. "Oh, I get it, Danny" she said. "I just want to know what's up. Call it 'Type A' policing." At that, she smiled and turned her attention back to Capt. Shoemaker and Lt. Perkins, who had remained after muster as well. The mood in the room was more expectant than tense, and the officers and detectives glanced at each other, and with several shrugs shared and received, they all settled back to wait for the room to clear. When the door closed, Shoemaker finally turned around to face the officers and spoke.

"We've had a couple of days since our last meeting people," he began. "What have we learned?" Then he quickly added, "Perk and I have been talking throughout, people, but we haven't shared everything together, so let's get everything out on the table." The captain waited, and seeing no one begin, rolled his eyes, then pointed to Novak. "Danny, what have you got?"

Novak consulted silently with Hart for a second, then addressed the group. "Well, Steve and I have been hearing continuing rumblings about Cobra and his operation." The other officers were confused for a while when Novak said "Steve," but quickly realized he was talking about his probationary officer. "In any case," Novak continued, "there are a number of drug dealers we know by reputation, most of whom have been in custody a couple of times on minor charges, but these are others who aren't part of any larger organized ring, you know, like Parker, Cobra and Spino." Many of the other officers nodded their heads in agreement.

"Well," Novak continued, "I don't know if you noticed but almost all of the people roughed up a couple of weeks ago were independents, and they were all located on the fringes of Cobra's territory"

"We knew that," said Moody.

His reply seem to hold no animosity, so Novak continued. "Anyway, that's exactly what we saw in the second strike: some of the people targeted were independents working dangerously close to Cobra's territory."

"And it looks like those independents from the first attack are wary about going back into business," Hart added. "We saw one just yesterday who was walking to school rather than dealing. It kind of shocked us."

"Who was that?" asked Porter. Hart looked at Novak, who answered.

"'Bracket' -- you know, Bobby Sims," Novak said.

"We know him," Porter said. "And that squares with what we've been hearing as well."

"Which is?" Shoemaker asked.

Porter turned to his partner, then glanced briefly at Hart and Novak. "We think that Cobra is gearing up for a really strong strike either against the independents or maybe even against the other two big trafficking groups in the city." As he spoke, both Novak and Hart looked at each other. They had come to the same conclusion, but had been afraid to voice it first.

"The point is," Moody added, "We think this could easily happen really soon, like in the next week."

"Why do you think that, Dave?" said Lt. Perkins.

Moody looked a little uncomfortable, but said. "Well, Siem and I --
we've been hearing something about Cobra and his main guys."

Perkins waited, then prompted, "And...?"

"Well, Perk, we can't find him, or we just don't know where he is."

"Can't *find* him?" Novak asked, shaking his head.

"Yeah," Moody replied. "You know he's always been somewhere
around the Old Christopher Docks."

"That's what I always heard," Novak said, "Though only second or
third hand." He looked carefully at Moody. "You had confirmation
of this?"

"Didn't need it, Novak," Porter answered. "We always knew
basically where he was, the problem was making anything stick to
him -- or getting him into an interview room long enough to get him
to talk before his mouthpiece arrived." Porter spoke out of
frustration. "So yeah, we pretty much knew exactly where he was,
but he's not there anymore, or at least that's what a couple of our
confidential informants told us."

"Reliable CIs?" asked Shoemaker.

Porter raised his hand in surrender. "As reliable as they can ever be,
Captain," he said. "The CIs were Johnny Davis and Spew, uhm,
Russell Martin, and they usually give it to us straight."

"I went to school with Davis, Captain," Novak said. "He isn't smart
enough to make up something like this."

Moody chuckled. "You got that right," he agreed.

Shoemaker stood and began to pace quietly. After one round of the
room, he turned again to the officers. "I don't know of anybody like
Cobra who doesn't have more than one place to hang," he said.
"What else have you heard?

"Actually Captain," Moody began, "we asked them what they knew about multiple locations, and we got the same answer -- no one has seen much of Cobra for about three days." Turning to Porter, he added "Three, right Siem?" Porter nodded.

"So anyway," Moody continued, "That's what we know." Novak had an intake of breath, and everyone looked at him.

"Danny," Shoemaker asked, prompting him to continue.

Novak turned to Moody and Porter. "Did you hear anything from the 12th Precinct?"

Moody and Porter looked at each other, then Moody asked, "What about?"

"About locations," Novak said. "I seem to remember one of his hideouts at one time was at the upper edge of Auburn, in the 12th. I just wondered if that's where he might have gone."

Moody and Porter looked at each other again, then turned back to the group. "I guess we can look into that," said Moody.

"Do that," said Shoemaker.

"Wait," said Hart suddenly animated again.

"Hart?" asked Shoemaker.

"Uh," she began, then "All Danny and I know about is what seems to be happening with the independents, and the detectives" she gestured with her hand "have heard some of the same things we have, plus about Cobra leaving his usual haunts."

Perkins leaned forward, impatiently. "And...?"

"And I was just wondering what we or anybody knows about the other two big drug trafficking rings in the city. Are they gearing up for this big battle or do they even know much about what Cobra's doing?"

Shoemaker was confused but nodded anyway. "I can see how that might be relevant, Hart," he began. "What I think you're suggesting is that we think we know what Cobra is doing, maybe to engage the other drug rings, but we don't know what they're doing in response, is that right?"

"Something like that, Sir," Hart said. "Cobra wouldn't need to abandon his usual hideouts to take on a few independents, but unless we know what the other traffickers are doing, we only have half of the story."

The room was silent for a moment, before Shoemaker turned again to Moody and Porter.

"You two need to check this out with narcotics division, since they haven't seen fit to keep me in the loop," Shoemaker said, with an obvious tinge of annoyance. "Maybe you can talk to some of our less secretive narcotic cops about this." Moody and Porter picked up on the tension and simply nodded their heads, writing down the directive in their notebooks. Shoemaker turned his attention back to the whole group. "Well, we all thought this might happen anyway," he said. "Let's have Moody and Porter do their magic with narcotics, and Novak and Hart, you work with Lt. Perkins and see what you can find out about where Cobra might be, thinking about things like fortification, access to roads, and maybe even access to the water for incoming shipments -- hell I don't know."

Shoemaker sighed again. "And I'll get on the horn and speak to some of the other commanders about the Parker and Spino gangs, and let's see where this leads us."

Chapter Forty Five

Novak and Hart left the muster room and walked to their cruiser. Novak started the car and quickly headed down Columbia Avenue.

"Where are we going?" Hart asked.

"Heaven's Home," said Novak.

Hart consulted her watch. "A bit early, isn't it?"

"Not really," said Novak. "I have an idea."

Once parked at the restaurant, they entered to find a surprised Ruth Williams. She started to show them to a table, when she noticed Novak's mood.

"What's on your mind, Danny?" Ruth Williams asked. She led Novak and Hart to a table and sat down.

"Work things," Novak replied. He and Hart sat down as Novak gathered his thoughts. "Ms. Williams, we've been trying to figure out what's happening with all the drug traffickers, and one problem we have is that we're trying to find out more about Cobra -- Louis Gray -- and we can't seem to find him. Have you heard anything about him lately?"

Ruth gave an offhanded gesture and answered with mild annoyance. "No, and I don't need or want to hear anything about that man," she said. He's a bad man, Danny, he's brought a lot of misery to this neighborhood."

"But do you know where his headquarters is?" Novak asked.

Ruth seemed stunned. "The last time I heard," she began, "uh, the last time I thought I heard he was at the Old Christopher Docks."

"But he's not there now," Novak said.

Ruth seemed genuinely surprised. "Oh," she said. "I mean I don't follow him but that's the only thing I ever heard, but I know that's not much.

Novak shook his head. "No, that's what we all thought, Ms. Williams," he said. Novak rubbed his chin, then looked around for something to write with on, when he looked up and saw a pencil in Hart's hand. He held out his hand for the pencil, then turned over his place mat. "Let me show you what we're trying to figure out," he continued. He made a crude map of the major streets in Lexington and Auburn, showing intersections and some major businesses. It look him only about three minutes, but both Williams and Hart were able to understand the map. When he had completed the map, Novak looked up. Pointing at the map, he said. "Now about here is his last hideout at the Old Christopher Docks." He looked up and saw general understanding on the faces of both women. Continuing, he said, "Now a couple of years ago, I think he was closer to Diamond Street in the back of an auto store, somewhere around," he searched, then made another X on the map, "here, I think."

"But I seem to remember another location maybe in between these two." He looked more squarely at Williams again "Do you know anything about this?"

"I know the neighborhoods, Danny," Ruth Williams said, "But I wouldn't know anything about where Cobra is working except for where he was last, at the docks." She frowned. "But Lester might know." Ruth turned toward the kitchen and called, "Lester! Can you come out for a minute?"

"Wait!" they heard from the kitchen. Lester stuck his head out of the kitchen. "What did you want, Ruth?"

"Can you come out for a minute?"

Lester looked again at the stove and shook his head, "Not for about 5 minutes, Honey."

"Tell you what," Ruth said. "Why don't I take over there for you?"

"Okay," Lester said, and he turned back to the kitchen to wait for his wife. Ruth left the table and Hart turned to Novak

"You have an idea," she said.

Novak shrugged, "Not much of one, but…."

Lester Williams arrived at the table, wiping his hands on an apron. He came with his own glass of water and sat down without fanfare.

"Danny. Stephanie." he said, then turned to Novak, calmly.

"Mr. Williams," Novak began. "We've been trying to figure something out about Cobra's hideouts, and I was trying to remember where he used to be." Novak explained the map on the table and the two locations he knew about, with the obvious question to Lester unspoken.

Lester studied the map for a while and turned it sideways once or twice before putting it down.

"I think you missed a couple of places, Danny," Lester Williams said. "Sometimes people talk too much for their own good," he said, and he leaned closer to Novak and Hart. "Now the way I heard it, this Cobra and his people had a place about" he checked the map and pointed, "somewhere on Poplar, see here, near 13th. And I seem to remember some place on Samson, but I don't remember where on the street it would have been."

Novak looked at his map, and picked out where Samson would extend and measured it with his hands, looking back and forth between the two ends. "I don't see any kind of pattern with these," he said, "but I would almost have to drive by them to really know, I think," Novak said. "Still, thanks, Mr. Williams."

"Um hmm," Williams replied. "But I do know someone you might want to talk to who knows more about real estate in all of these areas." As he spoke, Novak and Hart both perked up.

"Who?" Hart asked.

"Deacon Collins," Williams said. He got a cynical look in his eye. "If there's anybody who knows about making money off of real estate in this city, it's him."

Chapter Forty Six

Novak and Hart stood outside in Lt. Perkins office, and both were uneasy. Perkins noticed them as he approached his office.

"Novak. Hart," Perkins said, a little surprised. "You have something for me?"

"Yes, sir," Novak said. "We were talking with Ruth and Lester Williams, you know, from Heaven's Home Restaurant, and we talked about some of the other locations that Cobra has used."

"And?"

Novak pulled out the map he had drawn at the restaurant. "May we should just show you, Sir," he began. "Could we go to the table?" Perkins nodded and gestured toward his conference table. At the table, Novak pointed out the locations that he and Lester Williams had identified for Cobra. Novak also shared that Lester's recommendation that Perkins should call Ernest Collins, because he might know something about the properties Cobra was using. Perkins was impressed.

"This is good work," he said. "Both of you." He turned to Hart and smiled, holding out his hand. "Do you have some of those famous notes to share with me, Hart?"

Hart took out her notebook, paged through and then tore out several pages, handing them to Perkins. He took the notes, quickly scanned them, then examined them more closely. Finally, he raised his head looking at the two officers.

"I think the idea of calling Ernest is a sound one," Perkins said. Raising his hand, he added, "so as I understand it, we're going to ask him what he knows about the properties, perhaps ownership, that sort of thing, correct?"

"Right," Novak said.

"Why don't we just check with tax records?" Perkins asked. "That would be easier and more direct."

Hart and Novak looked at each other.

"That might be easier, sir," said Hart. "But the problem is we don't have exact addresses. We thought or at least Mr. Williams thought that Mr. Collins might know about whole blocks in these areas given his background."

"Exactly," said Novak. "This is just a head start -- we'll probably still need to look at the tax records after speaking with him."

"That makes sense," Perkins replied. "And I can definitely make that call." Perkins shifted to his desk and was just looking at his phone directory, when Dave Moody knocked on his door. Perkins looked up.

"Got a minute," Lieutenant?" he asked, then noticed Novak and Hart. "Hey," he said to them.

"Hey," Novak said.

"Come on in, Dave," Perkins said. He picked up the phone, then put it down, adding "do you have breaking news for me, too?"

"Why," Moody said. "Did Novak and Hart have something?" Perkins answered by indicating Novak with his head. Moody faced Novak and waited.

"We were looking at some of the former places we think Cobra has been using, Dave," said Novak. He pointed to the table, adding, "We even drew a map."

Moody glanced at the map. "Actually, we were doing the same thing," he said. "Siem and I have a couple of addresses that we wanted to look into before we did anything about it."

Coming from around his desk, Perkins said, "Let's see what you've got." The four officers huddled over the conference table and

Novak's map, eventually welcoming Siem Porter, and compared locations. Moody and Porter had identified one additional location, but it was an important one. Perkins stood up looking concerned.

"What's up, Lieutenant?" asked Hart.

"Not sure," Perkins said, quietly. He went slowly behind his desk again then added, "we may want to make that check of tax records now rather than later. Hart and Novak looked at each other while Moody and Porter just look confused.

Perkins picked up the phone. "I think we ought to have the captain here." he said. He made the call, his tone confusing all four of the officers standing around his conference table. Andrew Shoemaker soon arrived and Perkins got him up to speed, also sharing Hart's notes with him. Shoemaker listened attentively, gave Hart an appraising look after reviewing her notes, then turned again to his lieutenant of detectives.

"So," Shoemaker began, "What now?"

"One possibility Shoe," Perkins said, "is to check into these locations using tax records. "This one," -- he pointed to the property identified by Moody and Porter -- "is in a block that I remember seeing with Ernest Collins a year or so ago." Perkins grew quieter. "And as I recall, he may have owned much of the entire block, which means that I certainly don't want to call him to ask about this or any other property." The group became eerily silent, reflecting on what Perkins had said.

Surprisingly, it was Hart who spoke first. "Something tells me we don't want to make too much of a leap here," she said.

Shoemaker laughed. "Never knew you to be a diplomat, Hart," he said. "But you're right. We really need to tread carefully here." He turned to Moody and Porter. "What, if anything, have you guys heard from narcotics?"

Moody snickered. "They didn't say much, Cap," Moody said. "They did imply that there were more than the usual rumblings going on and that they were monitoring" he turned to Porter -- "is that they word they used, Siem?" Porter shrugged. "Anyway," Moody continued, "monitoring what's going on. We got the impression that they resented us being involved, but I think they know something is up." Turning to the captain, he added, "can you check that out with somebody, Cap?"

"I'm going to have to," said Shoemaker. "It's worth looking into." Turning back to Perkins, he added "So you think checking out ownership records will give us something?"

"Hard to say, Shoe," Perkins said, his low mood evident. "We can do that pretty independently, and I don't think it's a waste of time for Dave and Siem." The detectives rose quickly, understanding their assignment.

"What do you want *us* to do, Lieutenant?" asked Novak.

Perkins looked briefly at the detectives and Shoemaker, before saying, "Let me get back to you. I may have another assignment for you soon."

* * *

The officers filed out of Perkins' office, and for a while, Perkins and Shoemaker sat in silence. Eventually, Perkins sat back at his desk, and reclined in his chair looking skyward. Shoemaker watched him and waited, finally sitting down on the edge of the conference table facing his long-time friend.

Perkins looked up. "Obviously, you're thinking the same things I am," he said. "How would you handle this if you were me?"

Shoemaker smiled. "Well, you already know what you have to do, so it's not that," Shoemaker said. "The bigger question is are the conclusions we just jumped to the right ones?"

Perkins shook his head. "Damned if I know, Shoe," he said. "Though I suppose we ought to do this one thing at a time."

"That we should," Shoemaker said, "and hope to hell we're wrong.

Chapter Forty Seven

Kat Neely looked up from her desk and saw Angela Marin and Don Brown walking towards her. She smiled as they approached.

"What's up, Gee? Hey Brownie," Neely said. "You guys hardly ever come in together."

"Hey, Kat," Marin said. Brown just smiled as Marin continued. "Brownie and I just came in after seeing something we weren't so sure about."

Neely leaned forward. "Anything you can share?" she asked. "Something juicy?" Her voice was playful.

"Hardly," Brown said. "Just something we thought Moody and Porter might want. They're working the drug strikes, right?"

"Yep," Neely said, nodding. "They just finished up with Perk and Shoe." She turned toward the corridor. "They might still be in Perk's office." Brown and Marin looked at each other, shrugged, and started walking toward Perkins' office.

"Thanks Kat," Marin said.

Marin and Brown walked to Perkins' office and knocked. They were a little surprised to see both Shoemaker and Perkins in the office, and the commanders didn't seem too pleased to see them.

Shoemaker glanced at Perkins, who addressed the officers.

"Afternoon, Gee, Brownie." Perkins said. "Is there something you need?"

"Yes sir," Marin began. "Brownie and I were just patrolling and happened to come across something not far from the catacombs." Before Marin could continue, Novak and Hart appeared at the door.

"Sorry, Lieutenant, Captain," Novak said. "Kat said we should come to hear what Gee and Brownie had to say." Perkins waved the officers inside, then got up to come to the conference table. "Let's all sit why don't we," he said, his voice clearly strained.

Hart shot a glance to Novak whose face was his own question mark, and they all sat down.

"Actually, Gee and Browning were just talking to us, but speaking for myself, I'm not sure what it's all about," said Perkins.

"Sorry, Sir," Marin said. "We didn't get far enough to explain it to you." Marin sat up and quickly scanned the group. "We were just saying that we were stopped right around the catacombs, and…"

"Sorry," Hart interjected. "But I don't know the catacombs." She looked to Marin, but also to Novak.

Novak pulled out his makeshift map and spread it on the table.

"Talk about prepared," Brown said.

"You have *no* idea," Novak replied. He looked at the map, turned his head slightly, then pointed toward the right top corner. "The catacombs were from the old sanitation system, when the county ran it and not the city. There was an office and manufacturing complex there in addition to all of the tunnels." He looked briefly at Perkins for clarification. "Weren't most of the tunnels filled in a bunch of years ago, Lieutenant?"

"Far as I know Danny, around ten years, I think." Perkins looked to Shoemaker, who only nodded his head.

"So just who was at the catacombs?" Hart asked.

"Somebody we know pretty well -- Pepe Brantley," Marin said. "You know, one of Cobra's people." The other officers at the table quickly sat up.

"Just where at the catacombs did you see him?" Shoemaker asked. "This is important."

Marin frowned for a moment then said, "Well, we were at 2nd street and Tower, so at that corner." Marin looked around the table. "It wasn't for too long a time, and to be honest, I wasn't sure I saw him, but then Brownie said that he saw him too, so I was sure it was him."

"Silly question, Gee," Perkins said. "But are we talking about lurking around, or moving through quickly."

"Oh, quickly Lieutenant," Marin said. "Maybe a few seconds then he disappeared. Not like magic or anything, it's just that he went behind some buildings on 2nd, though I can't be sure which one."

"We can identify the block though," said Brown. "We're really sure it was Brantley, and we know that he's one of Cobra's people."

Perkins pressed his palms on the table. "Yes he is, Brownie," he said. "As far as we know, a central figure." The group was silent, then Perkins added, "often where Cobra is, Brantley and the others will be too."

Novak frowned. "The area that encompasses the catacombs is pretty big, Lieutenant," Novak said. "We may need to pinpoint it a lot better than just 2nd and Tower."

"Agreed," Shoemaker said, clearly again in command.

He turned to Marin and Brown "You two need to consult with any other officers who might have patrolled in that area in the last couple of days. When we break, head to the phone bank and see what you can find out."

"Yes Sir," both Marin and Brown said.

"We have to be sure where we're going to focus, Perk," Shoemaker said. "Do you think Moody and Porter have anything with those tax records yet?"

Novak said, "I can call them if you want. Do you want my phone?" As Novak was speaking, Perkins held out his hand. "Just check my contacts," Novak added as he handed the phone to Perkins. Perkins keyed in Moody's number and set the phone to speaker. After three rings, Moody answered.

"What the *fuck*, Novak?" Moody cried. "You can't wait for a little information?"

"No I fucking *can't,* Dave," Perkins said. The group in the office heard a muffled "Shit!" then, "Yes, Sir," from Moody. "What can I do for you, Lieutenant?"

After rolling his eyes, Perkins asked, "How far along are you with those tax records, Dave, and we already know you aren't done."

Perkins and the others could hear a hollow silence that suggested Moody had placed his hand over the phone. "Well," Moody answered, "we have some information, but we have to do it by block, which is not a problem, except we found that lots of the owners are corporations, and that's a different database, so we still don't know the actual owners." Moody paused. "That was the point, right?"

"Right on the money, Dave," Perkins replied. "And maybe I can help you with that. Plus" he added, "we have another string of addresses we might want to check out over by the catacombs."

"The catacombs?" Moody asked.

"Exactly," Perkins said, as he quickly wrote down Moody's cell number. "Tell you what, keep on with what you're doing and I'll call you back in about ten with some more things to check out."

"That doesn't sound good Lieutenant."

"You picked up on that really well, Dave," said Perkins, as he ended the call.

Chapter Forty Eight

The four officers left Lt. Perkins office, focused on their assignments. Lt. Perkins and Capt. Shoemaker were focused as well, but theirs was coupled with a tension that the officers hadn't picked up on.

Shoemaker looked at this friend. "This is going to be really difficult, Perk," Shoemaker said. "In fact, I should probably make a call up the line so they know our current thinking."

Perkins' eyebrows creased. "Try to hold off on that a little bit, Shoe," Perkins said. "We may have something and we may not, but we're not going to be hurt by waiting a couple of hours."

Shoemaker was surprised. "Only hours?" he asked.

"Absolutely," Perkins said. The officers are primed on this, Shoe, and that includes Moody and Porter. No, I don't think they're going to waste any time."

The two friends sat for a while, until Shoemaker, ever impatient stood up again. "We should probably spread the word internally about this."

"Meaning?"

Shoemaker sighed. "Meaning, we bring in the shift commanders and let them know what's going on, at least O. C. and Andrews." Shoemaker checked the time. "Andrews will clock in in about an hour anyway, so this won't be a big deal."

"How big do we want to make this, Shoe?" Perkins asked. "If we're going to keep some things quiet, we can't tell the world."

"Agreed," Shoemaker said. "We have to tell the shift commanders though, so we can let Ben Gore know what's going on when he gets on at midnight -- no sense calling him in early."

"Agreed," said Perkins.

"Good," Shoemaker replied. "In fact, let me call O.C. and Andrews in now and fill them in."

"Okay," Perkins said. "Your office in an hour?"

* * *

Sgt. O. C. Boyd and Sgt. Paul Andrews were already in Shoemaker's office when Perkins arrived a little more than an hour later. Boyd was sitting on the sofa rather than at the conference table, and he looked exhausted. By contrast, Paul Andrews, his fellow shift sergeant looked fresh and ready to go.

Perkins couldn't resist. "You look a little worn, O. C." he said. "You didn't have any fun during this shift?"

Boyd laughed. "I'm dealing with incompetents here, Perk," Boyd retorted. "What did you expect?"

Perkins returned the laugh. "Right, O.C." he said. "Incompetents all of whom *you* supervised and signed off on."

"That is a mere technicality," Boyd said, shaking his head. Pointing to his colleague, he added, "plus Andrews pressured me to sign off on the lot of them." Boyd stopped talking, and picked up on the tension in the room between Shoemaker and Perkins. "Guys," Boyd began, "You need to let us in on what's going on. You both look like somebody died or something." Perkins' and Shoemaker's eyes met, and before they could speak, Andrews interjected.

"Wait, did somebody here die?" Andrews asked.

"No. No, guys," Perkins said. He glanced and Shoemaker and continued.

"We're had a number of officers working on the drug issues in the precinct, like the two strikes, what's happening with Cobra -- all of it."

Boyd sat up, suddenly alert. "What have we found out, Perk?" he asked. "Last I heard it had something to do with Cobra's hideout, but that may have been wrong."

Andrews was confused. "Wait," Andrews said. "If it's at the level of the actual traffickers, why isn't narcotics taking the lead?"

"A good question, Paul," Shoemaker said. "The fact is that narcotics *is* working on it, but even though Moody and Porter have spoken with them, they're holding their hands close to their chests."

"Have they been picking up on the tension between the big gangs?" Boyd asked.

"Of course you would ask that, O.C.," Perkins said. "And the fact is that Moody and Porter believe narcotics just isn't letting us in on anything. On the other hand, we're going to keep sharing whatever we have with them." Perkins took a deep breath. "Look, the fact is, we think we have more going on here than just regular drug action." His tone caused both Andrews and Boyd to stare.

"Before we tell you all the details," Shoemaker replied, "we called you in partly to let you know how we're using some of your people. We've got Novak, Hart, Marin and Brown all working on aspects of this, in addition to Moody and Porter, and some of them are probably going to be working over today."

"And?" Boyd prompted.

"And," Shoemaker said. "This operation may require us to use Special Ops as well." He looked up. "We think we know where Cobra is hiding out."

"Whoa," Andrews said, clearly animated. "What's our source?"

"Gee and Brownie," Perkins answered.

"That sounds pretty credible Perk," Andrews said after a pause.

"We thought so too," said Shoemaker.

"So where is Cobra?" Boyd asked.

"Bottom line is that Gee and Brownie saw Pepe Brantley moving around the catacombs today," Shoemaker said.

Boyd first frowned, then nodded. "That kinda makes sense," he said. It's not that busy an area anymore."

"Plus it has access to the water, and as I remember it's not far from Cobra's primary territory." Andrews added.

"Exactly," Shoemaker said. The captain then filled in the two sergeants on the properties previously used by Cobra and the efforts of Moody and Porter to check tax and business registration records looking for patterns or common denominators. He also told them of the assignments given to the teams of Marin and Brown and Novak and Hart.

"Don't want to interrupt, sir," said Andrews. "But this sounds like an operation that might get dicey. When do we plan to cut Hart off from this and use only fully commissioned officers?"

Shoemaker looked to Perkins who briefly shook his head as if to clear it.

"We hadn't thought of that before, Paul," said Shoemaker. "And it's a good point." Thinking for a moment he added, "let's keep that in mind and play it by ear; Perk and I will stay mindful of that and make a determination later. Fair enough?"

"Fine with me, Shoe," Andrews said. "I just didn't want us to forget her status."

Shoemaker turned to Boyd. "O.C.?" he asked. "Good enough for you?"

"It's fine with me, Shoe," Boyd said. "I say keep Hart in as long as possible. Something tells me she can handle anything we can throw at her."

Chapter Forty Nine

Two hours later Lt. Samuel Perkins appeared at the door of Andrew Shoemaker's office carrying a small cardboard box by the handles, and a paper bag.

"What's that?" Shoemaker asked.

Perkins smiled. "Good coffee and cups." Perkins said. "We're going to need it, I think."

Shoemaker's lips pressed into a grim line. "I know, Perk," he said, "And I know this is probably harder on you than on anybody else."

"Maybe," Perkins sighed, "I imagine Novak isn't feeling too good now either, though." Shoemaker didn't comment. "Any word yet?" Perkins asked.

"Not yet" Shoemaker answered. Checking the time, he added, "Still a little early."

Perkins put the coffee and cups on the conference table. Turning to Shoemaker, he asked, "Did you decide to call Central?" Or Captain Jones from the 12th?"

"Yes on both counts, Perk," Shoemaker said. "Central just reiterated sharing information and they put out a notice to the other precincts, which is what I expected." Shoemaker checked the time. "I think we talked about a conference call at 1800, so we have plenty of time for our meeting." Shoemaker leaned on his desk. "The conversation with Leland Jones was challenging."

"How so?"

"That kid who was killed -- Manny? Well, he actually lived in the 12th, and they've been getting a lot more harassment of their officers than we have lately, so Leland is a little strained right now."

"But," Perkins asked. "He's on board with us?"

Shoemaker's voice was resolute. "Absolutely," he said. "Leland is - - well, he's just Leland, and when it comes to the bottom line, nothing really throws him off that far. He wanted me to give him a personal update either before or after the conference call."

"Sounds like the Jones I know as well," Perkins commented. He chuckled. "He is a tough son of a bitch, isn't he?"

"That he is," said Shoemaker, then he nodded with a smile. "Just an excellent man and cop, and mentor to me over the last few years."

"I'm hearing lots of sloppy footsteps," Perkins said. Turning to Shoemaker he added, quietly, "Moody." Shoemaker smiled, then looked to his office door as Detective Dave Moody and Siem Porter appeared.

"Hey, Captain. Lieutenant," Moody said.

"Hey," Porter said. "Do I smell coffee?" Perkins pointed to the conference table and Porter nudged past Moody to grab a cup.

"Plenty to go around, Siem," Perkins said. "Let's just relax until everybody else gets here." Shoemaker filled the detectives in on his phone calls to central and the 12th precinct, and as he finished, Novak and Hart came into the office, saying that Marin and Brown were right behind them. Marin and Brown soon appeared accompanied by the shift sergeants, and all ten officers, from probationary to precinct captain sat around the conference table.

Shoemaker told the officers about his conversation with Central and the upcoming conference call with the other precinct commanders including Captain Jones of the 12th. Once the officers were up to speed, he turned to Perkins. "Perk, how should we start this off?" he asked.

Perkins turned directly to Moody and Porter. "Guys," he began, "how far were you able to get with those tax and ownership records?"

Porter sat up straighter. "Well, all I want to say at first is that I don't want to spend any more time in financial records," he said, "this shit is complicated." Opening several papers onto the table, Porter continued. "We looked into the records, and like we told the captain before, most of the owners are corporations, which is why we had to look further into the ownership." Turning to Shoemaker, he continued "To be honest, captain, we only found the owner or I guess owners for four of the addresses you gave us." He looked to Moody. "Four?" Moody nodded. "Yeah," Porter continued, "the rest of them have corporate names, but we couldn't find the ultimate owners or I guess board members."

"We could probably find more with more time, Cap," Moody said. "But that's all we could come up with so far," he said. "Plus we would probably have to ask for more help maybe from fraud division to help us out."

"Don't worry about it Dave," Perkins said as he looked over the papers in front of him. "This is good work for the amount of time you had." Gesturing with his head, he asked, "so what properties *do* you have the ultimate ownership for?"

Moody turned to Novak. "You got that map of yours, Danny?"

"We've got better, Dave," Novak said, as he pulled out a larger official street map of Port Angel. He and Hart had already circled the properties discussed in the officer's previous discussion.

Moody smiled. "Yeah," he said. "That's what I'm talking about." Porter leaned closer to Moody, and began using his fingers to find properties on the map. "Give us a second, Lieutenant," Moody said, and both he and Porter placed pencil numbers on four locations on the map, then looked up.

"Okay," Moody continued. "These are the properties that we have the owners for." Looking down at his notes, he added, "now this one, number one is owned by Downtown Developers, and they have like a gazillion board members, but they're all out of town people."

Porter chimed in, "we know because they have to list the addresses of the board members, and none were even from this state."

"Why would a totally out of state company want to own properties in Auburn?" Hart asked. Looking around the table, she added, "it doesn't really make any sense."

"A good question, Hart," Perkins said. "Let's keep going, and maybe we'll get back to that." Turning back to Moody and Porter, he said "Guys?"

"Okay," Moody continued. "Property number two is owned by Diversified Development," he said. "In fact, they own property number four too." He pointed to both locations on the map. "They have a board, but only one person is listed, the Chairman, and he's some guy from Florida."

"How do you have a board with only one member" Perkins asked, "I mean, what's he chair of?"

"It's a shell corporation, sir," said Hart." Perkins waved his hand in a "come on" gesture. Hart looked around the table. "A shell corporation, meaning that it only exists to hide the actual owners. Companies do it when they want to buy something but don't want the actual owners' names to be revealed."

"Is that legal?" asked Porter. "Certainly doesn't seem like it."

"No, I get it," said Shoemaker. He looked up briefly then continued. "Let's say a really rich guy wants to buy a property, but doesn't want people to know that he's trying to. The shell corporation makes the offer, and nobody knows who really owns it, so when the final deal is made, it's all legal, but there isn't any pre-sale publicity that might screw it up." He leaned back. "I mean it doesn't smell nice, but it's definitely legal. All you have to do is search long enough and you'll find the actual owners."

Perkins turned quickly to Moody and Porter. "Which doesn't mean you didn't do your jobs, guys," he said. "It just takes a lot longer to sift through this shit than you had." He pointed to the penciled three on the map. "What about property three?"

Moody looked grim. "That was a little easier, Perk," he said. As his eyes met Perkins', the lieutenant knew his suspicions were correct.

"Ernest Collins," said Novak. Moody and Porter looked at Novak and stared.

"Well, actually a corporation owner by him, but yes -- Ernest Collins," said Porter.

"Don't be impressed, Siem," said Novak. "Steve and I were looking into properties owned just by Collins, and we found the same information you did." As Novak spoke, Hart took pages from her notebook, completely oblivious to the smiles of her colleagues, and consulted her notes before speaking.

"What we found was that same property you found, detectives," Hart began. "Plus we found five more, and they are already marked on the map; see the red marks?" Hart pointed to the map. All eyes looked to Novak's map, and they noticed that many of the red properties were aligned closely to the numbers previously marked by Moody and Porter.

"Plus, Novak added, "we found that one of these properties is owned by several shell corporations, but they ended with Collins as chair of the board." The group digested this information with the mood dropping. Samuel Perkins sagged slightly in his chair, but knowing his connection with Collins, none of the other officers wanted to ask him about it.

Following the report from the detectives and Novak and Hart, Marin and Brown reported that the drug activity in the area near the catacombs had changed from a few independents dealers, to a lot more action with people associated only with Cobra.

"There was something else you need to know, Captain," Brown said.

"Which is?" asked Shoemaker.

"An informant told one of our officers that he heard some of the drug dealers for Cobra talking about something big coming up, and he implied it was going to be nasty."

"That's what we were concerned about anyway," Shoemaker said. He turned to Moody and Porter. "Anything else from narcotics?"

Moody shook his head. "Nothing more," Moody said. "But they had the same impression Gee and Brownie have."

Shoemaker stood. "That's what we thought." he said. "People, I have a conference call in about twenty minutes, and then some more calls to make maybe to narcotics, the 12th and Special Ops. Which means you may need to work over for some planning tonight, so stand by.

"Can we take the coffee with us?" asked Porter.

Chapter Fifty

As Shoemaker and Perkins continued working in the captain's office, the uniformed officers assembled in the muster room. Boyd moved to the front of the room.

"Hey, before we all split up," he began, "let's see where we think we are." Andrews joined Boyd at the front of the room, and seemed very comfortable while the other officers were confused.

"What do you mean, O.C.?" asked Novak.

"Simple, Danny," Boyd said. "There are things the loot and captain are going to do and things we need to be aware of as uniforms."

"One thing we need to do," said Andrews, "is work through what some of the likely scenarios are, and how we think we ought to work with the other groups." He looked briefly at Boyd. "I don't know about you O.C., but the idea of doing anything with Special Ops, doesn't give me a warm fuzzy feeling."

"That depends," said Boyd. "They're decent guys -- well, some of them are. They just take over shit too much for my taste

"And we certainly want to work some things out as a group before things get more complicated than they already are," Andrews said.

Boyd shook himself. "You got that right," he said. "Those guys can be very messy. They don't impress me."

"Right " Andrews said. "Which brings up what we think we're going to be doing, and if there is any additional information we need so we can make some good decisions." The other officers took out their notebooks, and began to share what they knew. As they talked, it became clear to Hart and perhaps to others that they needed to know a lot more to pull off any kind of operation against Cobra.

"How is Special Ops organized here?" asked Hart. "They didn't really share anything about that in the Academy."

"They're essentially like the SWAT team for the city, county and Allen County, Hart," said Boyd. "Any operation that involves special weapons, significant danger, terrorism -- things like that -- is always relegated to them."

"Maybe I've not been fair to Special Ops," Andrews said, "they actually do a good job, and perform an important service." He looked up. "The problem is, some of them are cowboys, and they embrace that even more than they do the service." He turned to Boyd. "That about cover it, O.C.?"

Boyd smirked. "I'd say you were being generous, Paul," he said. "But let's not worry about that now. What I want...."

"I have another question," said Hart. "I want to know more about the catacombs?" Hart asked, looking around at the entire group. "Can somebody tell me more about them, like how extensive they are, more about the location?" Her voice trailed off.

Most eyes turned to Novak. "Well, I grew up not far from there in Auburn District," he said. Novak stood up and approached the whiteboard at the side of the room. Finding a marker, he drew a quick map of the area around the catacombs. Turning back to Hart, he said, "the catacombs, extended from here on 10th all the way to Front St. and most of the tunnels go under the streets. It allowed storm water and other things to go to the river, but at the same time, was a way to avoid flooding by holding waters below ground -- kind of like a dam."

Hart stood up and approached the board. "Didn't somebody say that some of the tunnels are closed off?"

"Right," Novak said. "But I don't know which ones they are." He turned to the rest of the group. "Anybody?"

"Not me, Danny," said Boyd. "That's one of the things we need to know more about." Turning to Hart, he asked, "Hart, can you take the master notes for this?" Hart frowned.

"*Me?*"

"Yes, *you*," Boyd replied. "And don't even think of asking *why you.*"

Andrews called their attention back to the front of the muster room. "Okay, which tunnels are open and which are closed off -- that's the first thing we think we need to know. What else do we want to look into before we hear from Shoe and Perk again?"

"What about power and light?" asked Marin. "Is that still being supplied?"

"Don't know, Gee," said Andrews. He looked at Hart who wrote down the question.

"If there's access from the river, we need to know if that's still open," said Hart.

"True," Boyd said. "Do you know, Danny?"

"Not sure," said Novak, shaking his head. "I know there's a big drain to the river, and it should be open, but I'm not sure."

The officers continued to generate questions and discussed what any kind of operation might look like. They also identified specific questions they wanted to ask informants and citizens along their beat to pinpoint what was going on.

"What about the detectives?" Brown asked. "Some of the things we're asking are things they can check into faster than we can."

Andrews waved him off. "O.C. and I will take care of that," he said. "Let's generate the questions first, then worry about who can answer them."

Hart frowned at her notes, and apparently made so much noise doing so that the other officers looked to her. She looked up to 5 pairs of eyes staring at her. "Whoa," she said. Regaining her composure, she added, "anyway… one thing we have to find out somehow and soon, is if we're striking on one front or three."

"Say what?" asked Marin.

"We're not in the Army, Hart," reminded Boyd.

"No," Hart said. "Right. What I mean is are we going to suggest a strike against Cobra -- one front, or do we have to do some of the same things against the other two gangs?"

The group was silent for a while. "Well," Andrews said, "from what I've heard so far, we're looking to Cobra's gang partly as a preemptive strike and because we think he's been behind the previous strikes and murder of Manny Johnson, right?" Most of the other officers nodded their heads.

"Well," Andrews said, "we don't have anything like that against Spino and Parker, as culpable as they may be."

"We may still have a three front strike to deal with, Paul," Boyd said. "Hart is right to ask that question so," nodding to Hart, "add that one to your list, Hart."

"Done," Hart said.

"Alright," said Andrews. "What else do we need to know?" The officers continued raising questions, answering some, and putting others aside for later. They finished about an hour and half later, and then dispersed to make phone calls. Only Boyd and Andrews remained.

Turning to his colleague, Boyd said, "What do you think, Paul?"

Andrews rubbed the back of his neck. "I don't know, O.C.," Andrews said. "If this goes down the way I think it might well -- it could be a real bitch."

"I agree," Boyd said. Inclining his head, he added, "What about Hart?"

"Hart?" Andrews said. "She seems to be handling it okay. She's pretty tough, especially for a probationary."

"Yeah, well this just might be her trial by fire," Boyd replied. "I hope she's up for it."

Chapter Fifty One

Capt. Andrew Shoemaker was already pacing the next morning when the group reconvened in the conference room. The group had swelled to include several uniformed officers, detectives, and command staff. The commander of Special Ops attended as well. Cyrus Winter was a lieutenant and a long time veteran of the department, of slightly above average height, but of clear and evident power and control in both his physique and manner. He did not appear to Novak or Hart to be a "cowboy," despite Paul Andrews' earlier assessment.

Shoemaker called the meeting to order. "Are we all here?" he asked.

"All here, Captain," said Andrews

"Very well," said Shoemaker. "Do we need to do introductions, here?"

"Already done, Shoe," said Boyd.

"Good," Shoemaker said. "Let's get started." He turned to Boyd and Andrews. "We have a number of things to follow up on, so I want to hear first from our uniformed officers, then our detectives, and then we'll engage Special Ops. Sound good?" Shoemaker looked around the table, and seeing no objections, pushed on. "Okay," he began. "What do we have?" The first to speak were Angela Marin and Don Brown, who had been gathering more information from officers and citizens near the catacombs. Everything they heard supported the notion that Cobra's operations seemed to have moved into that area, and had effectively stifled independent drug dealers as well.

Marin was particularly strong in her assessment. "All indications are that Cobra's people, you know some of the lower level and mid levels are just itching for something big. Everybody we talked to said they could practically feel it."

Shoemaker turned to Moody and Porter. "Before we go on, Dave and Siem, can you tell us where narcotics is on this?"

"Could be good news or bad news, captain," Porter said after a pause. "It sounds like narcotics believes what we're saying, which is good, but they can't do much about it particularly if we're worried about the Spino and Parker gangs getting involved, too."

"So which is the good and which is the bad news, Siem?"

"Oh, yeah. Sorry, Captain." Porter replied. "Well, they're pretty cool with us moving against Cobra. They just want to coordinate with us to close around the Spino and Parker gangs and keep them out of everything."

Shoemaker went to speak, but Perkins beat him to it. "So we still need to coordinate with them, correct?"

"Right, Lieutenant," Moody said. "But they don't have any need to control our operation, which I think is good." Perkins gave an approving nod toward Shoemaker, who said,

"Fine. Let's keep that in mind for later discussion." He turned next to Novak and Hart. "What do you two have?"

Novak explained about some of the properties around the catacombs, and how they could be secured prior to an operation. "There are a lot of them that are abandoned, Captain," Novak said. "So we don't actually know what's in them, if you know what I mean."

"Are we sure about ownership?" Shoemaker asked, knowing it was a sensitive subject.

Hart and Novak glanced at each other. "We're sure, air," said Hart. The room was silent.

Not knowing what was going on, Cyrus Winter finally spoke. "Are you guys keeping secrets from me?" he asked. "What do we know about ownership?" Moody looked at Perkins, who nodded and sat back.

"Ownership was check out by Detective Porter, with some back up by Novak and Hart" Moody said. "We found that lots of the properties are owned by corporations, but that an officer of many of those corporations is a local, Ernest Collins of Midtown Development."

Winter frowned. "Isn't he some big community guy?" he asked.

"For want of a better term, yes, Cyrus," Shoemaker said. "Collins has been known to put pressure on us for things, and is very involved in the community." He glanced at Perkins, whose face was impassive. "It doesn't seem possible that Collins doesn't know what's going on -- there are just too many coincidences."

"Which might make things very difficult around here," Winter offered. "I'm guessing in both Auburn and Lexington, am I right?"

"Understatement of the year, Cyrus." said Shoemaker. He sighed. "And now you know why there is a little more tension in this room than usual.

"Hey, I get it," Winter said. "I'm here to cooperate, not judge."

Before Winter could say anything else, Shoemaker cut him off. "Good," he said. Let's keep going here. What do we really know about the catacombs? I think Hart asked that yesterday, but we need a lot more information if we're going to go to Cobra's stronghold." He looked around the table.

"I may have some information about that," Winter said. He took out a rolled up map that most of the officers hadn't seen and spread it on the table. It showed the area around the catacombs, in addition to a sketchy map of the catacombs themselves. Everyone in the room leaned over the map, saying nothing until Boyd broke the silence.

"Winter gets the prize for the best map, Novak," joked Boyd.

"Point taken," Novak said.

Winter drew his finger along the map, explaining some of the access routes, in addition to identifying which had been sealed up by the city or county years earlier. "We don't have any intelligence that Cobra would have bothered to open these tunnels or access points," Winter said. "I mean he might have, but I wouldn't think it was worth it."

Perkins said, "That makes sense." He looked at the map for another minute, then asked "If you were Cobra, how would you fortify this place: what would you do to keep it secure and defended?"

Winter thought for a moment, tracing his fingers on the map as he did so. "Well, one area I wouldn't spend too much time on is the beach below," he said. "It's more of an exit rather than an access point, so it's unlikely to be defended." Winter kept looking. "The junction of some of these tunnels here and… here are likely to contain some kind of defense."

Boyd was impatient. "Look, you know we have no idea how long he's been in there," he said. "He may have almost no defense given he just got there."

"No," Hart said. As people turned in her direction, she added, "you're right Sgt." she said, "we don't have any real idea, but it makes no sense to take chances, especially in a location that can be defended so easily." Gaining confidence, she added, "my suggestion is that we think like him and decide to secure every point of defense we can; that way, we can figure out ways to get through each one." Hart stopped and waited.

Shoemaker broke the silence. "You may both be right," he said. "Though the safe thing is to assume the worst, so we present fewer risks to our officers." Boyd nodded his understanding, as did Winter.

"Plus, Captain," Winter said. "That's the approach we would be required to take in Special Ops anyway, so…."

"So, we need to look at every angle, and decide what we can accomplish," Shoemaker said. He looked at the officers, smiled and asked, "can somebody send out for some more good coffee?

Chapter Fifty Two

Coffee was ordered, and families called for those officers working overtime. Winter made several calls to his office, and had a brief conference call with his deputy commander. When returned to the conference table, his face was grim, but he was silent.

"Problem?" Shoemaker asked, picking up on Winter's mood.

Winter turned his head slowly toward Shoemaker. "Just a little personnel problem, Sir." Winter waved his hand dismissively, and smiled slightly. "It shouldn't be a big problem.

"Your look doesn't say that, Cyrus," Shoemaker said. "But I'll take it for now." Shoemaker then looked around the room. "People, let's get back to it." The officers returned to the conference table, taking out their notebooks. Shoemaker turned to Winter again.

"Cyrus, in looking at this facility -- the catacombs as they are -- how can we flush them out in the safest way possible?"

"Flush them out is probably the wrong way to look at it, Captain," Winter said. "The ideal operation is to get them neutralized so they simply walk out."

"I hear you, Cyrus," Boyd said. "But in looking at this map," Boyd pointed at the table, "there are at least three tunnels that access the outside and the beach. That's a lot of territory to cover."

"Didn't say it was going to be *easy*, O.C.," Winter smirked.

The room was silent again until Perkins asked another question. "How can we best determine their location *inside* the catacombs," he asked. "When I got here, they had already been transferred to the city and being closed down." Perkins shook his head to clear it. "I guess what I'm asking is how do we plan this attack so it's effective and gets those assholes out of here."

Winter sighed. "And that's problem or challenge number one -- we in Special Ops don't have problems, you know, just challenges." Boyd smirked.

Novak sat back in his chair. "How extensive is this map, Lieutenant?" he asked Winter.

"Extensive, meaning?"

"Meaning can you see all the rooms inside?" Novak asked. Turning to the entire group, he added, "I remember a couple of places we used to play in the catacombs when I was in my teens." Novak ignored the widened eyes of his fellow officers. "As I recall, there were very few places inside where you could gather, because they had deteriorated." Novak stood and leaned over the map, trying to identify rooms. "I think the only really big room was around here." Looking at Winter, he added. "If that's true, we should only have to focus on them being in here."

Winter stroked his chin, thinking. "I can't say that for sure, Novak," he said. "But I can check it out with the county or city." He turned to Shoemaker. "Let me check this out with them, Captain." Winter gathered up the map. "Come on with me, Novak," he said. "You may have some things to share. Can we take about twenty to thirty minutes now?"

Shoemaker checked his watch. "Do what you have to do," he said

"Good," Porter said, rising. "We'll just be here with the coffee."

* * *

Thirty five minutes later, Novak and Winter returned with an older man dressed in heavy work clothes. Winter introduced him to Shoemaker and Perkins, explaining how they had gotten to him. Winter was personally acquainted with the man, and tried to make him feel comfortable.

"Don't worry about these guys, Marty," Winter said as he introduced him to the officers. "They're okay."

Martin Wilson turned to all the officers. "Good to meet you all," he said.

Winter toward the map. "Novak's memory was pretty good," he began. "Marty Wilson worked both for the county and then the city when the catacombs were transferred." He turned to Wilson, asking, "Marty, can you describe the rooms in the catacombs and their condition?"

Wilson, still a little uncomfortable, stepped forward and leaned over the map. "Like Mr. Winter said," Wilson began, "There are only so many places in the catacombs that anybody could live in."

"Live in?" asked Boyd.

"Oh yes," said Wilson. There is a very large living suite in there for the people who used to manage the catacombs when they were in full operation. It had electricity, good water -- everything."

"But it's been closed for years!" cried Marin.

"Well, yes and no," Winter said. "Because the whole system had to be maintained regardless of power outages and things, it has a completely separate system and meters -- I've never even seen them."

"Meaning," Shoemaker began, "that we can't just cut off their electricity or water to flush them out, right?"

"No Sir," Wilson said. His eyebrow furrowed briefly. "I'm not even sure I know where the valves or controls might be, but my guess is they're internal, so we can't do anything about them.

"Given that they have their own power and water, where exactly *could* they be?" Perkins asked.

Wilson pointed. "Most likely in or around these two locations, sir," he said. "They're both big enough, but this one is the primary living

quarters. Like I said, it's a big as a small house." The officers
looked at the map with confusion on most of their faces.

"You know," Hart said, breaking the silence, "I can't see how the
rooms and tunnels go together. I mean, if we're going to walk into
this place, how would we get from place to place?"

"We need another map," Shoemaker said. A map that's eye level."
Turning to Winter, he added, "do you have one of them?"

"I can make one," said Wilson. "It might take me a little bit, but I
can draw one that's pretty good." He looked around at the faces at
the table. Sheepishly, he added, "I used to draw some when I was
little."

Shoemaker smiled. "Then, let's get it done, Mr. Wilson."

Chapter Fifty Three

The assembled officers looked at the map produced by Marty Wilson, and most nodded appreciatively. Cyrus Winter's face showed concern, the same concern he had shown a few hours before.

"Cyrus?" Shoemaker said. "Are you going to tell us what's going on?"

Winter looked briefly around the table. "Well, Captain," he began, "I'm trying to figure out how we to best make this strike, and I keep hitting a wall."

Boyd frowned. "Don't see the problem Cyrus, "he said, "I mean, how extensive is the beach area at the end of the 'chutes?'"

Winter shook his head. "That isn't the problem, O.C.," he said. "The square footage isn't that hard to cover, it's…."

"Then it seems to me," said Hart, "that's it's a simple matter of securing the beach, then cutting off the west tunnel and moving into the southeast and northern ones." Shoemaker sat back, then looked at Winter.

"That's technically correct," Captain, Winter said. "But that's not the real problem."

"Cyrus," said Boyd. "What *is* the problem? Like Hart said," Boyd inclined his eyes toward Hart. "cut off the west tunnel and enter these two, plus make sure the exit is secure."

In an exasperated voice, Winter said. "Look, guys," he said. "What O.C. and" he checked Hart's name badge "Officer Hart are saying is accurate. The problem is one of personnel. Even using non Special Ops officers, which is possible though not recommended, we don't have enough personnel to do this right."

Perkins looked again at the Wilson map. "Okay, Cyrus, he said. Tell me how you would divide the personnel."

Winter pointed to the map again. "Okay. The best way to secure the beach is with several officers, I would say five or six minimum and usually with one Special Ops officer per team." He could see Boyd and Hart nodding their agreement. "Now ideally, we want each of the strike teams to be three people, but two would be acceptable. That means four people for the two access tunnels, and I would still say three or maybe four to cut off the west tunnel. That's a minimum of six, and preferably eight Special Ops officers."

"How many are you down?" Hart asked.

"Two," Winter said. "We have two injuries, in addition to one who is deployed right now."

"What about other forces?" Hart asked.

Winter chuckled. "Remember we *are* the regional Special Ops force, Hart," Winter said. "We're the ones who are called in for these kinds of operations. There *is* nobody else."

Perkins look again at the map. "So six Special Ops?" Winter nodded. "Okay," Perkins added, "Where exactly would they be?" Winter pointed to the tunnels. "Ideally, I would like three at each of these two tunnels, but definitely three here, since it's the largest and easiest for the traffickers to use. Two can go in this tunnel, then I'd like the commander, either me or my sub commander out on the beach with the regular officers. The last Special Ops officer would be stationed with regular officers at the west tunnel." He looked up, "So, six minimum like I said but I would really like to put three on each of the access tunnels.

Boyd took a deep breath. "I just recertified, Cyrus," he said. "I can replace one of the Special Ops people."

Winter nodded. "I had forgotten that, O.C.," Winter said. "That would help, but it would still only give me two at the southeast tunnel -- that just won't work."

Hart cleared her throat. "I could do it," she said, quietly.

Winter turned to her, frowning. "Who are you, again?" he asked, before he re-checked the color of her badge. Winter gave a Hart a cold stare.

"*Probationary* Officer Stephanie Hart, Lieutenant," Hart said. "And former platoon sergeant in the Military Police." She pointed to the map. "This is classic counter-insurgency -- I used to teach this to junior soldiers, and took out several bunkers just like this one in Iraq. Want to see my certs?"

After Hart spoke, Andrews looked directly at Shoemaker.

"No," Perkins said. "Absolutely not." Then he glared at Novak. Hart kept leaning casually on the table, showing no emotion. Apparently, she wasn't inclined to back down.

"Did you ever wonder how Sergeant Boyd and I knew exactly which areas we should cut off versus the ones we should use for the strike?" She turned to Shoemaker, since he hadn't told her no yet. "You can't do this with book knowledge or theory, Sir. It has to be instinct, and I've got that."

Impatiently, Captain Shoemaker remarked, "This is not a discussion for the entire group." He stood. "I need Boyd, Andrews, Hart, Winter and I guess Novak to stay here with Perk and me. We'll call the rest of you back when we're ready." Shoemaker's tone was uncharacteristically harsh, and the officers and Wilson left the room quickly, leaving the smaller group. Shoemaker turned to the smaller group. "I'll be back in about ten, so take a little break, then we'll meet."

* * *

Shoemaker reconvened the meeting fifteen minutes later when he returned with a file in his hand. He gave the file to Perkins, then turned to the group. "There in an obviously correct answer here," Shoemaker began once the door was closed. "There is no provision in department policy to allow a probationary officer to be involved in an operation like this, which" he turned to Perkins "is probably one reason Perk objected." Perkins nodded.

Shoemaker turned his gaze to the officers. "What we are facing here is something unique, and I don't like it." He stood up again and paced near the end of the conference table. "I don't like the quick turn around on this, and I don't like being forced to even consider it." He stopped pacing. "On the other hand, I don't think we have the time to wait for someone else, because of what's brewing." Shoemaker sat down. "Thoughts?"

Paul Andrews began, looking at Hart and Novak. "I mentioned to the captain and lieutenant yesterday that I thought this was an operation that was going to get serious really fast, and I asked when we were going to exclude you, Hart, for the reasons the Captain said." He pressed his lips into a firm line. "Now I don't know what to suggest."

"Winter?" Shoemaker asked.

"My instinct is to do it without Hart," Winter said. "I don't know her, don't know her training, and never worked with her and that might compromise how I work with her." He looked at Hart. "It just doesn't feel right to me, Hart -- no offense."

"None taken," she said.

"Based on this personnel file, here," Perkins said, "it looks like Hart has had the highest level of counter insurgency training and was given a commendation for two operations in Iraq. Looking solely at experience, she's good." Turning to Winter, he added, "that's taking nothing away from what you said earlier, Cyrus. I get it."

"Let me shift the conversation a little bit, Cyrus," Shoemaker said. "How would you propose using O.C. in this operation?"

Winter looked down at the map again. "Probably since he isn't normally Special Ops, I'd put him as back up on the southeast tunnel, so he would be the third member of the team."

"And no way to go with two members on each team?"

Winter shook his head. "I couldn't recommend that in good conscience, Captain," he replied.

Perkins turned to Novak. "Thoughts, Danny?"

"Well I obviously trust Officer Hart as a police officer," Novak began. "And I think we all do even with that probationary title. But I don't know anything about Special Operations like this."

Shoemaker turned again to Winter. "What if Hart was the third officer on the three person team, Cyrus? Would that be more acceptable?"

Winter considered for a moment. "Captain, having either O.C. -- who I know -- or Hart as the third in the team might compromise the team if only because the Special Ops person hasn't worked with either of them before, nor trained with Hart before."

"But *I* have," said Boyd.

"What?" Winter asked.

Boyd turned to him. "I've worked with Hart and trained with her," he said. "What if we were the second and third persons on that team, with a Special Ops leader, you or somebody else? I know your entire team, and I know Hart." Boyd smirked before adding, "As much as anyone can know Hart, that is."

Winter's body language was saying no, even as he struggled with saying yes.

Shoemaker sought to relieve the tension. "Is there someone you need to call about this, Cyrus?" he asked.

"We're all in this room, Captain." Winter said, shaking his head. "You have to decide what you're willing to accept; as commander of Special Ops, I in theory don't have a superior when it comes to this stuff."

Shoemaker sat back, looking first to Perkins, who nodded. He turned his gaze next to Andrews who nodded as well. Finally setting his eyes on Boyd, he asked. "Are you really comfortable with his, O.C.?"

Boyd laughed again. "With the right supervision, Shoe," he said. "I trust Hart to do the right thing."

"Good enough for me," said Winter. Turning to Hart, he said, "Welcome aboard."

Chapter Fifty Four

Perkins was muted as he convened a meeting of Thomas Fair, Sharon Shore, and Captain Shoemaker in his office. "We all know why we're here," Perkins began. "Shore. Fair. This is one of those very uncomfortable operations that isn't going to be easy."

"I hear you, Perk," Fair said. "But it seems that it's going be toughest for you. I mean, we get it."

"You just tell us how you want to handle, Lieutenant," Shore said.

"I want to make this as informal as possible," Perkins said. "Call it 'respectable.'" Perkins gave a small smile.

Shoemaker looked look to Perkins. "Something tells me we ought to have a couple of patrol cars there -- no lights -- along with your command vehicle, Perk."

"That's how I thought it would go, Shoe," Perkins said, wearily. "Let's call in a couple of officers we know we can trust, and have them standby here at the precinct."

Fair checked his watch. "When do you want this to go down, Lieutenant?" he asked. "Just to coordinate with the uniforms."

Perkins looked up to Shoemaker. "I'm going to have to check on that with Winter," Shoemaker said. Turning to Fair and Shore, he added, "Lt. Perkins can fill you in on the entire operation. Our objective is to be there at about the same time the operation starts at the catacombs.

"Shall we call in the uniforms now so they're ready?" asked Shore.

"A good idea, Sharon," Shoemaker said. Glancing briefly as Perkins, he added, "why don't you two take care of that while I check in with Winter." Rising, he said, "we'll check back with you, Perk."

And Shoemaker led Fair and Shore out of the office, leaving Perkins alone with his thoughts.

* * *

Winter sat at the head of the conference table, somewhat tired but also energized by how well the planning had come together. The group at the table included not only Winter, Boyd, and Hart from the 9th but four other Special Ops officers summoned by Winter. The discussion had brought all the Special Ops officers up to speed on the operation, and then briefly reviewed the weapons and communications protocols they would be following. Boyd and Hart understood quickly and were quickly seen as competent members of the team.

Winter's deputy commander, Sgt. Ted Spear's job was to lead the team of Boyd and Hart on the southeast tunnel assault. After sizing up his team members, he looked at Winter. "I think it'll work fine," he told Winter. "So the question I think now is how do we make this happen in the best way possible, huh, people?"

Winter pointed to the map projected on the screen. "The Red Team will move into the southeast tunnel. That team will have Sgt. Spear, along with Sgt. Boyd and Officer Hart from the 9th. Blue Team using the north tunnel will consist of County Deputy Ross, Sgt. Jackson, and Officer Reed." He turned to face the group again.

"The plan is to place regular officers and Sgt. McKay from Special Ops at the west tunnel to secure it against escape for the drug dealers. It isn't the right size or configuration we believe for us to use it to penetrate the objective."

"What's the plan for the beach? Sgt. Spear asked.

"I don't think we need to worry about that, Ted," Winter said. "I'll he there with Captain Shoemaker and other officers." Pointing, he added, "I don't think we'll be able to scale it easily, but I may be able to place two officers above the outlet, but I'll make that decision once we get there for our final evaluation."

As the team finished working out the details of the assault and reviewed what they knew about the catacombs, they also developed a protocol for the team securing the beachfront. Boyd stood up.

"I think we ought to bring them in now so they can be briefed, Cyrus," Boyd said.

"I agree, O.C., Winter said. "Can you call them in, and find out what's happening with Shoe and Perk? Five minutes later, Captain Andrew Shoemaker returned to the conference room, and listened to the general outline of the plan Winter had developed. Since Shoemaker had less experience with strike operations, some of the plan was Greek to him, but he listened intently, asked questions to clarify, then waited. Boyd returned a few minutes later, saying that the other officers who would work on the beach were right behind him. Shortly afterwards, Angela Marin, Don Brown, Paul Andrews, Mike Canady and Carson Poole walked in.

"Welcome, people," Shoemaker said. "We appreciate your being here to take care of this operation, it's very important for this community." He pointed to Winter. "This part of the operation involves the catacombs, as you may already know - I guess I'm talking mostly to Poole and Canady, since you weren't here for the previous discussions."

"Gee and Brownie have given us a good intro, Cap, " said Poole. "I think Canuck and I get the general drift."

"What do you need us to do?" Canady asked. Winter checked with Shoemaker who nodded.

"Okay then," Winter began. "Let me give you the general gist of what's going on and what we need you all to do, particularly on the beach below the catacombs."

Chapter Fifty Five

Lt. Samuel Perkins stood at the door alone, with the uniformed officers remaining by their vehicles and the detectives at the bottom of the concrete steps. Perkins rang the doorbell, and was surprised when Collins answered the door himself. Collins looked at his long time friend, and stood by to let him pass. Before entering the house, Perkins turned to the detectives, signaling them to come inside the door and wait.

Collins led the way into a formal parlor, and turned again to Perkins. "I'd offer you a drink," Collins began. "But I suspect you'd tell me you couldn't have one anyway."

"You'd be right," replied Perkins. Collins waved Perkins to a seat, but Perkins stood where he was. Collins sighed.

"I suppose we should just make this simple and not pretend I don't know why you're here," Collins said.

"That would be refreshing," said Perkins. "But I still want to know why."

Collins just looked up at his friend, and took up an already poured glass of dark liquid. Taking a sip, he said, "it's a long story, Samuel."

Perkins sat on the edge of a library table in the room. "I have time," he said, gravely.

"But I don't, Collins said, "and no matter how much time we had, it wouldn't make any difference."

Perkins found himself growing angry. "I still think I deserve to know why, given who you are, and what you've been to this community; how could this happen?"

Collins bristled. "Do you really have to ask that given how much money is involved?" He shook his head in amusement. "And do you really think that Louis Gray --'Cobra' -- who barely graduated high school had the brains for this kind of operation?"

Perkins stared at his former friend. "You're right, Ernest: there isn't enough time in the world for you to explain this me." Standing up, he said "We need to go now. Ernest Collins, I'm placing you are under arrest...."

Chapter Fifty Six

Spear was fully prepared with his equipment in five minutes. It took Hart and Boyd around fifteen apiece. Still, Spear was impressed. "This is going well so far," he said. Touching his headset, he added "let me check in with Winter." He turned away from Boyd and Hart, who were adjusting their equipment, and checking the magazines of their assault rifles.

Hart noticed that Boyd had neglected to attach the armored skirt piece to his body armor. "Sergeant," she said. "You forgot your skirt." Boyd looked confused, until Hart pointed to the bottom of her body armor. "You may not call it that, but it's this armored piece that protects right below your hips."

Boyd waved her off. "Not important, Hart," he said. Then grinning at her added, "can't imagine me wearing a skirt, after all." He returned to his assault rifle.

"Not this time, Sergeant," Hart said. "The skirt or whatever you want to call it is department protocol. We can't go in there without it; we have no idea what Cobra or his people have."

Boyd was dismissive. "Not to worry, Hart," he said. "I can make my own command decisions."

"Right! And jeopardize the entire operation," Hart said, the annoyance in her voice unmistakable. "Not this time, *Sergeant* Boyd! We already had to practically beg to get you in this operation, let alone me," Hart continued, "And this is too important for us to screw it up now. We can't jeopardize the entire operation because of you."

"You know, Stephie, I…" Hart got right into Boyd's face.

"And if you ever call me 'Stephie' again, I'll make you go in there in your fucking underwear!" Hart breathed and controlled herself, adding sweetly, "now please put on the God damned armor, *Sergeant*."

By this time, Spear had heard the interchange. "A problem here, people?" he asked. Boyd and Hart looked at each other, and instead of answering Spear, Boyd said "I always thought you had bigger balls than any other probie officer, Hart." To this Hart just rolled her eyes. She turned to Spear saying,

"Everything's okay here, Sergeant." Spear looked to both of them, still confused, before turning away to confer again with Winter. After he left, Boyd turned again to Hart, whose gaze was still angry.

"You win, Hart," Boyd said. "I'll put on the skirt until we finish this operation. *Then* we'll talk about your insubordination." The challenge in his voice was unmistakable."

Hart maintained her stare, then said, "Fine with me," she said. Then she checked her own equipment and prepared herself mentally for the strike.

"All units in position?" Winter's voice came clearly over their speaker headsets.

Spear and his colleagues at the other positions reported in.

"Very well," Winter said. "Move forward, and be careful in there."

Chapter Fifty Seven

The noise coming through the chutes that led to the beach started low at first and then increased. As the first gunshots were heard in the inner suite, Sayles couldn't contain his fear.

"Boss!" he shouted. "There's cops on the beach! What are we gonna do?"

Gray put down his cell phone, and looked up. "That call was from Tommy," Gray said. "He said it looks like the police are at all three access tunnels, and are coming in."

Sayles walked around the suite, sweating.

"Sit down, Ricky!" Gray snarled. "You aren't helping!"

"But Boss!"

Gray rose and approached Sayles. "You need to control yourself, Ricky," Gray said. "This is a time for cool heads." Gray started deliberate, slow pacing in the suite. After one pass around the room, he looked up at Sayles. "Get Pepe and Emilio in here, Ricky," he said.

"I don't know where Griffin is, Boss," Sayles whined.

"That's why you *call* him, Ricky," Gray said. Sayles quickly called Brantley and Cabral, summoning them to the suite. As he finished the calls, Gray called him over again.

"Ricky," Gray began, "How many people are in the anteroom putting together bags?"

Sayles thought for a moment, counting on his fingers. "I'm thinking six since we wanted to get the bags out later tonight," Sayles said. "What is it you want to do?"

Gray looked at Sayles as though he was an insect. "What does anyone do when cornered, Ricky?" Gray asked. Standing closer to Sayles, he added, "just what are you made of?

At that moment, Cabral and Brantley entered, concerned. "Did we just hear some gunfire?" Cabral asked. "We weren't sure what was going on."

With surprising calm, Gray pointed to the chairs. "Sit," he said. Then he moved to his desk and sat behind it.

"We are under siege," Gray said. "The police are closing in from the beach and through the three tunnels." The other lieutenants looked at each other. "Tommy called me to let me know about the tunnels and we heard the gunfire from the area of the beach. Therefore, we can assume the police have secured that exit point."

"That doesn't give us many options, Boss," Cabral said. "I can't think of any." Cabral frowned. "You told me you had somebody outside who was going to keep the police away from us. What happened?"

"You cannot always depend on others, Emilio." Gary said. "The police are fools," Gray stood and began to pace. Looking at his lieutenants again, he said. "Don't they know that taking out our organization will just lead to anarchy, to more fighting in the streets than before?" He shook his head in disgust. "Who is going to keep order, who is going to take care of our people and their families with us down?" Gray stopped, and got full control of himself; his lieutenants could see him relax.

"Very well," Gray said, "that's the hand we have been dealt. How shall we handle it?" He looked at his three men. "Anyone?"

Sayles and Brantley looked directly at Cabral who looked down briefly, then up again. "What *can* we do?" he asked. "If we can't get out, we can't do anything."

Gray chuckled. "I'm surprised at you, Emilio," he said. "I've always seen you as a man who doesn't let people push him around."

"Boss, where can we go?"

"For the moment, we go *through* them, Emilio," Gray said. "And we make every inch of their advance cost them." Responding to the looks of the men around him, Gray added, "Don't be idiots. I have no intention of dying here." Turning to Cabral he said. "Emilio, your task is to head to the west tunnel we were excavating and see what we can do to use that to escape.

"Do you think we can get out that way?" Cabral asked.

Gray was impassive. "That's what you are to find out -- go alone so we have enough firepower in the main tunnels." Cabral quickly left the room.

The remaining lieutenants looked at Gray as though he was crazy, but they remained silent.

Turning to Brantley and Sayles, Gray added, "We need to seal off the product in the third room so it can't be taken by the police. "The less product we have, the less they will have on us." Turning to Brantley, he said, "Pepe, break out all the weapons and prepare yourselves. This is likely to be difficult."

Brantley left and went to the small weapons room. Gray directed Sayles to bring up the dealers, saying, "We will not go down like animals, Ricky." Sounding almost inspired, he added, "This will show the world who and what we are, Ricky." Gray was smiling and looking very noble as Sayles left the suite.

Chapter Fifty Eight

Gray and his people grouped again in the main suite, and Gray issued simple directives for teams to go to each of the tunnels to respond to the police action. Most of the lower level drug dealers were frightened, and if given the opportunity, would have surrendered, but Gray was having none of it.

"Emilio has gone to the west tunnel to see if we will be able to leave that way," Gray said. Our job is to ensure that we have time to do that." Standing tall, like a military commander, Gray added, "Be ready, gentlemen."

* * *

Spear nodded to Boyd and Hart and began moving into the Southeast tunnel. In the lead, Spear moved quietly and with grace. Hart was impressed by how nimble he seemed to be. They walked slowly and took the first turn easily. Spear called for them to halt, as he lightly touched his headset.

"First junction, Cyrus," Spear said. The three officers waited for a response.

"Continue advance," the voice of Winter said. After briefly locking eyes with Hart and Boyd, Spear advanced down the left tunnel. As she turned into the tunnel behind Spear, Hart glanced to the right, as did Boyd when he followed her. Spear continued his advance moving carefully, and trying to pick up the pace to prevent Cobra and his people from mounting a strong defense. Hart could feel the increased pace and she briefly glanced at Boyd before returning her attention to Spear and the advance. Right before she hit the next junction, she heard a loud "crack! and saw Spear go down.

Reacting immediately, Hart and Boyd moved to the limp form of Spear, ready for the counter attack. Hart got to Spear first, covering him slightly with her body as Boyd came behind her. Working solely on instinct and adrenalin, Hart began pulling Spear back into the tunnel they had just come from, as Boyd laid down suppressive fire. As Boyd continued firing, they could hear,

"Red Team, status!" then "Spear!" from their headsets. Hart pulled Spear more quickly than she could have imagined and only relaxed slightly when they turned the corner into the original tunnel. Boyd laid more fire until he felt they were safe. He and Hart locked eyes, then both grabbed Spear's shoulders to move him more quickly to safety. Once they had gone close enough to the tunnel entrance, they put him down and Hart began to examine him.

"Spear is down," Boyd said over the headset. On the beach, Shoemaker looked at Winter, worried.

"What happened?" Winter asked.

"At the second junction, we hit fire," Boyd said. He looked over at Hart, who was examining Spear's leg, holding her hand over this wound.

"Spear?"

"Hold on," Boyd said. He moved to Hart, trying to find out how Spear was. Spear started making voluntary movements.

"Hold still, Ted," Boyd said. He turned again to Hart.

"Just messy," Hart said. "It missed the femoral by a mile, but he's not walking or moving by himself anymore tonight."

Boyd turned from her, keying in his mike again. "Spear is semi-conscious," Boyd said. "Hart said the wound on his leg is messy but not lethal. He needs to get out." Boyd turned toward the tunnel entrance. "We're about 20 feet in from the first tunnel entrance."

"Got it," said Winter. Next to him, Shoemaker remained concerned.

"Do we abort?" he asked.

"A little too late for that, Shoe." Winter directed two officers to extract Spear from the southeast tunnel, and once they cleared, he spoke again to Boyd and Hart. "You two ready to continue?" Boyd looked at Hart, who nodded.

"Both ready," Boyd said. "At least we know where to look this time," he said.

"Alright," Winter said. "Proceed."

With Boyd in the lead, the officers walked carefully down the same tunnels they had already traversed, even more aware of their surroundings and sounds. They made the first turn successfully, and stopped before the junction where Spear had been shot. Before moving forward, Boyd turned to Hart who nodded her head. Boyd took a deep breath, and turned the corner. He made it down the tunnel and stopped; the tunnel should have gone straight for another thirty feet or so, then turn left. What they found instead was a "T" where they were forced to go left or right. Boyd signaled for Hart to stop.

Hart drew up closer to him and asked, "What's wrong?" But even as she asked, she noticed the "T." She looked up at Boyd with no answer, just a question. The officers pulled back slightly, and Boyd made the call.

"Problem, Cyrus," he said.

"Go," Winter said.

"What should have been a straight shot is a T and we don't know which way to go."

"Confirm?" Winter asked.

After giving an impatient look to Hart, Boyd said "Confirm what?"

"Confirm T rather than straight shot."

After rolling his eyes, Boyd said, "Confirmed."

"Stand by."

Boyd turned to Hart and neither of them seemed sure of which leg was best to take, as both should lead around rather than directly to the inner suite.

"Red Team."

"Here," Boyd said.

"Pick one, guys," Winter said. We have no way of knowing which is best, and both should take you around the suite. Just be careful."

"Affirmative," Boyd said. He turned to Hart again, who shrugged. Boyd then pointed to the left tunnel, and Hart nodded her head. Boyd keyed in again. "Taking the left tunnel," Boyd said. "Red Team out." He and Hart began moving down the left tunnel and had gone thirty feet before they realized they had chosen the wrong tunnel.

Chapter Fifty Nine

The first shot took Boyd down. Hart began suppressive fire immediately, to cover Boyd's exit, but the Sergeant couldn't move alone.

"Hart! Retreat!" Boyd shouted. Hart's only response was two more suppressive shots to keep Boyd's attackers from shooting.

"Hart! Retreat! Boyd repeated.

"Shut up!" Hart shouted. As she advanced slowly toward Boyd, she added, "Get ready with your sidearm!" Hart hoisted her rifle on her shoulder, moved quickly and grabbed Boyd by the shoulders.

"You can shoot any time now, Sergeant!" she said, angrily. Hart pulled Boyd as quickly as possible toward the tunnel junction, struggling with his weight. Boyd let out three rounds of fire just before they turned the corner to relative safety. Hart dropped Boyd after making sure he was completely out of the left tunnel, though she pulled him to the right side wall.

"Shit!" Boyd said. Looking at Hart, he continued. "Don't you ever listen to orders, Hart?"

Hart was checking Boyd's leg. "What do *you* think?" she answered. Looking at Boyd directly, she added. "Keep your sidearm ready." Hart inclined her head down the tunnel. "Where did that come from?"

"It looked like it came from a little opening in the left side of that tunnel, Boyd said. "It might be one of those old tunnels Novak talked about, you know, one of those that might be excavated." Hart's face was angry.

"Which could mean another means of egress," she said. Boyd nodded.

Hart checked Boyd's left leg where he was hit. "Hurt's like a bitch, doesn't it?" she asked.

Boyd chuckled. "Does that make you happy?"

"Ha!" she said, "you have no fucking idea."

Looking down at his own hip, Boyd asked, "What do you think?"

Hart looked up at him. "Blunt force," she said. "It isn't too bad, but it's going to make it tough for you to move." She pressed the area carefully, and Boyd jumped.

"Sorry," Hart said. "The shot didn't break the skin, but you're not getting up are you?" Boyd shook his head. He chuckled.

"Aren't you going to say you told me so?" he asked. Hart frowned in confusion.

"I think that shot hit me where the skirt attaches to the armor," Boyd admitted. "If I didn't have it on, it might have gotten my femoral."

Hart stopped and stared briefly at Boyd's leg, then his eyes. Slowly, she said. "Glad you know that, Sergeant." Just then there was a rustling sound in the left tunnel. Hart grabbed her sidearm, turned, and fired, knocking one man down."

"Jesus Hart, do you *ever* miss?" Boyd asked. Hart just smiled.

"Red Team. Status report!" said Winter.

"The left tunnel was the wrong one," Boyd said. "There seems to be a side tunnel off to the left and people either coming in or going out." Boyd stopped.

"And?" Winter prompted. Hart held up her finger to Boyd to silence him.

Hart thought for a moment, then keyed in.

Officer,…" Hart hesitated, *"Compromised."* Boyd mouthed "compromised?" and Hart shrugged.

"What does that mean, Hart?" Winter asked. "O.C., what the hell is going on?" After Boyd and Hart exchanged glances, Boyd keyed in.

"Nothing much, Cyrus," Boyd said, casually. "Temporary setback." Looking at Hart, he added "Just need to regroup is all."

"What does compromised mean, O.C.?" Winter said. "Do we need an extraction?"

"Negative!" Boyd cried. "Cyrus," he continued, "This tunnel is important." He glanced briefly at Hart's impassive face. "We need to keep moving forward."

"And can you do that?" Winter asked, after a pause. Boyd and Hart could hear Shoemaker in the background, though his words were indistinct." Without hesitation, Boyd said,

"Of course. As soon as I get off the horn with you."

Clearly wary, Winter pressed. "But what did Hart mean by compromised?" Boyd looked to Hart for help. She pointed first to her headset, then made a cutting gesture. Boyd smiled.

"Uh, Cyrus….I'm getting a little in…… so after…..Did you get that?" Then he clicked off his radio. Hart did the same. Boyd shook his head.

"We could get in trouble for this, Hart," Boyd said. "especially when they find out I can't even walk right now."

"Hey, I'm just following my commanding officer," Hart said. "So, what's the plan?"

"I think we need to get back in that tunnel" he pointed to the left "and keep people from going out by that little side exit."

"That makes sense," Hart agreed. "That's why I put you against this wall, so you could lay suppressive fire." Hart stuck her head out of the tunnel briefly. "It looks like maybe ten yards from that side tunnel is a projection in the right wall. I can hang there and keep people from the exit."

Boyd leaned to see down the tunnel. "I can lay some cover for you, but I can't do anything about the right tunnel," Boyd said. Then he glanced to his right. "And I can't move myself to cover both tunnels very well."

"I know," said Hart. "I guess, just do whatever you can."

Boyd sighed, looking up at her. "Are you ready to do this?" Boyd asked.

"Yep," Hart said, "As long as you have my back."

Boyd chuckled. "Well, you've always had mine, so I guess I can have yours."

"Alright," said Hart exhaling. "Here I go, Sergeant." Hart turned away, but Boyd grabbed her elbow to stop her. Hart turned back to him.

"You know Hart," Boyd said. "My friends call me 'O.C.'" Hart smiled and extended her hand.

"Mine call me 'Steve,'" she said. They shook hands, with no words spoken. Then Hart started down the left passage again.

Chapter Sixty

Hart advanced carefully down the tunnel, looking ahead for the opening to the left that Boyd had identified. While she was a little concerned about having no one protecting her from fire from the right tunnel, she was confident Boyd would do what he could. And given the poor lighting in the tunnel and her black attire, she pushed her concerns aside. Once in position she stopped, wary of advancing. Hart took a deep breath, and maintained her surveillance on the left tunnel. As she watched, a figure dressed in gray and black approached down the main tunnel Hart didn't hesitate.

"Police! Down! Now!" she said. The man raised his sidearm. "Pop! Pop!" The shots caught the suspect in the shoulder and side, Hart thought, and he seemed unlikely to rise on his own.

"One," she thought. Seeing a slight movement that was hidden to Hart, Boyd responded with two shots of his own, directed down the main tunnel. Hart briefly looked to Boyd, then returned her attention to the tunnel. She began to hear more action, distant gunshots and voices but she couldn't determine what was happening. Slight movement ahead of her helped her refocus. As the figure approached her full field of vision, Hart noticed the street sweeper in the man's hands.

"Pop! Pop!" These shots were to the shoulder and chest. Boyd didn't bother to provide additional cover fire.

"Two," she thought. "How many damn others do I have to deal with?"

"Hart?" Boyd asked. "Status?"

"Two down," Hart said. "And I have no clue how many more." She maintained her watch on the left tunnel, and thought she saw movement. When a boot slid quietly through the opening at the bottom of the passageway, she tensed. A figure in black entered quickly with a firearm.

"Police! Freeze!" Hart shouted, "Identify!"

The figure turned toward Hart, lowering its weapon slightly. "Hart?" the figure asked.

Recognizing the voice, Hart shouted, "Mike? Canuck?"

The figure answered by lowering his weapon completely, and raising his helmet. "You can stand down, Hart," Canady said. "We've got them -- all of them." Hart exhaled and smiled.

"Okay," she said. Then she laughed. "That was interesting."

"Yeah," Canady replied. "We caught up with one of Cobra's people -- Tommy Burch I think it was -- and he told us about this tunnel. We had just gotten there and started coming down when we heard two shots." Canady's eyebrows furrowed. "Didn't you hear the chatter?"

Hart remembered that her radio was off, and said, "We had some problem with the radio down here -- O.C. and -- oh shit!" Hart turned and went immediately to Boyd, checking his status. As she got to him, she motioned toward her headset with her fingers, saying, "We had some radio trouble, didn't we?"

Boyd took the hint, and he turned his radio on as well.

"Right," Boyd said. He motioned toward the figure in assault gear. "Who's that?

"Canuck."

"And it's over?"

"Seems to be," Hart said.

Boyd looked at Hart as she got ready to help him up. "You're not gonna get all mushy with me now that it's over, are you?" Hart laughed.

"What do *you* think?" she asked.

"Then tell them I want to see them now!" they heard on the radio. "Can they get out under their own power?" It was Andrew Shoemaker and he didn't seem very happy.

Hart and Boyd looked to Canady, who only shrugged.

"Wouldn't want to be you two," he said.

* * *

Boyd was complaining as he was loaded onto the stretcher, though he knew it wouldn't do any good. "Damn it" he cried, "you're making this worse -- who are you people anyway?" His reaction almost prevented Winter and Shoemaker from approaching both him and Hart.

"O.C.," Shoemaker roared. "What part of 'report in,' don't you get?" Turning to Hart, he shouted. "And just what the hell does 'officer compromised,' mean?" Shaking his finger in Hart's face, he bellowed, "Do you know how this is going to look downtown?"

"Shoe," Boyd said. Then a little louder, "Shoe." Shoemaker turned to Boyd.

"Shoe, we had to improvise in there," Boyd said. "Hart was just doing what I told her to do; we made a plan and carried it out."

"Against *all* protocols," Winter reminded them. "That doesn't fly, O.C." Looking to each officer in turn, he continued. "And when you get direct orders from me, I expect you to respond to and follow them."

"Well, you know we had some radio trouble, Sir," Hart offered.

Boyd agreed. "Yeah," he said. "Maybe it was the concrete or the steel, I don't know…" His voice trailed off.

"You do know Hart," Shoemaker said, close to her face, "that we can tell if a radio is turned off or not, right?"

Hart's face didn't change. "Really, Sir," she said, sweetly. "That's good to know, thank you." Shoemaker's eyes flashed briefly, then he glanced at Boyd, who was looking as sweet and innocent as he ever could. Shoemaker looked at each officer again, then shook his head and left.

* * *

Hart sat on the bumper of a police wagon, sipping water. Novak sat on another bumper facing her, smiling.

Hart frowned at him. "What?" she asked.

Novak kept smiling. "They're talking commendation or more, Steve," Novak said. "Pulling two fellow officers from harm, taking out three of the bad guys under fire -- it's storybook kind of stuff."

Hart shook her head. "That's only if Captain Shoemaker doesn't boot me," she said.

"Shoe would never do that."

"You didn't hear him five minutes ago, Danny," she sighed. "He may let O.C. off with a slap on the wrist, but I don't have his track record."

"Yet," Novak replied.

"So what really happened outside during our 'radio trouble?'" She smiled when she said radio trouble.

"Not much," Novak said. "That one tunnel was secured during the advance, and both teams got as close to the objective as they could. Your team's approach got cut off because of the map and tunnel problem, but it all worked out anyway."

"Cobra?" Hart asked.

Novak shook his head in amusement. "They took him in his central suite standing like some kind of weird general." Novak said. "The people who took him said it was surreal."

"How about casualties?" Hart asked.

"Not bad, really," Novak said. Three officers hit, but only one broke the skin, that was obviously Spear. O.C. and Smith from Special Ops just had blunt force injuries." Novak laughed. "Boy, O.C. is going to be hurting." He stood up. "Are you ready to head to the debriefing?" Novak asked. "O.C.'s not going to be there, so you're the only one who can talk about your team."

Hart sighed and stood up. "I guess," she said, "but when this is over that bubble bath is calling my name."

Chapter Sixty One

The Police Commissioner closed the ceremony by saying, "…and thank these fine officers for their exemplary service." The audience, including several family members, applauded enthusiastically, both welcoming newly commissioned officers onto the police force and recognizing the exemplary service of officers involved in the strike against the Louis Gray "Cobra" drug trafficking gang. Stephanie Hart, badge number 2086, stood smiling as she was welcomed into Sheryl Novak's hug.

"Great job, Steve!" Sheryl cried. "Full commissioning and the Medal of Valor!" Sheryl was positively beaming. "This is so awesome!" she said.

"Sheryl," Hart said, her face reddening as she touched the ribbon around her neck. "Part of this was just plain luck -- or basic survival, take your pick."

"Sure it was," Sheryl said, as Danny and O.C. Boyd approached.

Boyd held out his hand. "Welcome, Officer Hart," Boyd said. "To the full ranks of the underpaid and underappreciated." His smile and handshake were genuine.

Hart took his hand. "Thank you, Sergeant," Hart said. "I appreciate your support." Boyd smiled and walked away.

Novak briefly hugged Hart, then stepped back and said,

"Lunch?"

* * *

Danny and Sheryl Novak and Stephanie Hart entered Heaven's Home Restaurant and were seated graciously by Ruth Williams, who joined them at their table after serving drinks. Her smile was infectious. Finally, Danny Novak couldn't stand it.

"What?" he asked. Ruth pointed to Hart's uniform.

"I'm just happy to see Stephanie with that new badge," Ruth said. "You certainly earned it, Child."

"Thank you, Ms. Williams," Hart said. "I had some great teachers along the way."

"Mmm hmm," was Ruth's only response.

"So tell me," Sheryl began," how this whole scholarship thing for Harold is going to work."

Still smiling, Ruth Williams turned to Sheryl. "It's fully paid including housing and includes a small board plan. Harold will need to work for spending money, but that's not really a problem. We're all very excited."

"How do you feel about him going so far away?" Sheryl asked.

Ruth paused, and for a moment Sheryl thought she had opened a wound. "Mostly good," Ruth said. "Harold's worked so hard for so long, it's nice that he has this opportunity. But you know," she continued, "I think Harold will be back after college. He has an awful lot invested here."

"I agree," said Danny. "He's done a lot of good for a young man, but I have to tell you Ms. Williams, it'll be nice for him to just be twenty years old without having the world on his shoulders." Danny could see Ruth's eyes moisten, but she remained smiling.

"You're right, Danny," Ruth said. "He does deserve that; we're just going to miss him." Ruth turned her attention back to Hart. "So is tomorrow your first day solo?"

"Yes it is," Hart said. "I'm not really nervous, but there's something about the first day, you know."

"I know, Stephanie," Ruth said. "But you really have nothing to worry about."

Hart smiled. "Okay," she said. "So if I come here tomorrow for my first day solo lunch, what are you going to serve me?"

* * *

Captain Shoemaker stood at the head of the muster room with Lieutenant Perkins, and shift supervisor, O.C. Boyd.

"Good morning, people," Shoemaker said. "We have a lot of things to cover this morning, so listen up." Shoemaker raised his head from the podium, and smiled. "First, let us welcome our two newest commissioned officers, Officer Susan Elliott, badge number 2120, and Officer Stephanie Hart, badge number 2068. Welcome, Officers." Shoemaker stepped back from the podium and led the applause.

"Okay, probably the last time you'll get *that* kind of reception," Shoemaker said to general laughter. "Now, here is some of the latest in terms of incidents last night -- O.C." Sgt. Boyd took over the meeting, informing the officers of incidents that had occurred the previous day and individuals of interest. As Boyd spoke, Hart noted with interest that four other officers were writing in notebooks that made copies without carbon paper. She smiled to herself and kept writing. Boyd finished, and yielded the floor to Lt. Samuel Perkins, who crossed to the podium with a confidence that had been missing weeks earlier.

"Good morning, people," Perkins said. "I wanted to give you a few updates this morning all of which are related to our successful operation against the Cobra drug trafficking gang." As he spoke, several officers gave mild cheers. Perkins smiled briefly before continuing. "First, 'Cobra' -- Louis Gray -- was indicted as were his three surviving lieutenants for trafficking, several counts of ADW, possession, and other charges. Frankly, the list is extensive, and even if only some of the indictments stick, they won't be seeing daylight again. The same goes for Ernest Collins: I think we've seen the last of him."

"And" Perkins continued, "you may remember a few weeks ago we were getting pressure from the Rev. Archie Price of Greater Mt. Zion AME Church about the lack of police activity to clean up the drug trade, especially in Lexington and Auburn." Perkins lifted his head and made a grand gesture. "Well, the Rev. Price came to see me yesterday to thank us for our efforts -- your efforts -- in ridding the neighborhood of the Cobra gang and," he paused, "he apologized to us for the tone of this rhetoric a few weeks ago." Perkins smiled as the room erupted in cheers. Ever the diplomat, Perkins called for calm after a short while.

"Now, the third thing I wanted to let you know," he continued, "is that the Rev. Price also expressed his concern about what he sees as an increase in drug violence from many places in our neighborhood, particularly what he terms 'low-level' violence, such as fist fights over turf. This has ironically occurred as an unintended consequence of the Cobra group's demise."

"So in other words," Shoemaker interrupted, "no good deed goes unpunished."

Perkins chuckled. "Pretty much," he said. Hart and Novak and many of their colleagues rolled their eyes, as Perkins yielded the floor to Boyd.

"Last minute things, people," said Boyd. "With the full commissioning of two new officers, we're going back to our old sectors for patrol. Those of you who are experienced know your sectors, *I assume*." Checking his list, he continued. "Elliott will be in sector three, and Hart in sector nine. Facing first Elliott and then Hart, he said, "head down to the motor pool for your vehicle issue."

Boyd addressed the entire group again. "If there are no further questions, let's get to work." He left the podium, gathered his papers and began walking out of the muster room. As he neared Hart, he said, "That silver shield looks good on you, Hart," he said, smiling. He noticed that she hadn't attached the medal of valor wing to her uniform. "Where is your wing? I thought you were really good with sewing and stuff."

"I am," Hart said. "But I figure for any formal ceremony, I can just wear the ribbon and medal: I'm not really into wearing extra stuff on my field uniform."

"Me either," Boyd said, and something in his voice caused Hart to turn back to him.

"Wait a minute," she said. "Here I was feeling all bad that you didn't get the Medal of Valor for the operation, and you already have one, don't you?"

"Actually," Novak intervened, "he's won the medal twice and this was his third commendation."

Hart shook her head and laughed. "Live and learn, huh?"

"Hell, Hart, you'll have more than that the way you're going," Boyd said.

"I'll remind you of that later," Hart said and she smiled.

"Have a good first day, Steve," Boyd said.

"Thanks, O.C." Hart replied.

As Hart left the muster room, Novak caught up with her.

"*O.C.* and *Steve*?" he asked with a smile.

Hart shrugged. "You had to be there," she said.

"I guess I did," Novak replied, and he followed her out on patrol.

The End

Did you like this book? Great! Head to my website fjtalley.com and tell the world! I would sincerely appreciate it. You can also access the site by this QR code

FJT

Made in the USA
Columbia, SC
13 February 2018